THE PYTHAGOREAN PATH...

The

PYTHAGOREAN PATH...

AN ENNEAGRAM TALE

SECOND EDITION

by Julia Twomey

The Pythagorean Path...
An Enneagram Tale
Copyright © 2023 Julia Twomey
Second Edition

This book is a work of fiction. Any references to historical events or real people are used fictitiously. Other names, characters, places, and events are products of the author's imagination, and any resemblance to actual events, places or persons living or dead is entirely coincidental.

ISBN 979-8-218-12975-0 (paperback)
ISBN 979-8-218-12976-0 (ebook)

Cover design: Madeline K. Davy
Photograph: Peter J. Schuette
Shift & Shadow sculpture/ back cover: Steven R. Davy

Dedicated to Owen, Aden, Sam, Luca, and Gabriel

Much thanks to the Off Campus Writers' Workshop,
and to Fred Shafer.

Thanks also to many friends who made suggestions.

And to my editor, Goldie Goldbloom

CONTENTS

Chapter One	Evanston, Illinois 1
Chapter Two	The Choice 25
Chapter Three	The Challenge. 33
Chapter Four	Numbers 53
Chapter Five	Say What? 71
Chapter Six	Slick 89
Chapter Seven	Achilles' Heel vs Kryptonite...
	Lake Geneva, Wisconsin 97
Chapter Eight	Lincoln Park. 111
Chapter Nine	The Visitation 121
Chapter Ten	The Mirror 127
Chapter Eleven	Party Girl 135
Chapter Twelve	Tattoo Girl 143
Chapter Thirteen	Namaste 153
Chapter Fourteen	The *Anamchara Text* 171
Chapter Fifteen	All Vehicles, Big and Small 195
Chapter Sixteen	Debriefing 201
Chapter Seventeen	Vincent Marcov 207
Chapter Eighteen	More News. 217
Chapter Nineteen	Armageddon 239
Chapter Twenty	Integration 249
Chapter Twenty-One	The Future 255
Notes	 257

CHAPTER ONE

Evanston, Illinois

T he white envelope sat on the hall table.

Fearing his quarterly grade report, Jack tore it open, like he was ripping off a Band Aid. His eyes scanned for a list of classes and the dreaded number codes.

But, no, this was something else. Jack let out a sigh, feeling he had dodged a bullet.

He was late, and so he stuffed the papers that were not his grades in his backpack.

The angry words with his dad from the night before still weighed on him. There would be no driver's license until his grades improved. What good was it to be sixteen if you couldn't drive?

Jack needed to get out of the house. Closing the front door, he hopped on his bike. While he longed to sit behind the wheel of a car, this morning his old bike offered a welcome escape.

Four months ago, a COVID infection had put Jack in bed for three weeks. While he mostly had recovered, his stamina and focusing skills had not returned. Preparing for tests and writing papers now posed a major challenge.

The sting of a red D on his last math test was still raw. And, his dad's reaction had been unsympathetic. Jack had felt close to his dad, and so this lack of understanding felt like a rejection. It seemed his parents only liked him when he performed in a way that was up to their standards. School always had been easy for him until the weeks of coughing and fever had left changes that no one could explain. Book learning was a big deal in his house, and his parents found it difficult to accept his struggling. They felt he needed to try harder.

He coasted down the familiar street, gliding up to Grace's house, where he saw her sitting on the porch with Mike. The three friends had bonded over a decade ago, and they had spent pretty much all their free time together. However, they often wondered about how different they were, almost like they hailed from alien planets.

Typically, in a situation, Grace moved to take control, assuming the role of boss. Mike, on the other hand, looked for ways to dial down any conflict. Jack was the careful one, the one who followed the rules. Or, at least he *had* been the careful one. Since the rift with his parents, Jack found it easier to drift outside their rules—coming home late, forgetting to do chores, and taking unauthorized trips into the city.

And, there was another change. As close as Jack felt to Mike and Grace, lately he'd been hiding his worries, fearing they saw him differently now that he had slipped off the honor roll. Ever since his illness, he had been more on edge. And, to complicate matters, Jack had found a shift in his feelings toward Grace. Up until recently, she had been his buddy, someone to compete with for a better grade on a math quiz or land the better comeback.

But it was different now; one look from her unsettled him. Maybe it was her deep blue eyes that looked up at him now, along with the strands of blonde that fell out of her carelessly clipped hair. Why did these simple things make him feel so nervous?

"Hey," said Grace.

He nodded and dropped into a chair, feeling his face flush.

"Did your grades come yet?" Grace asked.

Mike and Jack shared a look. Leave it to Grace to bring up a thorny topic.

"*What?* Ellen got hers yesterday," she shot back.

"Thanks Grace. Just what I needed first thing in the morning," said Jack.

"Geez, Jack. I'm sure you did better this time." Grace said.

"I'm telling you. I'm still not the same." said Jack.

"It will happen. Just needs more time," said Mike.

Jack wanted to change the subject. But, he wondered, if he wasn't smart anymore would Grace rule him out as boyfriend material? Maybe he'd take up track if his stamina improved. She might go for an athlete, he thought.

"Anyhow, I'm starving. Grace, do you have any cereal?" Jack asked.

He grinned and pushed his wavy brown hair off his forehead… the move he'd practiced in front of his mirror.

"Get it yourself. I'm not your mom." Grace said.

"Nope, much cuter," he said to Mike's hoots, while he headed into the kitchen.

He returned a few minutes later with a bowl of steaming oatmeal.

"*Mom!*" Grace yelled. "How come you cook for this yokel but not for me?"

"*She* loves me," Jack smirked.

"It's those weird green eyes of yours," Mike said.

"No, mate. It's my incredible physique," Jack said.

Grace threw a magazine at him, barely missing the cereal.

"My mom *does* think you guys are cute," she said with disgust.

"Hey, what can I say?" he said, as he scooped up another spoonful.

He glanced at her. Her cheeks were red. A tiny kernel of satisfaction registered inside him.

Grace changed the subject back again to his least favorite topic.

"I thought that last English test was rough. Gunderson picked all those stupid questions from the footnotes," she said.

Jack was losing his appetite. He stared at his cereal. Why couldn't she shut up? Just give it a rest. So impossible. If things were going smoothly, Grace found a way to cancel the peace.

"And the paper we had to do for History, needing all those references, "said Grace.

"Yeah, I spent the whole weekend at the library," said Mike.

Jack could feel his face redden, his hand gripping the spoon.

"You just won't let this stuff go. You're both complete losers," said Jack.

Grace glared at him, got up, and went into the house. Mike looked away.

Jack fumed, then closed his eyes. It seemed he was fighting with everyone in his life.

Grace came back with her own bowl of oatmeal.

"I'm sorry," Jack said, turning to his friends. "When we talk about grades, it makes me *crazy*."

"I know," said Grace. She touched his arm. "I'm sorry too."

Mike opened his laptop and said, "Grades seem like nothing compared to the *really* big disaster going on in the Arctic. Did you hear about the gigantic ice shelf that's now floating toward the Gulf Stream?"

It was just like Mike to change the subject.

"It was on the news this morning. I don't understand why nobody can stop this climate mess. It's not like any of us can escape. Don't those old senators in Washington have grandkids?" Mike said from behind his open laptop.

The collapsed ice wall was news to Jack, so he scanned the report on his phone.

"Everything is going to be floating or burning up in the heat," Jack said.

"Sounds like the Bahamas," Grace said. "Not the worst thing in the world."

"Grace!" both boys said, tossing pillows at her.

Nothing was sacred with her. Anything to get everybody riled up. Stirring the pot is what Jack's grandmother called it.

It was then Jack remembered the papers in his backpack. If not his grade report, what could be in the letter? He pulled out the crumpled stack of pages and began to read.

When Grace saw the concern on Jack's face, she said, "Read it out loud."

"This has got to be some kind of scam," said Jack.

"Let me see." Grace pulled the papers out of his hand.

Jack sat back, confused, trying to make sense of what he had read. Grace scanned the page.

"You need to show this to a lawyer. Bet your dad would help, Mike," and she handed the sheets over to him.

After reading the cover page, he agreed.

"Oh yeah, dude. You do need a lawyer. I'll call my dad," said Mike.

"Yeah, I better check this out," said Jack.

The day that had started with a scary white envelope and an argument with his friends did not seem to be settling down. Anything but.

Mike pulled out his cell phone and in moments his dad picked up.

"Hey, if you haven't left yet, can we come over now to talk? See there's this legal thing that Jack got in the mail," said Mike.

Ten minutes later they threw their bikes on the lawn of Mike's house on Lincoln Street, and walked up the stone path to the door.

* * *

Dr. Vincent Marcov's Compound

Vincent Marcov sat in his armchair and reached for the brandy, pouring himself a drink. A contented look settled on his face as he thought about the progress made by his satellite's strike above the Arctic that morning. The gigantic ice wall smashing into the Arctic Sea had been the lead story on CNN.

Won't be long now, Marcov thought. The melting ice would create conditions ideal for a record devastating hurricane season. Marcov planned to track the cold water as it entered the patch of ocean off the west coast of Africa. This breeding ground for storms would send hurricanes dancing across the Atlantic and spinning into the Caribbean and Gulf of Mexico. Marcov's only disappointment was that someone else would get to name the tropical storms. That didn't seem fair.

* * *

Evanston, Illinois

The teenagers kicked off their shoes inside the front door of the Farrells' house. Usually, Mr. Farrell would have been downtown by this time, so it was lucky that Mike's dad was free on such short notice to look over Jack's letter.

The lawyer had often been called in to help over the years. There was the time Grace had run up against the school board for petitions she was gathering during lunch hour. Then there was the incident when his son and Jack had been accused of hacking a manual for a robot. The kids had been innocent, but it was Mr. Farrell who had come to their defense. Now the three teenagers sat on the edge of their seats in front of his desk. Jack handed over the letter and waited.

An unsettled feeling rocked Jack's stomach. He liked routine, and this letter certainly was not that.

Mr. Farrell took his chair, sat back, and began to read, raising his eyebrows as the contents of the letter began to register.

After a few minutes, he took off his glasses and turned to Jack. "Well, young man, this is quite a surprise, I'm sure."

Jack cut him off.

"It's a scam, right? Has to be."

"Nope, not a scam. I know this law firm well. Bottom line, you have been named the heir to the Joseph Spencer Estate. A trust is set up to manage the property and business interests, but it's all yours."

"That's impossible; I barely knew the guy," said Jack.

Memories of last summer flooded his mind. An invitation to a family reunion. Based on DNA his mother had submitted to trace their genealogy tree. His protest at spending an afternoon with a group of random folks who happened to be third cousins. His mom prevailing. The event in Barrington. Hundreds of people from fourteen states. Meeting an older man. Joseph Spencer.

Mike's dad continued.

"I heard on the news last month that Spencer had passed away. He spoke once at the Chicago Bar Association, and I remember his message on climate issues. He must have raised tens of thousands of dollars for his foundation during that single lunch hour. What a legacy," said Mr. Farrell.

Grace leaned over and gave Jack a hug. Any other day he would have loved this closeness, maybe touching her hair. But today? Now? It all seemed unreal.

"This has got to be a mistake," Jack said.

He felt faint. Mr. Farrell's mouth was moving, but the words no longer registered. Was the office tilting? Grace's hand was still on his arm. But he viewed it all outside himself. Jack looked at

Grace, seeing her admiration, which, for the moment, overshadowed any inheritance.

"You must have *really* impressed this man, Spencer." Grace said.

"I only talked to the guy for a while." Jack heard his voice, but felt detached from his words.

This all sounded too good to be true. What had he ever done to deserve an inheritance? Somebody was going to find out this all was a big mistake. Some relative would show up. Maybe Spencer was crazy when he wrote that will. None of this made any sense. Grace would find out he was a fraud. A bead of perspiration rolled down his temples, soaking into his collar. And, he had met Spencer before his bout with Covid. He was not that same kid anymore. Not the honor student.

"Dude. Couldn't happen to a better guy," said Mike, punching Jack's shoulder.

"We should call your parents. Stay for lunch because this calls for a celebration. I'll cancel my morning appointments and order some food," said Mike's dad.

Well, Jack thought, maybe now, at least, his dad would stop harping about his grades.

* * *

Several Weeks Later... Lake Forest, Illinois

The Abernaults' car made its way around streets lined with ivy-covered stone walls. Charlie, now awake from his nap, fussed in his car seat. Over the back seat, his mom gave him a cracker. The baby reached for the snack and Jack picked up the water bottle that belonged to his little brother. Charlie's cheeks were flushed. Everyone said he looked like a small version of Jack.

"What a slob. Charlie eats like a flock of pigeons." Despite the mess, it was clear, Jack felt a special bond with Charlie.

The baby took a bite then scattered the crumbled cracker with delight.

"Charlie, you little rascal. You did that on purpose. I'm on to you, hiding behind those sweet cheeks." Grace said.

The baby responded by batting her face playfully, sending more crumbs her way. Grace smiled. Then her gaze shifted out of the car window.

Jack stared at her profile for a moment, her pale yellow curls falling on her cheek. He hoped Mike wouldn't notice the object of his attention. If his friend figured it out, it would mess everything up. It would change the friendship. Moments like these tangled his feelings with his loyalties.

Grace said, "Wow, that house has a tennis court."

"Look at that campus," Mike said. They rounded a bend circling Lake Forest College.

"We should have dressed up," said Mike.

Jack tossed his cap at Mike's head. The three sixteen-year-olds firmly embraced the fashion code of bus station at midnight. Grateful for this distraction, Jack punched and dodged Mike, the boys wrestling in the back seat like two bear cubs.

"Stop it!" Grace and Jack's mother both snapped at the same time, sharing an exasperated look.

"You guys are clowns," said Grace.

"It never ceases to amaze me how these two can regress to the third grade," said his mom.

The commotion stopped as they passed a Tudor clock tower, the car coasting to a slow roll at Lake Forest's Market Square. Boutiques with awnings and heritage-colored doors bordered a green lawn. Under a colonnade, a string of sparkling windows displayed eighteen carat gold jewelry, imported ceramics, and high-end housewares. In the last window, a mannequin glared at would-be shoppers, daring them to enter her exclusive shop. An oversized scarf of Italian silk draped over one shoulder.

In contrast, the car his dad was driving was old and dusty, a pale brown minivan. There was duct tape holding the bumper to the car's frame. Jack squirmed in his seat. Everyone they passed turned and frowned at the van. He felt embarrassed. They didn't belong. The shoppers on the sidewalk all seemed dressed for brunch, wearing tweed jackets, or wrapped in handwoven shawls. Nobody wore jeans, sweatshirts, or old sweaters with stretched-out sleeves.

Just then, a black SUV with tinted windows pulled up alongside them and stopped long enough for a shadowy figure to check them out. After a moment, the driver made a U turn, speeding off in the opposite direction.

"Well, now that was totally weird. Are the paparazzi following you already?" said Grace.

"Yeah, totally creepy. Haven't you noticed the *National Enquirer* tailing us two cars back?" said Jack sarcastically.

Despite his joke, Jack sensed trouble. Maybe that driver was a detective. Hunting him down. Hired by one of Spencer's disgruntled relatives.

The Abernaults' car turned toward the road leading down to the lake. The faint smell of applesauce wafted up from Charlie's jacket. He noticed the frayed sleeves on the baby's hand-me-down. Clearly, they were misfits in this fancy village.

As his friends talked, Jack felt Grace's jeans brush next to his legs. The scent of lilac wafted off her curls. Sitting this close usually would have excited him, but he felt too anxious to relax. All these sensations unsettled him. In his body, in the car, in this unfamiliar town.

Mr. Abernault swerved around a bend, almost missing the entrance tucked in a tall hedge of arborvitae. Putting the car in reverse, he backed up and they made their way under a wrought iron arch that read *Morningside.*

"Woah," said Jack's dad, "This is a *huge* estate."

"Crap. It's a freaking castle. Is there going to be a drawbridge, too? Just call me Richie Rich," said Jack under his breath.

His friends were silent. The worst possible reaction.

At that moment, he felt alone. As if life as he knew it was floating away. A year ago he had felt secure, with a plan to study science or engineering, like his dad. But then Covid happened, and his future faded. So, where did he belong now, in comfortable Evanston or in this unfamiliar village filled with estates?

While the attorneys had assured him that the property transfer to his name remained all in order, he still worried that there was something they had not told him. When he had voiced his concerns, his parents only had rattled on about how this was an astonishing turn of events. But Jack, a doubter by nature, began to look for a downside. He figured there had to be a catch.

This inheritance was nuts. After all, he had only met the Spencer guy once.

And why him? Maybe Spencer was mad at his legitimate heirs, and so had left the estate to him out of spite? He had seemed like a nice old man. With green eyes, like his. The guy hadn't acted crazy. But maybe he had a stroke or something. Started doing wacky things?

Their van pulled up in front of a 1920s mansion with a slate roof and walnut front door. The house, built of fieldstone, blended into the landscape and evoked a sense of quietness. His dad parked the van and then the group stood on the gravel, taking in the house.

"Holy cow," said his dad.

"This is out of this world! Gorgeous!" His mom said.

"At least it's peaceful. And no drawbridge," said Jack.

His friends laughed.

"You're going to need some Dobermans for security," said Mike.

The thought of himself walking two shiny black animals made Jack smile.

"Maybe I'll get a smoking jacket and silk scarf," he said.

"And a manservant named Rodney," Grace said.

"Can I apply for that job?" asked Mike.

"Sure, but you better have references," Jack said.

They laughed.

High above their heads, heavy branches shifted in the breeze, casting a maze of shadows on the lawn. A blast of cold came off the lake, and the group quickened their steps. Jack's parents said they would let the teenagers take the first look inside the house. They would follow after Charlie had a ride in the stroller, otherwise he might take an unscheduled nap.

"Remember. Meet us at noon in the front hall," his mom said.

"OK, twelve noon," Jack said.

Fishing the key out of his pocket, Jack turned the lock, and with his friends following, they entered. The teenagers found themselves in a large hall with a wrought iron railing curving up a wide staircase. Walnut paneling covered the walls and ceiling. The richness of the interior was interrupted by an unexpected modern light fixture glowing above their heads. A thick carpet cushioned the floors under their feet, and the smell of polished wood filled the air. Jack turned and stared at a painting in a burnished gold frame. Was that an original Georges Braque? The interior of this estate was like something out of a dream.

Jack could almost feel the house breathing.

Grace let out a slow "Woah!"

Jack felt a flood of hope. With all this money now, Grace was impressed. However, it occurred to him that now he would never know if she liked him for himself.

His gaze shifted to the array of items in the room. The furniture most likely was brought back from Spencer's travels, but the room felt warm, like a family home.

Wonder if his family would move up here? Sell the house in Evanston? Would he switch schools? Eat lunch with new kids? It would be hard to leave his friends. There would be the weekends. But Grace might meet somebody.

And this place was huge. Charlie could get lost in here. Have to childproof all these rooms. On the other hand, with all these resources, he could just write a big check. Maybe he wouldn't qualify to study science or engineering, but would all the doors fly open for him anyway?

It was hard not to feel the presence of Joseph Spencer and his extraordinary achievements within these walls. He tried to put this house in the context of the pleasant man he had met just that once. Maybe it was the responsibility that bothered him. Because Jack now sensed an obligation, a burden, resting on his shoulders. Could he live up to everyone's expectations? How could he follow in the footsteps of a great man's legacy?

Mike brought him back to the moment. "Wow. This place is awesome."

Grace was quiet. Jack wondered what she was thinking. Maybe that he would turn into a jerk now that he was rich? He didn't know how to act.

Then he thought about Joseph Spencer's will. How the wording had been clear that Jack was *to do the next right thing* with Morningside. That phrase in the legal documents posed both a challenge and a promise of unlimited opportunity.

He saw Grace watching him.

"This is too much. I don't need all this pressure. Everyone is making a big fuss. And for what? Yeah, this house is great, but I have enough going on, without dealing with all this stuff," said Jack.

She took his hand.

"Hey, the house is *beautiful*. And Mike's dad said the foundation will manage it. It's not like you're all alone," she said.

They continued walking through the house while he thought about the choices that lay ahead. Jack caught a thin whiff of something burning, but he shook it off. Probably embers from one of the fireplaces.

Swigging a gulp from his water bottle, he looked around. On the walls of a long hall, murals with mythological creatures glared at him.

"You don't deserve all this. What have *you* ever done?" A goddess seemed to whisper from the ceiling.

Jack looked down to avoid her gaze. When he looked up, he was confronted with more eyes glaring from the faces in the shimmering mosaic. The images pressed down on him as he craned his neck. It was impossible to tell how far away the tiles were. One minute, the glistening figures seemed distant. In the next, they felt close in, accusing and judging him.

"Fine," he said, talking to the walls and startling Grace. "I'm not worthy of *any* of this. I don't belong here."

"Uh, no kidding," she said. Then seeing the look on his face, she said. "It really *is* yours, Jack. *Calm down.*"

Jack let out a sigh. They sat for a moment on a bench in a hall until Grace broke the silence.

"Hey, I'd live here. Think of all the stray animals I could take care of. Maybe start a little zoo," she said.

"You don't even feed your cat," said Mike.

"Snickers doesn't like me, so I let the boys handle him," said Grace.

"Does his dislike have anything to do with the costumes you forced him to wear?" asked Mike.

"There weren't *that* many," said Grace. "And, as I recall, I didn't hear any complaints from you guys. You both loved it."

"Ah yes. The memory of Snickers, his grey hind legs stuffed in red satin briefs, a matching cape tied around his neck," said Jack.

"You *are* bad, Grace," added Jack.

"Yeah, and you love it," she said.

"I must," and he hugged her playfully.

Jack caught a look on Mike's face.

Uh oh, Mike maybe was picking up on something.

Wanting to escape, Jack said, "Wonder if my parents are letting Charlie crawl around in the main hall? I'm going to go check."

Jack traced his steps back the way they had come, but his parents were still outside. Then he heard the faint voices of his friends now coming from another floor. He moved on quickly at first, but found more frescoed walls depicting famous scientific moments in history.

On a table, a photo of Joseph Spencer receiving the Medal of Freedom at the White House caught Jack's eye. Before COVID messed up his brain, that could have been him, he thought. Honored for engineering or physics. Wearing a tux. Walking the red carpet. Maybe winning a Nobel Prize? Shaking hands with uniformed officials. Over his shoulder, a sash filled with medals. Grace smiling at his side.

Then Jack's thoughts returned to the day he had met Spencer, recalling the well-attended family reunion. He had found the older man at the buffet table, trying to decide between a chocolate torte or apple pie. Spencer had looked up, asking which piece looked better. And he had responded without hesitation that apple pie never disappoints. Spencer had served them both a slice. As they ate, they had talked about how the turnout for the event had been great, but that the crowd was a bit overwhelming. Jack had noticed the elderly man looked tired, so he had pulled up a chair for him, and fetched him a bottle of water. It was then Spencer had confided that his wife had passed away, and that she generally was the one who enjoyed these big shindigs. Jack had admitted that he and his dad had been less than enthusiastic about the reunion.

"My mother insisted. She wanted to meet people that our DNA turned up."

"DNA often holds some interesting surprises... about how we're all connected," said Spencer, his eyes twinkling.

"I guess," Jack had said.

Spencer had asked several interesting questions. One, in particular, had stuck in Jack's mind: *What activity allowed him to lose track of time?*

Without hesitation, he'd responded. "I tinker with robots and computer programs. Hours fly by when I have a problem to solve. Must be following in my dad's footsteps. He's a mechanical engineer."

The older man smiled, and then leaned back in his chair. At the time, Jack thought Spencer looked contented as the man gazed up into the branches of the massive oak tree.

Now, apparently, because of that single conversation, he was the owner of Morningside. Most people might have felt they had won the lottery. But Jack asked himself, why hadn't Spencer left the fortune to some environmental group? It didn't make sense that he would sign over the whole deal to a sixteen-year-old. Only things he had in common with the man were green eyes and the family DNA.

Jack suddenly noticed that burning smell again. He'd have somebody check the wiring in the house.

A few minutes later, he found his friends on the second floor. They were coasting through the rooms, eager to see everything.

"Can you believe this place?" Mike said. "Man! The parties we can throw. There's an indoor *and* an outdoor pool."

"Better keep the parties outside," Grace said. "This is no place for a bunch of rowdy kids."

"Pool parties outside all summer then," Mike said.

"This isn't a frat house, you know. No pool parties," said Jack.

"Yeah, this place *is* kind of magical. Not a place for horsing around," said Grace.

"Oh, so now your friends aren't fancy enough," said Mike.

"Look, you guys can swim, of course. But I can't have a big free for all," said Jack.

"Whatever," said Mike, annoyed.

They walked back into the hall, but Jack again fell behind. He wished he knew more about his benefactor's early life, and what led him to study engineering. All he knew was that Spencer was a self-made man. Raised in a working-class family in Chicago, Spencer earned a scholarship to attend university.

It was incredible that someone with so few resources could build up this kind of legacy in one lifetime. Jack's parents, educated, with professional careers, still drove a crummy van. How had Spencer managed his way through a tough city high school and into an estate on a Lake Forest bluff?

Jack found his friends in the library, a room filled with leather volumes. In the center of a paneled wall, a portrait of a kind-looking woman in a black gown hung over the fireplace. Jack moved closer to view the engraved plate... *Elinor Kaye Spencer-1982.* Joseph's wife, he knew.

"Aw, she's pretty," said Grace.

"Yeah, definitely a babe," Mike said.

"I think she looks serious. They must have been quite the couple," said Grace.

Jack thought of a portrait of him and Grace hanging in the room. But Grace, he knew, would never sit still long enough for an artist. It would have to be a photograph.

Jack surveyed the collection of ticking antique clocks. "Wow, this is amazing," Jack said.

Making a mental note to return later, he knew these time pieces were early machines that had led to the industrial age.

Mike, on the other hand, was content to get lost in the moment, seldom pressured by deadlines or demands.

"Earth to Mike," Grace said sharply.

Jack snickered at the clueless, but classic, expression on Mike's face.

"What? Isn't this cool?" Mike said.

But Grace was checking out each clock, and then moving on.

She *was* something else, seemed determined to plow through this place. Jack again found himself stealing glances at her as she worked her way around the room.

But, as it turned out, Jack was not the only one sneaking a peek. Because, as the three friends took in the clock collection, they couldn't have known that at that moment, they were being observed. Behind the west wall a tall figure peered through a peephole hidden between the books. His gaze rested on Jack, sizing up this kid who seemed tall for his sixteen years.

When Jack moved to get a closer look at something on the shelf, Vincent Marcov's skin paled, registering the youth's serious green eyes.

Unaware of the intruder, but suddenly feeling unsettled, Grace called out, pointing to her watch.

The rogue scientist backed away from the peephole. Had the girl sensed his presence? Fleeing through a hidden passageway between the walls, Marcov exited through a back hall. His black

SUV with tinted windows was soon speeding away from the rear of the coach house.

Back in the library, Grace was impatient.

"Come on. We need to move on," said Grace.

Mike groaned, but she shot him a look. Ignoring the rebuff, he turned to follow her out the door. Once they were in the hallway, Mike looked around. "So where's a restroom?"

Jack pointed the way, and Mike started down the steps.

"Hey, so feeling better?" Grace asked Jack while they waited for Mike.

"This is a lot to take in," he said.

"*Stop worrying,*" she said.

He wished she wouldn't use the word *worry*. Made him sound like a nervous old lady. He shifted his weight and changed the subject. "Yeah. Think I'll hire a bunch of hot assistants to whip this place into shape," Jack said.

"I bet you will." Grace shoved him, laughing.

Jack smiled, and playfully pushed her back. Happiness flooded him.

Surprising her, and himself, he landed a kiss on her cheek.

"Oh, OK," and she returned the kiss on his cheek.

Mike caught up just in time to see Jack pull in Grace, kissing her on the lips. "So, I leave you two alone for *five* minutes, and *this* is what you get up to," Mike said, an unmistakable edge to his voice.

"Oops, Grace can't keep her hands off me," Jack said.

"Very funny," said Grace.

"I know what I saw," said Mike.

"Oooooo, the hall police, are we now?" said Jack, hoping to deflect.

"Whatever," said Mike.

Jack started to howl like a wolf at the moon. And Mike chased him down the hall. They were eight years old again.

Grace smiled at her two idiot friends. Their childish behavior seemed to push the reset button on the three of them. The boys, with their horsing around antics, and Grace with her sarcasm, returned them to a simpler time before the pressures of high school, the pandemic, interest in romance, and now this inheritance. These playful moments reloaded their trust in the friendship. After some more chasing, and eye rolling from Grace, they continued exploring the house.

It was then they arrived at a hall with a gold leaf ceiling hung with chandeliers. A marble floor glistened in the sunlight.

"And just when I thought we had covered the first floor. There's more," Mike said with some frustration.

"This place only keeps on going. Looks like a whole new wing," said Grace.

"Sorry if this is wearing you out, Mike," Jack said.

"No, only I've never been inside a house this big," Mike said.

Jack knew Mike was ticked off. But about what exactly? He had never mentioned any interest in Grace. But neither had he, come to think of it. A pairing with Grace likely would mess up the friendship. On top of having this big house, now he also might have a girlfriend. Mike couldn't be pleased with all the change. He'd be odd man out.

The sunlight blasted into the hall, igniting the gold leaf ceiling, beckoning them forward. Grace and Mike, drawn into the gilded hall, quickly walked on. But Jack paused, noticing another door... with simple grey stonework. On a whim, and maybe partly to process the tension with his friends, he called after them. "Hey, go on ahead. I want to check out this side door. I'll meet you at noon in the front hall," said Jack.

Mike and Grace glanced at each other. It seemed Jack needed some alone time.

Jack couldn't have known that the next time he saw them, things would be exceedingly different.

Because millions of light years away, another story was playing out that soon would change all their lives.

* * *

Planet Sophia

At that moment above the Morningside estate...up in the sky...way, way up in the sky...and through a space/time portal... in another galaxy, on the planet Sophia, the Council assembled. Rushing into the gallery and dressed in brown robes, they took their places around an ancient oak table.

The chairman banged his gavel and called the meeting to order. He told the group that Vincent Marcov had struck again. This time, the Council's archenemy had launched a second attack on the Earth's polar ice cap with his laser equipped satellite.

Alarm filled the room, as the members pounded their fists on the table. These attacks marked an escalation in Marcov's campaign to ruin Gaia's environment. And what happened on Earth eventually would impact Sophia, as Earth's population would rush to leave their dying planet. Already, Marcov's space vehicle had managed to travel to Sophia. And now that the rogue scientist had secured his escape route from Earth, there was nothing to stop him from destroying the planet.

"The time has come to entrust Earth's people with the ancient book of wisdom, the *Anamchara Text*," said the chairman.

The Council broke out in debate.

"It's about time," said an elderly man who was known as the Philosopher.

"I worry the book will be used to manipulate the population," said a member with wild curly hair.

"Things are too far gone. We must take the risk. They can't seem to fix their environment," said a young woman with a baby on her lap.

"Marcov has sleeper cells ready to block any progress with green technology," said the man sitting to the chairman's left.

The chairman's gavel banged. "In the hands of a fiend, the *Anamchara Text* could be weaponized. Centuries ago, it was decided that only special masters would have access to the knowledge. They feared the wisdom would be misused. But, with the destruction escalating, it's time to act."

"Joseph Spencer's heir has the potential to save the Earth's climate. If this young man accepts our challenge."

"Why is it a sixteen-year-old?" objected a thin man with a balding head. He looked around to see others agreeing with him.

"Because he has the hallmarks of a champion. Even if he doesn't know it yet," boomed a voice.

The Council turned to look at the newest member, Joseph Spencer. His serious green eyes scanned the assembly, quieting the complaints. They all knew the exceptional circumstances that had brought Joseph and his wife to live on Sophia.

The gavel sounded again.

The room hushed, and the chairman's eyes rested on the table's carved inscription, *For the Good of Humanity*. This manifesto, cut into the oak, memorialized the founding charter that had ignited an enlightenment on Sophia, much like Earth's Renaissance. Sophia's awakening had also been seeded by the writings of Pythagoras, a newly diverse population, and trade connections.

"We know Marcov alters the brains of individuals so they do his bidding. He does this with tiny nanobot technology. It's time to act. The discussion is closed, the matter decided. Two agents will meet Spencer's heir this morning at Morningside. This young man, Jack Abernault, is in imminent danger because Marcov will go after him."

The Council pounded on the table, signaling the group's consensus. Then one voice spoke up. "So which two agents did you send to deliver our letter to the Abernault kid?"

The Chairman's eyes lowered, as he shuffled papers in front of him. "Uh…I sent Max and Izzy."

A massive groan erupted in the assembly.

"I know, I know…but they have to start taking on some responsibility. And, they were running around here this morning, making a ruckus. I was afraid they would wake up the Old Man. And we *certainly* don't want that," said the chairman.

The grumbling abruptly subsided. They certainly did *not* want that. Children had been taught, from the time they could walk, never to open the large door with the letter *P* carved into the surface. The old man had left specific instructions that he did not want to be disturbed. But, it was clear, the Council members thought more experienced agents should have been sent, with the stakes so high.

CHAPTER TWO

The Choice

As Mike and Grace walked down the gold leaf hall at Morningside, they wondered about their friend.

"I wish Jack would stop worrying about this inheritance. All this is amazing," said Mike.

"I know…right? He overthinks everything. It's good that he's careful, but geez. Sometimes I want to shake him. That COVID infection really tripped him out. School was always so easy, and now it's not." said Grace.

"Yeah, but now he could retire when he finishes school. Coast for the rest of his life." Mike sighed wistfully.

"He'd never not work. Knowing Jack, he would start building something. Or think of how many polar bears he could save," said Grace.

"So, Grace. What's with you and Jack?" Mike asked.

"Don't know. Only fooling around," she said, twirling a strand of blonde hair.

"But Jack's not a fooling around kind of guy," said Mike.

"Maybe he is now," said Grace.

Then she pointed out the tennis court visible through a window, changing the subject. The two friends continued down the hall, coming up with more and more ways for Jack to spend his money. Ducking into rooms, they took photos of items they found, including a meteor fragment and a model of a Japanese tea house.

Meanwhile, Jack was investigating on his own.

After entering the simple stone passageway, he saw a stenciled triangle with an eye in the middle. This painted eye looked toward a section of wall.

He moved closer.

To his surprise, he found a door camouflaged by a mural of tall ships.

Tentatively, he opened it, and crossed the threshold.

He found himself in a small chamber, and there, before him, were two strange little boys sitting on a rug. Silver and moss green curls framed their faces. Jack assumed they must be the ground-keeper's kids. But what was with the hair?

The older boy jumped up. "Hello, sir. I am Max. This is Izzy. We are brothers."

The boy's speech had a strange mechanical cadence, with an overlay of high-pitched clicks and chirps.

The younger one whispered in his brother's ear, "Are we not supposed to call him Master Champion?"

Max quieted him, "Not yet."

Izzy's face brightened, "Oh, I forgot."

"Are you hiding in here?" asked Jack.

"Noooo…we were *hoping to* meet you," said Izzy. He chirped and clicked out the words.

"Did you know I was coming up to Morningside today?" asked Jack.

"Uh huh," said Izzy, staring at Jack.

Jack assumed he had stumbled upon a game of Star Wars. He used to act out these scenes with Mike and Grace when they were in second grade. These boys looked to be about nine and seven years old, dressed in crisp white tunics. The speech pattern, he thought, was downright impressive. These kids had skills.

"I am hungry. Do you have any food?" Izzy asked.

Max moved closer to Jack.

Jack thought, maybe too close, and he stepped back. But he pulled some granola bars out of his pocket.

He offered them to the boys, and their eyes lit up as they ate. They seemed surprised at the crunchiness of the food.

When they were finished they handed the empty wrappers back to Jack.

That's odd, he thought, but he stuffed them in his pocket.

Max spoke. "Good. You passed the first test. Sharing is the sign of a hero," Max said.

"We hoped you would come down the stone hall," said Izzy.

Jack wondered how the boys would weave him into their plot. He was surprised that these kids could keep up the pretense, not breaking character, but maintaining the mechanical talking pattern.

Max gestured for him to sit down.

After Jack complied, the two little boys explained that they had come from the planet Sophia and that they needed his help.

These boys were going off script from Star Wars. But, Jack decided to play along with their game.

"Tell me more," said Jack.

The older boy said Morningside Estate rested under a small sliver in the spacetime fabric. As a result, a porthole existed directly above the mansion that allowed passage, outside the galaxy, to neighboring planets...that is, if you had the right vehicle.

Max let his words register with Jack.

Then the boy admitted that he knew it sounded crazy, but he told Jack that they had a way to move through great distances outside the galaxy.

"Say what?" said Jack.

These kids were *amazing*, he thought. Then, to humor them, he said, "No way." He wished Grace was here to see this.

"Who is Grace?" asked Izzy, pulling Max's sleeve.

Had he said that out loud? Jack didn't think so.

"Be quiet, Izzy," his brother said.

"Again, we have a special space vehicle." Max said.

These little guys were too much... maintaining the clicks and chirps in their speech. Maybe they took acting lessons?

"Well, we will show you how we travel. We can even have you back by noon." Max said.

Jack smiled. "Sure you will. OK. Let's go."

As soon as the words were out of his mouth, Jack noticed the little boys' silver and moss green hair had soft tendrils around their faces, not like wigs from the party store.

"Come on. Follow us," Max said.

They led Jack outside where he noticed the sky had changed. Heavy grey clouds now bore down on the estate. Jack shivered as an icy chill travelwed up his spine. He wrapped his jacket tighter around his middle. Jack considered turning back, but then the boys entered a maze with eight-foot high boxwood. Spurred on, he followed them. The brothers giggled, zipping through the turns and curves.

Odd statues seemed to lean into the path, and little stone faces peeked out of the shrubbery.

"Here he comes?" Jack heard in a raspy whisper.

Jack whipped around to see who was speaking. Did that stone head turn? No, of course not. Must be the younger boy messing with him.

"Shh...Don't move. We don't want to scare him off," whispered a voice.

"Get a grip," Jack whispered to himself.

"Get a grip, get a grip," mocked the stone cherub.

He took a deep breath. This was *not* happening.

Jack moved on, but Max and Izzy had disappeared. He heard them rustling somewhere ahead in the maze. Their muffled voices punctuated with the high-pitched chirps. Jack paused a moment, noticing that everything seemed kind of other worldly. Snow began to fall on the mossy path.

"Here we go again. It's supposed to be spring," said Jack.

In spite of the falling snowflakes, the air suddenly seemed warmer. The boxwood that brushed the back of his hand had a feathery feel, like a bird's wing grazing his fingers. Jack noticed the scent of blossoms. A silvery haze settled in his path.

"Max? Izzy? Where are you guys?" said Jack in a worried tone.

All he could hear was a whooshing sound, like a strong wind.

What was going on? Where were those kids? They were here a minute ago.

Then, startling him, an old woman with kind eyes emerged from the mist. She looked like the portrait of Elinor Spencer that he had seen in the library, but decades older. She wore a simple black gown with a shawl and a veiled hat.

"Hello, young man. I see you have met Max and Izzy. Darling boys when they aren't getting into mischief." Her eyes sparkled with amusement.

Her unexpected appearance should have rattled him; however, she had a calming effect on him once she began to speak. He tried to introduce himself. But she hushed him.

"Oh, I know who you are. Joseph and you have so much in common. As time goes on, you will see. And, you would do well to keep an open mind. Be patient. Over time, you'll get your answers. You know, you're on the hero's journey, choosing the stone hallway, avoiding the flash of the golden corridor. Keeping it simple is always a good idea." Elinor said.

Jack apparently wasn't going to get any answers beyond what she wished to tell him. He wondered how she knew what had happened in the house. Maybe this was all a dream. He felt a cold breeze, then snow, then warm again. Surely, he'd wake up soon.

So, resigned, he listened as the woman continued. "I used to tell my darling Joe, do the next right thing, and you will be fine. It's a process that cannot be hurried."

Then, as quickly as she had appeared…she vanished, stepping back into the heavy mist that evaporated like a page had been turned.

"OK, now. That was totally weird," Jack spoke to the air.

Was a theater company putting on a performance at Morningside? And how had the woman quoted Spencer's will?

Jack looked around, but the two little boys were nowhere to be seen. Checking his phone, the time showed 9:30 a.m. Were Max, and Izzy, and the old woman actors or odd hallucinations? Maybe due to dehydration, or a funky vitamin pill?

Then he felt the empty granola wrappers in his pocket. Bewildered, he thought, No, they were real.

Well then, where were they? He looked around.

Exiting the maze a few moments later, Jack looked up and saw a huge glass cube resting in a low branch of a massive oak tree. A rope ladder dangled from the lower limb. While his instincts told him to hesitate because it didn't look too secure, his curiosity took over, and he climbed up. It seemed odd that he could not see through the glass, but his hand found an indentation that responded to his touch. A panel slid open, and there, smiling from ear to ear, stood Max and Izzy.

These kids certainly had a kick-ass treehouse at their disposal. Jack acted against his tendency to pause and leaped in to join them. Rocking in response to his added weight, the glass cube moved up and then down. The boys laughed, but with a staccato quality that sounded chirpy, and a little creepy. He was about to ask about their parents.

But before he could get the words out, a seat belt snapped over him.

And the cube **began to fly!**

Jack screamed as they jetted straight up like a rocket so that he could see Morningside, and Lake Michigan recede in the distance below him. They blasted through the clouds.

"Help! Stop! No!" Jack yelled.

Moments later, the cube floated through the sliver of a space/ time portal. Jack's stomach had flipped over at least six times. The pressure in his head was massive. He could hear himself screaming, his body in full-on revolution.

Where was he going? And why?

Max reassured him, trying to deal with Jack's panic. "We will have you back by noon."

But Jack's eyes were wide with fear as he yelled even louder.

"Make him stop screaming," said Izzy.

Max waved his hand in front of Jack's terrified eyes. But there was no calming him.

Their little faces hovering over him were the last things Jack registered… before passing out on the silver cushions.

CHAPTER THREE

The Challenge

When Jack came to, the boys reassured him that they flew this cube all the time and it had a perfect safety record.

"There really is nothing to worry about," said Izzy.

"What the hell!" Jack said.

"We will explain, but you need to stay calm. Let your body adjust to the flight," Max chirped.

Jack's heart rate settled, perhaps due to his hope that this was only a bizarro dream sequence. He would awaken any moment now and laugh about his crazy nightmare. His mind could not accept what he was seeing.

But the view was dazzling... amazing, with planets and constellations blinking like jewels tossed against a velvet backdrop.

His senses now seemed to be doing a systems' check of some kind. He heard a humming sound. There was the smell of ozone, also the sense of propulsion through space, and lights flashing. Would this happen in a dream? No, his sensations were real.

What should he do? Pretend to be asleep and then pounce? Wrestle them? There are two of them. But he was bigger. Then again, he didn't know how to control the flying cube...so, basically, he was trapped. The motion sickness returned, flipping his stomach. Weakened, he begged. "What's going on? Where are you taking me?"

"You'll get some answers. But, right now, you need to settle down."

"Settle down? Are you kidding? I've been abducted by two kids in a flying treehouse. Going who the hell knows where!"

Izzy looked stunned; tears welled up.

Max turned and frowned at Jack. "See what you've done? Izzy is not used to yelling. Who raised you?"

Surprised by the reprimand, Jack felt bad. Tears, like Charlie's, always had this effect on him. But he quickly shook off this thought. **Wait** a minute! These kids were criminals. Hadn't they abducted him? He would *not* feel bad for them.

Izzy blew his nose, and sniffed back a tear.

With his brother settling down, Max now seemed ready to talk.

"Look, we've been sent by a Council commission to enlist your help. You were correct when you thought there might be something more to Morningside than just a big house."

"I *knew* it!" Jack said.

Then, Max passed him a large envelope with *Jack Abernault*, written in silver ink.

"Open it," said Max.

Jack unsealed the envelope. Unfolding the letter, he read:

> *Max and Izzy hail from the planet Sophia, beyond the Milky Way galaxy. We are an evolved population of Homo sapiens, with advanced science that has resolved the issues around climate. Our world has a similar atmosphere to earth.*

Trying to process this incredible information, Jack looked at the two little boys.

They grinned, showing too many teeth to look totally innocent.
"This has to do with Earth's environment?" Jack asked.
"It is not that simple," said Max. He gestured to keep reading.
Jack returned his attention to the letter:

Our planet now shares a serious problem with your people. A rogue scientist, Dr. Vincent Marcov, discovered the space/time portal that allows him to travel to Sophia. For decades, this troubled genius has blocked attempts to fix climate problems in your world. Sometimes his attacks directly poison the air and water, but often, he sabotages climate agreements and green policies. Currently, he is working against the development of a generator for atomic fusion that would solve much of your energy crisis.

"Dr. Vincent Marcov?"
He could see the fear in Izzy's eyes.
"One sick dude," said Max.
"*So* mean," chirped Izzy.
Jack read on:

Earth's climate will shrivel unless your people evolve... and do it fast. As it stands now, your population seems immobilized by Marcov and his collaborators. To counter his activities, we need to raise the consciousness of Earth's people.

The answer lies within the pages of a special wisdom book, the Anamchara Text. *The writings hold an ancient formula. While there remain other avenues to enlightenment, this book holds a special set of insights.*

Not everyone will absorb this knowledge, but if enough people take the teachings to heart, they will mobilize to heal the climate.

At present, a number of your great minds and hearts live with us on Sophia, and we feel a special connection to Earth.

So, we have a challenge for you, and if you accept, it will entail three tasks:

First, begin a quest to meet certain individuals. Observe, and listen closely to them, not only with your ears, but with your head, with your heart, and with your gut.

Second, learn the teachings of the Anamchara Text, *and explain the book's contents to your people.*

And then, lastly, neutralize Vincent Marcov.

The path, dangerous and demanding, requires courage and cleverness. Our future and yours remain bound together in this endeavor.

We await your response.

The Council...Sector 41 ...Planet Sophia

Dropping the letter on his lap, Jack stared at the brothers.

Finally, he spoke. "Why me?"

Max looked serious. "I do not know."

Jack fell back on the cushions.

Izzy handed over a carbonated drink, and Jack chugged the liquid. He closed his eyes and wished if only the cube would stop spinning.

Max and Izzy watched him, and waited. They chirped and clicked in their strange language, a chatter that sounded like the bird house at Lincoln Park Zoo.

Reaching out his hand, Jack signaled for quiet.

Thankfully, the boys stopped talking.

Then Jack picked up the letter, re-reading it.

"This is nuts," said Jack.

"Look, you should know. Vincent Marcov has a laser capable satellite that slices off ice mountains, causing the sea to rise and hurricanes to form. And Marcov will see to it that atomic fusion technology never is linked to a workable generator," Max said.

Jack was well aware that the earth was running out of time; however, he was sixteen years old. A champion? He'd thought of himself as a worrier, not a warrior. What was this Council thinking?

But at least he had been right about something. He *had known* something was fishy about Morningside.

Jack sat slumped, a pile of sour insides, hurling through space. Everything felt upside down, flipped from a gravity-respecting world to a wild and wooly universe that spun his guts in a cosmic blender.

"Home. I want to go home," said Jack. Pleading now.

"Not yet. We have to show you something," said Max.

Jack moaned.

If he accepted the Council's challenge, he and his family would be in peril. Jack felt as if a menacing tattoo artist was searing his back with an indelible bullseye.

Jack squeezed his eyes shut, hoping to erase all of it.

But when he opened them again, nothing had changed. The strange children, in their white tunics, stood in front of him, looking expectant.

How was he even supposed to find Marcov—much less neutralize him? And what did that word *neutralize* even mean? Did they expect him to kill the guy? Why didn't they pick someone else?

Reading his mind, Izzy responded. "Well, we do not know. *Somebody* found you full of potential."

"Maybe it has something to do with your green eyes. Just know the Council is depending on you. Max and I are apprentices, not privy to the decisions made by the Council."

"Just take me home. I can't help you," Jack said.

"We will, just not yet," said Max.

Cold sweat rolled down Jack's temples. How could he believe these precocious children who had lured him into this flying glass jail? Were they even human with the green and silver hair, the avian voices? The letter from the Council claimed they were human, but clearly there were big, big differences.

Then Jack considered a darker outcome. If he said *no* to the challenge, would they toss him out of this cube, his body floating until it burned up in space?

Jack tried to calm himself, but inside, an internal circuit board seemed to be sparking and spitting.

He managed a breath.

Then, bubbling from the depths of his being rose something familiar. And, although COVID had muffled its presence, this core value of loyalty and responsibility returned with a new clarity.

Jack recalled the veterans in his family, and how they had stepped up. Hadn't he seen the photos in the family album, and heard the stories? There was the Civil War Pennsylvania enlistment record for his great-great-grandfather, Francis McGlohin. And, when Francis was only fifteen years old, he had left Donegal, enlisting as a mercenary soldier in the Crimean War. This boy, younger than he was now, had traveled to Odessa. With the money he earned from this venture he had paid for his family's passage on a ship to America.

Then Jack recalled the photo of Joseph, his great grandfather, dressed in the white uniform of a naval officer in World War Two.

Jack imagined entering a battlefield. Images of Gettysburg came to mind. He'd seen the photos. They had served, despite their fear.

Now, the planet was at stake. And it was *his* turn.

Jack understood climate was the world war of his generation. This battlefield looked different from other conflicts, without foxholes or conventional weapons. Rather, the instigators remained hidden in their offices, up in silvery skyscrapers. Battle plans filled their computers designed to dismantle environmental regulations, or extract natural resources to maximize profits for a select few.

Jack knew the average citizen was also to blame, ignoring conservation and recycling, and by failing to vote for candidates who supported climate measures. He thought of Charlie and Grace, and the air they would all breathe.

Then a wave of fear returned, and he pleaded with the brothers. "How am I supposed to do any of the things in that letter? In case you haven't noticed, I'm sixteen years old! I don't even have a driver's license!"

"No driver's license? That is surprising," said Max, shaking his head.

"All I know is we have this old book to give you, the *Anamchara Text*. It supposedly has some answers. We tried to read it, but it will not open. You will have to figure that out for yourself. But first, we need to show you where we live, so you can see how different life can be, compared with your soon-to-be gasping planet."

Jack now knew how Houdini felt under water and locked in chains. Next, he thought, they would be telling him about three fire branding dragons he would have to slay.

"So, explain how I'm supposed to neutralize this space traveling engineering genius, Dr. Marcov?" Jack asked.

"Look, we keep telling you, the Council made the choice. They didn't pick an army general. Or a Nobel Prize winner. They chose YOU. You will have the *Anamchara Text*. You will learn from some key people on your quest. We do not have the answers. We only have a single question. *'Will you step up?'* "

Jack considered his predicament.

A thought crossed his mind.

If he *could* muster the courage to accept this challenge, he'd be a hero. He might be a dead one. But he'd be remembered. For a moment he pictured his flag-draped coffin. Surrounded by Grace and his family, weeping. Sad, but proud of their patriot.

Then he became aware that Izzy was staring at him. Was he reading his thoughts?

Izzy frowned; Jack's cheeks reddened.

Jack tried to push away his dreams of glory. He had to focus.

Could he accept this challenge? It all boiled down to overcoming his doubt and finding his courage. Fears had always haunted him, been his *classic* nightmare. Not anger, not sadness ... fear. Jack always searched for certainty in situations. This was his life strategy for warding off worst case scenarios. But now, Jack felt he was cornered. Hurling through space, he had to decide.

Could he take on this responsibility? See it through? Sign on to a commitment of this magnitude? A quest? A dangerous scientist? That touched all his vulnerabilities?

Then he recalled Joseph Spencer, and how this man's life had mattered. The engineer had set up an environmental foundation and left scores of patents. Jack couldn't deny he had given plenty of lip service to climate concerns. He *wanted* to help... but without the danger part.

So, bottom line, the question remained. Would he live a consequential life?

Max and Izzy waited anxiously as Jack considered his answer to the Council.

Izzy whispered to Max in a worried tone. "What if he says no?"

Max squeezed his little brother's hand.

Jack would say later that it was loyalty, deep in his core, that tipped the scales. He realized that in small ways, he had been preparing for this moment all his life, practicing simple habits, like being on time, putting in the work, and taking on challenging tasks.

Then he had gotten COVID, and the infection had upended his life, steered him off his path. This seemed an opportunity to change direction, to return to his plans.

A look of resolve settled in Jack's eyes, as he thought of Joseph Spencer's words to *do the next right thing*. The moment felt like he was jumping off a cliff.

"Fine, I'll do it," said Jack.

The two little boys saluted him.

But as soon as these words were out of Jack's mouth, a tiny part of him began to waffle. There remained too many unknowns. So while Max and Izzy were confident that they had their guy, Jack noticed a sliver of doubt. He worried that Izzy might sense his hesitation, but the boy looked overjoyed.

So Jack realized that for now, anyway, he would have to live with this tension. He would see how far he could go.

Soon the glass cube slowed. Ahead, floating in space, Jack saw a gorgeous blue planet with green land masses. The north and south poles of the sphere glowed with a rosy light.

"We wanted to give you a tour of Sophia so you can see what sustainable life looks like," Max said.

Within minutes the craft floated over miles of rolling hills covered with fruit trees. Jack had never seen so many kinds of vegetation growing together on American farms.

A large mountain range loomed ahead, and Max explained that it was formed from composted materials. The peaks looked like a series of whipped cream cakes in a bakery window.

"Is that a ski resort?" Jack asked, his eyes widening.

"It is. Sophians vacation up there most of the year," said Max.

Then he steered the craft, veering around the left side of the mountain.

A glistening body of water rose on the horizon.

"Salt water from the ocean is sent up the mountaintop with those pumps," said Max, pointing at a silver tangle of pipes.

"Looks like your Niagara Falls. The force of gravity breaks the chemical bonds, desalinating the water. Then the water irrigates the crops," Izzy said.

"What powers the pumps?" asked Jack.

"Would you believe, squirrels, and rabbits?"

"What? That's like from a cartoon," said Jack.

"Yeah, well, it works. The woodland creatures are moving around anyway. When their paws hit the ground, sensors capture the energy. And we made this huge habitat designed for their pleasure."

"Also, we use solar, hydrogen power, fusion, and wind. And pipelines transport flood water to areas low on rainfall thousands of miles away," said Izzy, proudly.

Within minutes, the glass cube landed with a soft thump. The panel opened, and the boys jumped out.

"Watch your step, the lawn is still damp," said Izzy.

"Too late," Jack said as an icy chill raced up his body, his shoes soaked.

Izzy produced a canister that looked like a giant saltshaker. "Here, shake some of this over your shoes and socks."

Jack took the container and followed Izzy's directive. In moments, his feet were dry.

"Wow, that's good stuff. What's in there?"

"No clue...but my mom makes me carry it with me as I tend to find all the puddles," said Izzy.

"So, you guys have parents?" Jack asked with surprise. It seemed hard to imagine these independent beings belonging to a regular family.

"Of course we do, dummy," sassed Izzy.

"Hey, don't say *dummy*," Max said, "Not nice, remember?"

Izzy looked at his shoes, frowning.

Jack noticed that the boys' speech sounded less mechanical, and that they were using contractions. Maybe they were nervous when they first met him? Or he was acclimating to their speech pattern.

Jack was mesmerized by this place that looked as if a botanical garden had exploded with tree-sized flowers. Tall as sequoias, they towered over him, making him feel like a tiny being in a magical forest. He looked up through the umbrella sized petals that filtered the sunlight. The giant blossoms cast shapes on the ground around his feet. The light from the sky came from another sun. Jack couldn't be sure of the season.

The older boy led them over to a café, choosing a table with a view of the water. Robots with silver trays glided through the diners, serving meals prepared from the gardens. Jack stared at his plate filled with unusual foods. He took a bite.

For the first time in his life, Jack understood the word *ambrosia*. He would weigh a thousand pounds if he lived here. Sweet and savory didn't begin to cover it.

Mind bending, Jack thought. Space/time portals. Bunny powered irrigation. Tree-sized flowers …

Izzy, mind reading again it seemed, responded to his thoughts. "Yeah…space/time portals…it has something to do with parallel planes, but I can't explain it," said Izzy.

Jack knew Mike and Grace would be amazed. All this would be impossible to describe. Would his camera phone work?

But Izzy, reading the teen's thoughts, shook his head. Jack frowned. "You are freaking me out, little boy," said Jack.

The corners of Izzy's mouth began to tense and droop. Tears welled up in his eyes.

"Oh no, don't cry," said Jack.

Too late. Lines of tears streaked the little guy's face.

"Sorry, but it's weird to have someone reading your thoughts," said Jack.

But Izzy had already turned away sobbing.

"Don't worry about him. He needs to toughen up. So sensitive," Max said.

"He reminds me of my brother. Charlie freaks out if he can't find his stuffed rabbit. Or if he needs a nap," said Jack.

Max left to soothe Izzy with ice cream, which apparently also worked with kids on Sophia.

As Jack waited for the boys to return, he stood and surveyed the landscape. He considered the logistics of his current location. While he knew physics allowed for parallel planes, the distance he had traveled was impossible to process. This space/time leap made him think of a Super Mario game with the figure suddenly jumping up a level.

All this was disorienting, as if he was walking up walls and across ceilings.

"I'm *so* tired," said Jack when the boys returned with ice cream.

Izzy whispered in Max's ear that their visitor required a nap.

Max explained that travel through the portal increased fatigue and hunger, creating a jet lag so severe it caused a type of shock.

Max and Izzy each took one of Jack's arms.

Where were they taking him? But, too tired to protest, Jack followed along. He seemed to be swimming out of himself. So when he saw the bed, he collapsed on the fresh sheets, passing out as soon as his head hit the pillow.

It was not long before a dream unfolded, like gossamer wings opening a portal. Jack's body floated through space, until he found himself in a huge hall with a circular table. A carved inscription on the oak surface caught his eye.

For the Good of Humanity.

Shadowy figures dressed in brown robes materialized, and Jack recognized them from his textbooks. Winston Churchill, Harriot Tubman, John Lewis, Rumi, William Blake, George Washington, Ada Lovelace, Cezanne, Galileo, Rosalind Franklin, Marie Curie, Confucius, Albert Schweitzer, Martin Luther King, Alexander Hamilton, Siddhartha, Tesla, Sojourner Truth, Jonas Salk, Benjamin Franklin, Gutenberg, Francis of Assisi, Marconi, Abe Lincoln, Albert Einstein, Eleanor Roosevelt, Hildegard of Bingen, and Leonardo Da Vinci were a few of those assembled.

Then his gaze met the serious green eyes of Joseph Spencer. Elinor sat next to her husband. She smiled at Jack, but his mind filled with questions. The group began to speak with one voice, telling him that when the time was right, he would find the courage if he remained faithful. Along the way he would meet individuals who would advance his understanding.

"Why me?" asked Jack.

"Answers will come when the time is right."

A tall red-headed woman, wrapped in rose-colored silk, stepped forward. Resting her green eyes on Jack, she extended her arms toward him. A small vial of oil appeared above him, and she proceeded to pour something over his forehead. Jack tasted the oil, feeling a warmth fill his body. At that moment, the delegation faded, and Izzy appeared in the dream. The child bowed and gave him an engraved golden cylinder.

Jack noticed a quickening in his being, like he was walking into his true self. A fortifying substance coursed through his veins—an infusion of something? Then the dream faded away, and, rolling over, he fell back into a deep sleep.

When the sun came up, Jack found he was holding a gold cylinder. A series of engraved numbers on the metal surface caught his eye. Shaking off his sleepiness, Jack noticed he felt different... maybe more solid? And he was famished.

The boys sat around a breakfast table. An unusual woven mat rested under the plates. Izzy noticed Jack staring at the texture.

"So, do you like our table covering? It's modeled after shark skin so that it naturally repels germs. No need to launder," said Izzy.

The robot waiter appeared and served them waffles. After they finished the meal, Max checked the time and motioned it was time to go. They escorted Jack to the glass cube, and they all climbed aboard. The panel closed with a hiss. The cube levitated and then jetted up, leaving behind the beautiful planet Sophia. They flew in darkness until they slipped through the space/time portal.

Jack tried to broach the topic of the dream and his anointing by the woman in rose silk.

"Oh, yeah, she's the Druid Prophetess who sometimes serves as a muse," said Max.

Jack wondered for an instant if the boys were related to her. However, it seemed clear they had said all they were going to reveal. Jack showed the gold cylinder to the boys, but they only smiled, their eyes twinkling.

"What do the numbers mean?" asked Jack.

"Your first task, I guess," said Max. Then he picked up a huge book.

"OK, one more thing. The *Anamchara Text*. It should fit in your backpack. But good luck with opening it," he said.

And, with that, Max handed over the weighty looking volume.

Jack prepared to receive the heavy book. But shock registered when the massive volume weighed less than a lettuce leaf.

"What the...!"

"It's a surprise, isn't it? Something odd to remember us by. You see our periodic table is expanded...lots of cool materials with interesting properties," said Max.

"Look, there's earth," said Izzy, pointing down through the cube's glass floor.

Jack saw an astronaut's view of his home planet. From this distance the earth looked so gentle, so peaceful.

Then he worried. What if we land in a hostile country?

Izzy caught his eye, shaking his head.

"We'll land in the old tree. You'll see," said Izzy.

Jack shivered. That mind reading was so weird, so unsettling. Even creepier than the chirpy talking.

Izzy frowned.

Sorry, Jack thought. The emoji with the sheepish smile flashed in his mind.

Then he put the *Anamchara Text* and golden cylinder, in his backpack, taking extra care to zip the bag.

"There's Morningside. Prepare for landing," said Izzy.

Jack wrapped his arms around his center. The cube dropped like a duck shot out of the sky. But, just before landing, he sensed some flaps engage that slowed the final descent.

The glass vehicle fell into the old tree, with the branches rocking them back and forth in a tug of war. Finally, the rolling ceased.

Jack's head was spinning, his middle section flipping. Max slid open the panel, and the boys climbed down the ladder. They seemed fine, moving steadily as if they had just flown business class. Jack weakly hauled his backpack, following them down the rope ladder. Immediately he dropped to the ground, curled up on the grass, hugged his knees and closed his eyes.

Thank God. It's over. Balled up, his body seemed to be running a system's check to see if he really was all there.

After a few minutes, Jack got to his feet and looked around, but Max and Izzy had vanished, and the glass cube was gone!

Jack wobbled over to the mansion, trying to adjust his legs that felt jelly filled. He entered a porch door, making his way down a side hallway. A window was open, and he drew in a deep breath of air as he got his bearings. He heard voices.

Turning the corner, Jack found his mom, dad, Mike, and Grace. Charlie smiled sweetly from his stroller.

The large clock in the hall dinged the noon hour.

"Oh, there you are! Grace told us you went down a different hall, but that you'd find us. Anyone hungry?" Mr. Abernault smiled.

"Yeah...*here* I am," said Jack, reassuring himself, as much as to greet them.

His dad led them out to the driveway where they piled in the car and drove to the Deerpath Inn. Jack, still in shock, followed along into the restaurant. They settled in a corner booth with a high chair for Charlie, and focused on the menus. Jack drank from a pitcher of water the waitress had left, filling his glass multiple times.

The friendly waitress returned with her order pad ready.

"I'll have a Caesar salad," said Grace.

"Make that two, please," said his mom.

"Hmm...I could really go for a grilled cheese, and add some tomatoes," said Mr. Abernault.

"Yeah, same here, thanks," said Mike.

"Rice and vegetable bowl, with a side of potatoes," Jack said, closing his menu.

His mom gave him a look, but withheld commenting on this unusual choice.

The waitress smiled, taking their menus.

"Looks like somebody was thirsty."

She walked off with the empty water pitcher.

Thankfully, his friends went on for a full hour about all the amazing rooms at Morningside. Only Charlie seemed to notice his older brother seemed different. But they all left him alone. Maybe they figured he was overwhelmed by the visit to the estate. But he couldn't muster the energy to care what they thought.

Mike, oblivious to his friend's mood, now was talking about his sisters, a pair of scrappy girls. He described how dinner time was a nightly drama. Jack thought this sounded awful, getting an inkling of how his friend felt. After all, he only had this cute baby in his house.

Grace complained about her two younger brothers who spent a sizable amount of time looking for ways to bother her. But to Jack, because their problems took a different shape, his friends' lives sometimes looked easier. It could be annoying to be on alert for small items that Charlie might choke on. Gates and doors needed to be secured, and Jack found it tiresome to keep the noise down in case his brother was napping.

Shoveling in the rice dish, Jack hoped to bury the whole flying cube odyssey under a mountain of food. He started in on the loaf of bread, but suddenly the hastily eaten meal revolted, and Jack excused himself.

He found the restroom in the back and pushed open the door. He looked in the mirror and saw his pale face. He needed to get a grip. Pull it together. He knew if he started talking about the glass cube, his parents would take him to the closest emergency room.

Splashing more water over his eyes, he wondered if he could get through this day. He plastered a neutral look on his face and willed himself back to the table. As he made his way through the dining room, he saw his dad sign the tab and then slide his credit card into his wallet.

"All set?" Mr. Abernault asked the group.

They gathered their stuff, and filed out, wading through the tables filled with diners.

During the car ride home, Jack dropped off to sleep, exhausted and overwhelmed.

"I think he's coming down with something," his mom said.

"There's a bug going around. My sister had it last week," said Mike.

"Yeah, maybe. But what's with that bowl of green beans and rice?" Grace asked.

Charlie's eyes closed, and the car quieted for the remainder of the ride. The Abernaults dropped off Grace, and then took Mike home. When the car rounded the corner at Orrington Avenue, Jack awoke with a start.

"What a nice day," said his mom.

"Yeah, great," said Jack, but his voice didn't sound convincing even to his own ears.

They entered the house, and Jack took the steps two at a time up to his room. Soon he was dead to the world, after the shock of space travel and the Council's letter.

Four hours later, Jack awoke with a start. Could he tell his parents about his wild adventure? There was no way they would believe him. His parents were in the family room. Charlie was making headway in his efforts to stand.

"Oh my gosh. Get a photo of this. Is this cute or what?" said his mom.

His dad moved closer with the phone, clicking the shot, and then starting the video.

Sometimes it was hard to be a big brother. Turning around, he walked into the kitchen and made himself a sandwich. Then, as if an invisible linebacker had taken him down, his body craved his bed.

From the other room, he could still hear them fussing over Charlie.

Jack called out that he was going up to bed, but he didn't think his parents even heard him. He returned to his room. Flopping on his bed, he screamed into his pillow. His body felt heavy, as though he was still hurling through space. He pulled the covers over his head.

CHAPTER FOUR

Numbers

At seven the next morning, Jack awoke to the sounds of a crying baby. Flipping over in bed, his eyes landed on the golden cylinder.

He stared at it for a moment in confusion. Then, like an out-of-control eighteen-wheeler, the shock of the previous day hit. Jack gripped his mattress, as it all came back. The sensation of propelling through space returned with a vengeance, as his body felt caught in a speed trap.

"Why can't it all stop?" he begged his pillow.

However, the Council's challenge, the space travel with the two boys, dropped on him like a colossal anvil. Overwhelmed, he pulled his pillow around his head. Drawing up his knees, he curled into a ball.

Sometime later, Jack sat up in bed. The house was quiet now. Pulling on a sweatshirt, he hauled the backpack with the items from Sophia down the stairs. His parents were in the kitchen, and with the baby down for a nap, Jack had their undivided attention.

Could he tell them about his frightening experience? The burden of the events felt too heavy to carry on his own. Before he could decide, he found himself talking.

"So, I have to tell you something. But can you promise me you will just listen until I finish?" Jack asked.

"So *more* failing grades?" His dad looked angry.

"I wish," said Jack.

"WHAT!" said his dad.

His mother touched her husband's arm.

"Let the boy speak," she said.

"I'm freaked out enough," pleaded Jack.

"What then?" said Mr. Abernault, impatiently. "You're scaring your mother."

"You're the one who needs to settle down," said Jack's mom.

"Go ahead, honey. Just tell us," she said.

Her face, however, suggested she was running through all the possible troubles a teenage boy might be having.

Jack swallowed. "Yesterday morning, I had the most unbelievable, crazy experience that I'm still trying to process. And I don't expect you to believe this until you hear me out."

"After I left Mike and Grace in a hallway, I met two odd kids who I thought were playing Star Wars. I assumed they were the groundskeeper's kids. They talked funny, with clicks and chirps, and they claimed to be from another planet. They reminded me of when Grace and Mike and I would act out Star Wars all day long. So, of course, I played along. Anyway, I followed them outside. They were hiding in what seemed to be a glass treehouse, but when I entered, it jetted up millions of miles, through a space/time portal."

Jack's dad slammed his fist on the counter, his face flashed with anger.

"OK, right there! Stop! You're afraid to tell us you're failing. You're grounded for a month. Did you think telling some crazy story would get our sympathy, make us back down, so you can get that driver's license? Go to your room. Just because you have this estate does not mean you get to give up on school, COVID or no COVID," barked his dad.

"I *knew* you couldn't just listen. Don't you think I *know* this sounds crazy? But here's the thing, I was given two items that will prove what I'm saying is true. The fact is..." Jack drew in a deep breath. "...I visited the planet Sophia."

Lifting his backpack off the floor, he unzipped it, pulling out the gold engraved cylinder and the large volume. It was the unexpected weight of the *Anamchara Text* he knew provided evidence of his bizarre story.

"Here, take this," and he handed the book to his dad.

"What the ...!" Jack's dad exclaimed.

His dad's expression changed from anger into disbelief as his arms estimated the impossible lightness of the text.

Jack's mom took the book. Surprise flooded her face. "Whatever is this made from?"

"Sophia has new materials...an expanded periodic table. I told you. I went to another planet. *Now* do you believe me?" Jack asked.

They were quiet, clearly trying to make sense of what they'd just heard and experienced.

"I'll tell you the whole story. But look at this other thing I got," said Jack.

They examined the gold cylinder.

"This looks like solid gold. It's worth a small fortune. What do those numbers mean?" asked his dad.

"I don't know...yet," said Jack. He felt he was finally gaining the upper hand. "So NOW. Can you two just listen?" he said.

"I have to say this reminds me of that incident at O'Hare airport back in 2006. Remember, those airline pilots witnessed a flying disc that jetted up, punching a hole in the clouds. It happened right above one of the terminal gates. People reported seeing a circle of blue sky left in its wake. CNN and NPR covered it," said his mom.

Jack's dad lifted the *Anamchara Text* again, too confused to comment.

His parents sat dumbfounded as Jack described the encounter with Max and Izzy; meeting the old woman in the maze, the ride in the glass cube to Sophia, the Council's challenge, the Anamchara Text, and the engraved golden cylinder.

Jack hesitated now. Afraid of confessing the most disturbing part.

About Vincent Marcov.

Hearing about a genius rogue scientist who used high tech methods would be terrifying.

But Jack had to get out the whole story. It felt like now or never, and the words rushed out of him, as if he was being exorcised.

After he finished, his parents sat slumped on the sofa.

His dad finally rose and walked over to his desk. Shuffling papers in the drawer, he pulled out a document from Spencer's law firm.

"We got this letter after you signed the estate documents," said his dad.

"The letter predicted that you might find yourself at the center of major cultural advances." His dad waved the letter in the air.

"We certainly had no idea about space travel or a dangerous scientist. We assumed it meant you would serve on some cultural boards. What you're telling us changes everything. Spencer should have left his estate to a government agency, somebody with security, or to someone who actually owns a spacecraft," his dad said.

This was bad. His parents were feeling guilty now for not being more careful. But they should've listened to him. Hadn't he questioned the inheritance? Repeatedly?

Jack could see his parents felt hoodwinked, wishing they had been more diligent. He couldn't help but feel sorry for them.

"So," Jack summed up weakly, "*not* a bad grade report."

His parents moved in, wrapping their arms around him. When his parents finally released him, he could see the worry in their eyes, for him and for the family.

Jack sat with his parents, feeling overwhelmed. How could this have happened? They felt they had been tricked. Who was this Spencer, really?

"The challenge I accepted is a done deal. I said *yes*." Jack said. "I can't get out of it, Really none of us can. The planet is at risk," said Jack.

The ceramic globe sat in the corner, a birthday present to Jack from his grandparents. Was it glaring at them?

Mr. Abernault looked pensive as he knew that a clock was ticking on their planet. Some said the earth had twenty years, others ten, but if the polar ice cap melted, all bets were off.

And he was aware of growing evidence that the universe was not a closed box. Parallel universes were possible according to string theory. Lurking in these corners of the universe could be pretty much anything.

Dr. Marcov's sinister interference explained factions in the population who ignored science, in favor of spin and greed. This rogue scientist, maybe the most powerful man on the planet, sounded downright terrifying. Now that Marcov could escape to Sophia, there was nothing to stop him, with his satellites and latest technologies at his disposal.

Jack looked at his own arsenal, a fat book that weighed next to nothing, and a golden trinket with some numbers. And the stupid book wouldn't even open.

"I'm supposed to figure out how to open the text and to find out what the numbers mean." said Jack.

Jack had hoped to get some relief by telling his parents. However, sharing had only made it all *more* real, adding a deeper and darker weight... his family's safety.

The next morning, Jack sat on the edge of his bed, examining the numbers engraved on the golden cylinder. What could they mean? Maybe a bike ride would help clear his mind. He went out to the garage and got on his bike.

But dark thoughts rode alongside him, like a demon on a speed racer. On some level, his parents probably blamed him for putting the family in danger. And he felt tricked. First by Spencer. Then by the two bird-like kids.

The sign for the Skokie Lagoons loomed ahead. This collection of ponds, northwest of town, was created in the 1930s to drain swamp land. Following the bike path, Jack breathed easier as he rode into the forest, the foliage muffling the sounds of civilization. But soon the chirping of the birds brought back the memory of Max and Izzy's weird talk. And the line of trees reflected in the water mirrored an upside-down version, like the oddities he'd seen on Sophia.

The sights and sounds in the forest were setting him off, taking him back to another galaxy. So when Jack encountered an unfamiliar bend in the waterway's trail, he took a wrong turn and rode deeper into the woods.

Finally, he stopped to check his phone, but there were no service bars. He was lost.

* * *

Through the open window, Margaret Mason felt the sun's warmth as she scrubbed the sink for a second time. A line of glasses sat on the sideboard waiting for the dishtowel that hung on the hook. Her jaw set, Margaret scoured the counters. Pulling open a drawer, she frowned at two wayward spoons. After straightening them, she lined up the cookbooks. Finally, she grabbed the mop, thrusting it like a bayonet, attacking an invisible film on the kitchen floor.

Margaret surveyed her work, training her eye on the windowpane. A smudge highlighted by the sun's rays caught her eye. She sprayed and polished, stepping back to check the glass.

While she worked, she noticed someone approaching the house from the edge of the forest. Must be the postman, *finally*. She wiped her hands on her apron, feeling her irritation rise.

* * *

Coming out of the trees, Jack found a brick walk that led to a cottage. Who lived in such a remote area? The place looked like the home of industrious elves.

What if he met an elf this morning? After his recent encounter with Max and Izzy, there was no telling. And how had he gotten lost? And in a forest? This couldn't be good. But the choice now was getting more lost, or trusting that he might find help from the people, or elves, who lived here.

Jack walked his bike slowly toward the cottage, still considering if he should turn back. Then he saw a girl about his age in a checked apron standing in an open door. He was taken aback when she hollered at him.

"You're late! Every time we have a substitute, the schedule is off. Don't you know I've got chores. This poor service just won't do," she sniffed.

Then the girl seemed to settle down. "Oh, I see you're a kid, like me, so YOU can't be the mailman."

Surprised by the scolding from this bossy girl, Jack said hesitantly, "Uh…Hi?"

"What are you doing way out here?" asked the girl.

"I'm lost. I was trying to make a call, but there's no cell service in the lagoons," said Jack.

"You *should* have thought of that possibility before you came traipsing up the lagoon trail, said Margaret."

What a nag! He didn't need this. He'd turn around and leave.

However, Margaret Mason, relenting, told him that he could stand in the yard and try for cell service.

Jack pulled out his phone. Nothing... maybe a dead zone in the cell network?

Margaret's dad walked in the garden.

"Who do we have here?" asked the man, carrying an armful of books.

Margaret explained about the cell phone.

"How did you get way out here?" he asked.

Didn't these people ever go on a bike ride? At least they weren't elves. And they didn't chirp. But what's the big deal? He wasn't trying to sell them anything. Not very nice. No wonder they live way out here in the sticks.

Jack said, "Well, that's the thing.... I was riding my bike, and then I got lost ...so tried to make a call, but...no cell service."

After faltering through this explanation, Jack's mouth was dry, and he tried to clear his throat.

"Let's get you some water," said Mr. Mason.

They ushered him into the cottage and told him to sit on a wooden pew in the hall.

As he waited, Jack saw the living room through an arched doorway. An embroidered sampler hung prominently on the wall, with an inspirational message ...

There must always be room for improvement.

Windows with starched curtains circled the room. A hint of vinegar hung in the air, and floors shined with a coat of wax.

Not a speck of dust sat anywhere. Jack thought this orderly space, must be the cleanest house he had ever seen. He figured the Masons must not have any younger kids or sloppy pets. He wondered what Charlie and his crackers would do to this place in ten short minutes.

Margaret returned with a glass of water. Then Mr. Mason confirmed that he didn't have cell service either.

"I'll draw you a map so you can ride back out of the lagoons," said Mr. Mason.

"That would be great: thanks," said Jack.

Mr. Mason left to get paper. Jack drank his water. To make small talk, he turned to Margaret. "So where do you go to school?" Jack asked.

"I'm home schooled. Regular classes are too easy. I like math because there's a single correct answer. Subjects like English Lit have too many interpretations and I find that unacceptable. And my parents both teach math." Margaret said.

Mr. Mason returned, handing Jack a paper with a crudely drawn map. "Here you go," said the father.

Then it dawned on Jack. This family, devoted to numbers, might solve his problem. So he pulled out the gold engraved cylinder. Showing it to the pair, he said, "Any idea what these numbers might mean?"

Mr. Mason and Margaret looked at the odd trinket, seeing eleven digits.

"Well, now *this* is interesting," said Mr. Mason.

Margaret closed her eyes and seemed to be running through some possibilities in her head.

"Let's write them down." She handed Jack a pen and paper.

Jack scribbled them on the sheet.

"Could be a formula? A phone number? Or a lockbox at a bank? A combination to a storage unit? Birthdays?" Margaret said.

Suddenly, Mr. Mason spoke. He sounded upset. "I know what this means!"

Margaret looked alarmed. "So what do the numbers mean?" Margaret asked.

Her father looked at her, pointing to the map on the wall.

"Those numbers describe the coordinates, latitude and longitude, of OUR HOUSE!"

Jack looked at the father and daughter with confusion.

"What? I had no idea!" Jack said.

Just then they were startled by a large *bang!*

A giant book had fallen off the top shelf of a bookcase. Embossed on the leather cover of the volume was the title, *Pythagoras*, and rolling out of the book's spine, a gold cylinder, identical to Jack's, landed beside his shoe.

"Now, how did that get there?" asked Margaret, astonished.

They examined the engraving on the new cylinder, finding a different set of numbers etched into the surface. More coordinates? Mr. Mason handed the gold trinket to Jack. It seemed the man's anger had changed to amazement.

"It seems no mistake that you ended up at our door this morning. Unlikely, but possible, given the law of probability," Mr. Mason said.

Jack felt the cold metal of the cylinder. It now dawned on him that the Masons must be the first stop on his quest.

He felt the hair on the nape of his neck stand on end.

Mr. Mason's phone rang. When he saw the caller's name on the display, worry crossed his face. He answered. Listening, he responded to the person on the other end in a low voice. "Yes sir, I understand. Right away, sir." Mr. Mason said. He put down the phone.

"Can I polish those cylinders for you?" said Mr. Mason, his voice cracking.

The golden tubes looked fine to Jack. However, cleaning and shining things up seemed a high priority... a Mason family value. So, he handed them over.

A few minutes later, the father returned.

"Here you go, no more *cosmic crud*." Mr. Mason said heartily.

Jack put the two cylinders in his pocket.

Meanwhile, Margaret turned pages in the *Pythagoras* book. Jack looked over her shoulder and saw an interesting triangle, laced with dissecting lines and contained in a circle. The diagram was labeled *enneagon*, with nine points. Somehow, it reminded Jack of a sand painting he'd seen at the Field Museum. He knew that for thousands of years people fashioned circles, mandalas, to contemplate and to open up their minds.

"Pythagoras made some interesting speculations about the nature and relationship of things," said Mr. Mason.

"Can I take a photo of this diagram?" asked Jack.

They nodded, and he snapped a shot of the image. Then Mr. Mason's phone dinged with a text message. He frowned.

"We have to go. Margaret, in the car. Now!"

Mason's voice was urgent and demanding.

Margaret hurried out the door. Jack followed.

Jack overheard the girl ask her dad if the buzzing had started again. Jack didn't hear much of the father's response, but he did catch the word *nanobot*.

Father and daughter drove off, dust billowing down the lane.

Jack got on his bike, feeling shaky. At least there had been no elves to deal with or space travel. However, the mention of nano-bots, now *that* was concerning. He remembered an issue of *Scientific American* that described how these miniscule capsules entered the bloodstream and delivered medicine to a specific body part. But in the wrong hands, they could re-program parts of the brain.

Jack had sensed something "off" about the Masons, so rigid, and obsessed. Their place reeked of perfectionism, but nanobots took his concerns to a whole new level.

However, right now, Jack needed to find his way out of this forest. He still had no phone service, but he checked the hand-drawn map that showed three pine trees with an arrow to the right. He scanned the forest and spotted the trio of giant evergreens. Riding toward them, he veered right, and soon the lagoon came into view. Then he found the main bike path.

Would all the people on his quest be as weird? Then his thoughts returned to the nanobots. Scary scenarios looped through his mind. What if he was attacked by them? Would he even know? Had it already happened? He pushed hard on the pedals. He needed to put some distance between himself and the freaky clean house in the woods.

Soon he found he was riding through a neighborhood lined with mid-century homes and kids on bikes. His thoughts turned to the Council's instructions. Had he followed their direction to listen to the Masons? Maybe, he thought, but maybe not. He had heard the words, but had he really "gotten their beat"? His gut intuition still felt murky. Fear scampered around in his head, and anxiety was growing in his chest.

Finally, he passed the signpost for Evanston, and turned down Lincoln Street. Although this was a familiar route, he had the uncomfortable feeling of being watched, sensing eyes on his back. However, when he looked around, he saw no one there. Pedaling faster, he fought off the paranoia.

When he reached his street, he saw his mom unloading groceries. His dad appeared and Jack joined them, hauling brown bags into the house. While his dad deposited the milk in the fridge, Jack grabbed a bag of chips, tearing open the top. The strangeness of the forest house had creeped him out, but the crunch of the salty chips somehow felt grounding.

"Well, it seems my quest has begun. And I heard about nanobots," said Jack.

"I don't want you chasing down any more clues. This is just too dangerous," said Mr. Abernault.

"But I promised," said Jack.

"You were kidnapped; it doesn't count," said his dad.

"Space travel, aliens, rogue scientist, and now nanobots!" his mother said.

"Yeah, I totally freaked," said Jack.

Jack's dad said, "The last thing you need is a quest, but we need some answers. I'm looking into how to pull in the authorities. Problem is, if I tell the wrong person, or go to the wrong agency, I could have my security clearance at work pulled, maybe lose my job, and in the end, not be believed by anyone. All we really have is the impossible weight of that book. For all we know, the government might have some new material, recently discovered, that could explain the book's weight. So that's not enough proof. Not yet."

Jack understood this situation could ruin their lives. It was all dangerous. But could he abandon his quest? Go back on his promise to the Council?

So, rather than confront his dad, Jack changed the focus of the conversation.

"Yeah, it was weird how this Mason guy recognized the numbers on the golden cylinder as location coordinates of their cottage," said Jack. "And look at this image from the *Pythagoras* book. Reminds me of those sand paintings at the museum."

"Art often predicts advances in science. You know I always loved how Cubism forecast the splitting of the atom," said his mom.

"One can't deny the artists have a special vision," his dad said.

"William Blake certainly was tuned in to something beyond the rational, with his poetry and mystical drawings," his mom said.

It had worked. He'd avoided a showdown. His parents were off on another tangent—the connection between art and science.

Jack backed out of the kitchen and went to his room. He pulled out the golden tube that had fallen out of the *Pythagoras* book. Then he entered the numbers etched on the surface into Google maps. The pin dropped off the coast of New Zealand!

"Well, that's not happening," said Jack to himself.

It seemed it wasn't just his parents that wanted him to stop the quest. This new location was on the other side of the world and underwater.

Hitting a dead end, Jack turned to the old text that Max had given him. Maybe he'd have better luck with the book.

He did a web search of Anamchara. It was a Gaelic term, sometimes appeared as *anam cara*, meaning *soul friend*.

Soul friend, he repeated to himself. He'd take one of those.

That night Jack slumbered under his down comforter. As midnight ticked away, a dream began to play out on the stage of his sleeping mind. At first he was annoyed, hoping to find a new episode of *Jack Loves Grace*. He tossed in frustration, but his dream resisted, insisting on another story line.

Jack found himself in a room with oversized doors that opened to a balcony. Shadowy shapes began to materialize. Jack recognized his great grandparents, great aunts, and uncles from the family photo album. All of them had Jack's green eyes. They gathered around a table with the *Anamchara Text* resting in the center on a fine linen cloth.

Suddenly, the table whirled, and when it stopped all his relatives had transformed into children. They looked like their photos from an even older family album. The kids danced around, happy to be young again, without stiff arthritic joints.

"Look at this mess. Hand me a dust cloth." Aunt Betty glared at the text.

Great Grandma Louise served lemonade, making her rounds with the pitcher. "Opening this book may take a while and I want everyone comfortable," she said sweetly.

Uncle John consulted a manual for effective ways to open an old book without damaging the spine.

Uncle Francis worried that Dr. Marcov might find them, and so he wanted to call an adult for protection.

Each offered a different approach for solving the problem of the sealed book. Then his Uncle Tom stepped up.

"Prepare to be dazzled. Watch this!" And with a flourish, he jerked the tablecloth out from under the book.

The children clapped with delight. However, Aunt Betty snapped at them. "Cut that out."

Grandfather Mike ignored Betty and prepared to hurl the book over the balcony to break the seal. But the kids blocked his path. Jack knew Mike eventually learned to control his temper, becoming a labor union leader who could stare down any team of adversaries.

After Mike settled down, Uncle Richard took a turn. Known in the family for his low energy and calm personality, he yawned. Then he suggested the kids all close their eyes and just breathe. Nothing else had worked, and they knew Jack's dream was about to end, so they all closed their eyes. Taking in deep, slow breaths, they all slowly exhaled.

Four long minutes passed.

Then Richard reached over and lifted the book's cover.

The children clapped, looking impressed.

The volume was written in a strange language.

Then the letters scrambled, settling in a fancy scroll, as if they had been penned by a wizard.

Jolted out of his dream, Jack sat up in bed. Realizing it was still night, he rolled over and went back to sleep. Soon, Grace, riding a chestnut horse, galloped into his dream. He climbed up behind her and they rode a short distance, into a forest.

Hours later the morning sun blasted into his room. He awoke feeling groggy, and he was halfway down the steps when he looked in the dining room. Open on the table, sat the *Anamchara Text*.

"Hey, come down here. The old book is open!" He called up the stairwell.

His parents marveled at the mystery of the open book.

Jack described his dream. Not the one with Grace.

"That's incredible," said his mom.

"Yup, Cousin Richard, did it. After all the others tried," Jack said.

"Wonder why it was only your mom's side of the family?" asked his dad.

"Hmm…that's odd, but they all had the green eyes," said Jack.

His mother shared that many scientific solutions happened because of clues that appeared in dreams, and in half-awake states.

Jack carefully turned the first page. The paper had an oily parchment texture, like vellum.

"Oh, no. Some of the text is missing," said his mom.

"Wonder if the space travel affected the book," said his dad.

Only phrases here and there were legible.

Jack began to read aloud.

"*…all people, by the age of seven …*"

Then the text faded. On the next page, Jack saw the phrase...
acting like a taproot... then more faded text.

"This is pretty useless. I can't even read it," said Jack.

"Maybe it's for the best. This is all way too dangerous. We don't want you involved," said his mom.

"OK, but I'll explode if I try to hide this from Mike and Grace," said Jack.

Jack could see his dad's reaction.

"I understand you want to share this experience with your friends. But do you think they can keep a secret this remarkable? A secret, that if it gets out, could put us in more danger?"

"Yes, when they understand it's about the climate, they won't say a word," said Jack.

Jack's mom was a psychologist, and she knew that asking her son to carry this secret about Sophia might be too much. He needed a support system, but in this case, there was too much at stake.

"Your dad and I have already discussed this. I'm sorry but you can't tell them. It's too dangerous for our family, and you would be risking their safety as well," said his mom.

"OK, I understand," said Jack.

But he didn't.

Jack knew he would burst if he didn't tell Mike and Grace. And he also knew he was going to need help.

That evening his friends came over after dinner, expecting an evening of video games. Jack suggested they take a walk over to the park. He couldn't have his parents overhearing anything.

When they reached the bleachers near the field house, Mike and Grace heard a story that eventually would turn their lives upside down.

CHAPTER FIVE

Say What?

" *Very* funny, Jack. What makes you think we need to hear a stupid story like that?" said Grace.

"We're not eight years old anymore. And I thought Grace was the one who made up stuff to rile her parents," said Mike.

"OK... Hold on a minute," Jack said.

He unzipped his backpack.

Mike and Grace looked confused.

"You've been spending too much time on video games. I've heard of this happening, a dude just gets sucked in. Next thing you know...delusional," Grace said, folding her arms across her chest.

Mike's expression showed he was wondering if Jack had suffered a head injury or a mental breakdown of some kind? The inheritance, the COVID, and all the attention at the school maybe had been too much.

"You'll see. I'm *not* crazy," said Jack.

His eyes were gleaming, too brightly maybe. His speech sounded pressured, and so not really helping his argument.

Jack handed the old text to Grace. As expected, she prepared for a heavy volume.

"What the hell!" she said.

Mike took the book. "Woah!" he said. "You're scaring us, Jack."

"That scientist has nanobots and satellites? And the planet is even in more danger than we knew!" said Grace.

"I know. But I need you to promise that you won't tell *anyone*. My parents want me to drop the whole thing. Not say a word. Because if this gets out, we all could be targeted. They could lose their jobs. And they don't think you two can keep a secret. They told me not to tell you. Understand?" Jack said.

The teens looked stunned and afraid.

Maybe he shouldn't have told them.

"OK," said Mike slowly.

Jack could see his friend's heart pounding in his neck.

"Yes, yes, of course. We won't tell," said Grace, her eyes widening.

Jack continued, "I knew I could trust you guys. See, it's like I'm in a science fiction film that won't end." Jack said

"Are you at least OK *physically*?" asked Grace.

"Physically, yes. But it's like I have a parallel existence. Like I'm on a train, and *another* train is riding on another set of rails, but I'm on *that* train, too," Jack said.

Grace said she had noticed his odd behavior, but had chalked it up to his feelings about the inheritance, and worries about his grades, and not having his driver's license. She could never have guessed Jack had traveled to another galaxy!

"Explain it again. We want to hear everything," Grace said, taking his hand.

"We're here for you," said Mike.

So Jack told them again about his meeting with the space kids, the Council's letter, and Vincent Marcov. His friends were astounded that this odyssey began moments after Jack turned into the plain doorway on that first visit to Morningside.

Finally, Grace sat back. "Wow. After all our talk about the climate, your mission calls for *real* action. Any help you need, I'm *all* in," she said, her eyes full of fire.

To hear Grace describe the Council's challenge as a *mission* surprised Jack. But it *was* a mission, wasn't it? For an instant, the image of Grace and him dressed in tall boots and hero capes flashed in his mind. He blinked; after all, this was *not* Comic Con.

Mike, however, looked uncomfortable. Finally, he spoke up. "See, I'd like to help, but this sounds *really* dangerous. We could all end up dead, put our families at risk. My sisters are a pain, but I can't put them in the crosshairs of a crazy genius. I'll help you with logistics and computer stuff. But the dangerous parts, no way." Mike looked down.

"Hey, we can't let Jack do this alone. And we're already in trouble. Wake up, Mike. There's no place to hide. The climate is on life support," said Grace.

Jack intervened. "Look, guys, I don't want to be in this mess either. And I don't expect you to put yourself in danger, Mike. Just keep this a secret," said Jack.

"Thanks for understanding. And, I promise I won't tell anyone. They wouldn't believe it anyway," said Mike.

Grace wrapped her arms around Jack, and he closed his eyes. Her support gave him hope that there might be a path through this minefield of trouble and chaos.

The kids returned to Jack's house. His parents were already upstairs in bed.

The mantel clock dinged ten o'clock.

Jack watched his friends walk down the street. Grace was ready to take it all on. But Mike, clearly spooked, looked over his shoulder as he passed under a streetlight.

* * *

Wednesday 9 a.m. Chicago Loop

Sitting in his office overlooking Millennium Park, John Franklin shuffled papers, confident that he would close a deal this morning that would make his career. The plan to marshal the central banks into green investments felt like nothing short of genius.

His friend, Bob McCaffrey, had come up with an idea that plotted out a profitable transition from an oil-based system to a green economy. John had purchased the idea from Bob at a fraction of its worth. Then Franklin went one step further, failing to pay several installments.

John set out to gather venture capitalists and environmental experts. The business plan resolved the objections that had stalled reform for decades. A cascade of investments, cleverly situated to benefit the environment, moved money through a series of industries. John's only problem remained the worry that Bob McCaffrey might interfere if he got wind of the project's significance. Knowing he had failed to compensate his friend according to the terms of their original deal, he hoped that by the time Bob found out, it would be too late. He wondered now why he had chosen to cheat his friend over a relatively small sum of money.

At ten o'clock the board room filled with the businessmen and scientists. The meeting proceeded smoothly and by eleven o'clock, with the papers signed, they were about to adjourn. Just then, the board room doors flew open. Bob McCaffrey stormed in with his lawyer, slamming the cease-and-desist order on the table.

"Gotcha! You snake," hissed McCaffrey.

"There's been a misunderstanding here," said Franklin. However, his scarlet face betrayed him.

The individuals in the room expressed shock about the fraud accusation. Then members of the press arrived, and the businessmen and scientists scurried down a back staircase to avoid seeing their faces on the evening news.

Down in his black SUV, Vincent Marcov grinned at the ease of derailing this project. All it had taken was a phone call to McCaffrey, and a tip to the *Sun Times*. Not to mention the nanobots delivered to John Franklin's condo in a pizza. Soon the tiny bots worked their magic on Franklin. They entered his bloodstream, turning on the deceit in his brain that lay just under the talent for deal making. The environmental plan, now in ashes, would have changed the future, offering a road to a brighter, safer world. And Vincent Marcov knew he could not sit by and watch *that* happen.

* * *

The following Monday at lunch, Mike left the table to buy a bag of chips. Jack took the opportunity to ask Grace if she wanted to take the train up to the Lake Forest house over the weekend.

"We should've gone last week, when we were on break, but the next few days are going to be warm. We can bring our bikes on the train. It'll be fun. We can look over some of Spencer's files. I've got the password for his computer. And we can swim after," said Jack, trying to keep his voice steady.

"I've got debate practice at 8:00, but then I guess I could go. Doesn't Mike have allergy appointments on Saturday?"

"I think he's got some family thing," Jack said, trying to sound casual.

"OK, but I can't stay too long. I'm meeting up with Jimmy at seven," said Grace.

"Oh sure, we can be back by five," said Jack.

What was this Jimmy thing? Never thought she'd go for that type. Dopey grey eyes. Wonder if they've gone out before. She never said anything.

Then Grace said she would meet Jack at the station.

* * *

Saturday morning, they stood on the train platform with their bikes. They heard the rumble of the approaching train, warm air blasting them as the giant engine glided into the station. They locked the bikes, and found their seats. The Midwest on a day like this was magical, the air brimming with possibility. Through the train windows, they saw branches with baby green leaves beginning to pop with fresh color.

Within the hour, Grace and Jack stood in the main hall at Morningside.

"This place is *so* amazing," said Grace.

"Come on, let's get to work," said Jack, thinking of a revised plan for the day based on the *Jimmy* information.

"Do you think we'll meet any little space boys?" Grace asked.

"I sure hope so. But if they take us for a spin, you might not make it back for Jimmy."

Grace laughed.

They headed up stairs. When they reached the second floor, they opened large double doors, and entered an office paneled in teak. Woven screens filtered the light, casting soft shadows on the carpet. A collection of Japanese ceramics glinted in the sunlight.

"Someday I want to go to Japan," said Grace, running her fingers on a vase's rim.

"I'll take you," Jack said nonchalantly.

"That's a date," she said.

Jack moved toward the desk with a ring of keys.

"Hopefully one of these is going to fit," he said.

The second key turned in the lock, and Jack pulled a laptop out of the drawer.

Grace watched as he entered, *Smogdiamond1#*, the password provided by Spencer's attorney. In a flash, green leaves flooded the screen. A file labeled *Smog Diamond* rested in the center.

"This looks promising," Jack tapped the icon.

"Cool password, but what's a *smog diamond*? Sounds like the name of a band," said Grace.

"Here we go. Into the mind of Joseph Spencer," said Jack.

First up, he found a design for pulling carbon dioxide out of the air, showing a tower with propellers. Powered by solar and wind, the structure sucked carbon dioxide down a piping system, and into an underground facility. Pressurized air pollutants transformed into smog diamonds.

"Wow, that's so cool. I've never heard of that before." Grace said.

"Look, there's an attachment," said Jack, clicking on the file. The pdf showed a necklace with a single smog diamond.

"That's gorgeous, so simple. Even I'd wear that."

"Well, maybe *Jimmy* will get you one," said Jack.

She swatted him.

"His mom hired me to tutor him in math, but maybe I can get her to pay me in diamonds," she said.

Jack's jealousy evaporated.

Clicking on another file, he found other uses for captured CO_2; making soda carbonation and gravel.

But Jack now was finding it hard to pay attention. He sensed Grace leaning in to see the screen. He could smell the scent of flowers coming off her hair.

Grace seemed unaffected by their closeness as she clicked on an image. This file described the Mississippi Delta with sea grass that functioned as a natural filter for CO_2. A second photo showed millions of clams absorbing ocean pollution.

"Look at all these inventions. There seem to be patents attached to these designs," said Jack.

Grace pulled open a long drawer that housed drawings of faux plants on reforested land.

"I've never heard of mechanical trees. Look, they perform photosynthesis," said Grace.

"Here's a water conservation project. Giant ponds with floating balls reduce evaporation. And another design for harvesting heavy metal rocks from the ocean floor," she added. "I saw a TV show about how those rocks power electric car batteries."

Jack found a satellite design that tracked methane leaks.

Grace was so close now. He wondered if he should make a move.

Then he hesitated. What if he'd only imagined her interest in him? Maybe that kiss that Mike had interrupted was *a one-off?* What if she got mad? He'd feel like a fool.

Unaware of Jack's dilemma, Grace moved the mouse on the laptop, opening another file labeled "brightening."

"Look at this. A man-made cloud produced by spraying particles above the coral reef. The design is based on jet printer technology," said Grace.

"The particulates capture the sun's light before it hits the ocean's surface. Like a giant marine umbrella protecting the reefs," said Jack.

"So amazing. A group of retired scientists in Palo Alto, California worked on this project, because they hoped to save the climate for their grandchildren," said Grace.

Jack pushed her hand aside, taking over the mouse. He wondered if she sensed the tension.

But she was focused on reading about the Gates foundation. Their project used a field of mirrors trained on a point that heated materials to intense degrees. This produced a way to manufacture cement or steel in a carbon neutral process.

Another discovery showed a fungus that consumed radioactivity. It seemed Spencer planned to add this fungus to clean up nuclear dump sites.

"Wow. Here's a special recipe for animal feed that reduces methane produced by cows."

"Wish Mike was here. He'd have a fart joke about the cows for sure," said Grace.

"Oh yeah," agreed Jack.

Then he opened another file.

"Look at this," Jack said.

"Here's an amazing project that uses 200 lasers aimed at two atoms. It creates fusion, a limitless source of clean energy," said Jack.

"It seems they recently made a breakthrough, but they need to build a generator to make it work for the energy grid," said Jack.

She read over his shoulder. "A super PAC political group that lobbies for sustainable technologies …"

"I wonder how many of these designs were ever built?" Jack asked.

"Let's Google them." Grace said.

They looked up *smog tower, smog diamonds, mirror technology, cloud to protect the reef, harvesting seabed, diet for cows to reduce methane, radioactive eating fungus, satellite detecting methane,* and *seagrass riverbed.*

"*Woah.* They're *all* here," she said.

"They've *all* been built?" Jack sat, confused.

"Yup." Grace said.

"Why haven't we heard of them? And why aren't they available in more places?" Jack asked.

"Some powerful folks don't want change. Remember Greta Thunberg, the environmentalist from Sweden? She talked about this problem." Grace said.

"She's amazing. Speaking truth to power," said Jack. "And so focused, the advantage of being neurodivergent."

"Let's wind up in here. Enough to think about for one day," said Jack, checking his phone.

"We can swim and then grab lunch near the train station afterwards." Jack said.

"Great," she said.

They made their way to the wing that housed the pool, and Jack pulled open the doors. The sunlight hit the pool, and undulating shapes of silver, and star glints sparkled on the water's surface. An undercurrent sent another rush of geometric designs twirling in a stream, making the water appear to be dancing with the sunlight. Jack felt a rush of excitement, pulling his clothes off, down to his swim trunks.

Grace stripped down to a bikini that looked awfully like underwear and dove in the pool.

"So Grace, are you *trying* to make a move on me?" Jack said.

"Oh yeah. That's it," she splashed him.

Jack dove in, and feeling encouraged, began to splash her, working his way closer.

Grabbing her playfully, his instincts took over. His mouth found her lips. Embracing her tightly, he felt her return the kisses.

They moved to the edge of the pool.

A door slammed. "Oh, sorry, sir. Didn't know anyone was here today."

The two looked up, and pulled apart. The groundskeeper was backing away, out the door.

Grace laughed after the guy had gone. "Well, we just made his day, I'm sure."

But Jack was not amused. Why hadn't he messaged the groundskeeper? Should have seen that coming. *Bad*, bad planning. He was an idiot.

It was getting late and with the mood broken, they climbed out of the pool, toweling off with terrycloth robes.

Thirty minutes later at the station, they climbed back on the train, hauling the bikes through the doors. They ate their sandwiches and Jack put his arm around Grace's shoulders as the train headed south.

When they arrived back in Evanston, they rolled their bikes off in different directions. Jack felt happy. And he hadn't given a thought to Vincent Marcov or the nanobots for at least a few hours.

* * *

A week later

Jack sat in his room trying to study, but he couldn't seem to focus. Daydreaming about Grace and worried about Vincent Marcov, Jack's thoughts marched off in unproductive directions.

The words of the Council also haunted him. He sensed he had missed something. What was *the next right thing*? Had he listened to the Masons, learning all he could from his visit?

His quest had ground to a halt, and he couldn't read much of the *Anamchara Text*.

Lying on his bed, Jack closed his eyes, replaying the scene at the Mason's freakishly clean cottage.

Outside his bedroom door, he could hear a folk song drifting down the hallway.

Brrrrring….. Brrrrring

A ringing phone brought him back.

Suddenly, Jack sat up with the memory of Mr. Mason's ringing phone.

The man had been agitated after picking up the call. Jack remembered how a shift inside his body had signaled trouble. Was that his gut intuition?

Sun streamed through his window. He glanced over at the cylinder now glistening in the shaft of light.

Something was off.

Picking up the gold tube, he looked closely at the surface.

There was a distinct *difference* in the quality of the engraved numbers.

Why hadn't he noticed this before? The first three numbers were sharply etched, however the next two digits had right angles that didn't match the other grooves. These lines looked crudely scratched, turning number *ones* into number *fours!*

Writing down the new sequence, he opened his laptop, entering the new coordinates. The map zeroed in, locating a place in Rogers Park, not far from Jack's house!

He thought about how mad his parents would be if he followed this clue. Should he bring Mike and Grace? No, he decided, he'd go it alone.

* * *

The Next Morning   Rogers Park Neighborhood

The St. Ignatius Church tower cast a shadow on Lindy Simons as she made her way to the animal clinic. Fumbling with the keys, she juggled her shopping totes and entered the vestibule. Phillip, the pet rabbit, hopped over and nuzzled her frizzy ankle socks. Lindy scooped up the angora bunny, planting a kiss on his head. Then she stashed her bags behind the counter and bustled around the clinic. After filling the water bowls, she splashed water on the linoleum and threw down some rags to absorb the mess.

"Can't have customers slipping on a wet patch of floor," she said to the rabbit.

She knew the phone would be ringing soon, and that her assistant Jen would clean the cages in the back. Unfortunately, Jen often arrived late, coming up with all kinds of excuses.

But Lindy knew she would just smile in response, secretly hoping the girl would do better next time.

After wiping off the counters, Lindy looked through a growing stack of unpaid receipts. She didn't have it in her heart to say *no* when an animal was suffering. And she pushed aside the thought that these people took advantage of her sweet nature.

Suddenly, a heavy shadow crossed her face. Lindy grimaced, experiencing a whirring sound in her head.

Something sinister now looked out of her eyes.

Lindy turned calmly, locked her gaze on the rabbit, and viciously kicked the bunny across the room. The animal hit the wall with a thud.

A moment later, her eyes fluttered, and she frowned, wondering why the rabbit was cowering in the corner.

Just then, Jen ran in the door.

"My roommate used up all the coffee and I had to go the long way to get some caffeine. You know I'm useless without my morning Joe."

Lindy smiled, her eyes soft now, and continued to polish the front counter. Jen picked up the hose, but Lindy stopped her.

"Oh I already did that. Can you check the backdoor for deliveries?" Lindy asked.

Jen disappeared. Twenty minutes later Lindy found her on the phone with her boyfriend.

"So, I'm not sure I want Thai food again. How about the Lebanese place on Devon? We can ask Andrea and Mark to meet us there," Jen said, evenly making eye contact with Lindy.

"I can make the reservation," said Jen.

Lindy interrupted, asking Jen to straighten the waiting room.

Jen nodded, but then, seeming in no hurry to comply, proceeded to discuss menu options.

Lindy thought, "She only needs more positive reinforcement," and she left Jen to her phone call.

* * *

A few miles away, Jack hopped on the "L" train at Noyes Street. Twenty minutes later he got off near Glenwood Avenue and walked several blocks to the Burton Animal Clinic. He pulled open the glass door and a young woman with a flowered headband and matching apron smiled at him.

"Good morning. It's getting warm out there," she said brightly.

Jack greeted the girl, showing the slip of paper with the street number.

"I think maybe I'm supposed to meet you this morning," Jack said.

"Be back in a minute," Lindy said.

That was odd, Jack thought, and he looked around the waiting area. The furnace kicked on, and the unmistakable sharp smell of animals filled the room.

Then he saw the rabbit, cowering under a chair. It hopped away with a limp, and Jack saw the animal had been resting on a golden cylinder, just like the one from Sophia, and the one from the Mason's *Pythagoras* book.

He reached over and quickly put it in his pocket. Taking it felt weird, but somehow right. Must be meant for me, he figured.

Lindy returned, dabbing her eyes with a tissue.

"Sorry, I'm all turned around today. How can I help?"

"I'm following some directions on a kind of quest," said Jack.

Before he could explain, Lindy cut him off.

"That's wonderful! I'm sure I can help. I have flashlights, lanterns, actually any kind of camping equipment," she said.

Jack stepped back, holding up his hands.

"Whoa, hold on," he said.

What was with her? She was trying to be nice, but it felt smothering, like she had no boundaries.

Lindy saw his discomfort.

"I get that a lot. Honestly, I wear myself out. Trying to wait on everybody. Sometimes, I think people avoid me because I'm too much." Lindy said.

Hearing her pitiful confession made Jack cringe. He couldn't help feeling sorry for her. Maybe he would end up like her, saying *yes* too often. Like when he accepted the Council's challenge. A knot tightened in his stomach. Grace would probably get sick of him, too. It was hard to know when to help, when to stand down. He didn't want to be a doormat. Girls would walk all over him.

"Don't go yet," said Lindy, grabbing his arm.

"Let me explain," she continued.

"You see, a year ago today I was attacked by some high tech nanobots. I haven't been the same," Lindy said.

Jack felt the hairs on the nape of his neck stand up. Nanobots again! With *mind altering capacities.* It made his skin crawl. Could he get infected? Standing here? He knew how COVID had changed him. But a nanobot? What could *that* do to his brain?

Lindy continued.

"An angry customer upset about some expired pet food made a scene in the clinic. He tossed a bag filled with these tiny bug-like things. Within days I had vertigo. My doctor diagnosed neurological damage, and the brain scan showed evidence of a nanobot. I had balance issues and difficulty focusing. But, most of all, I became more needy, couldn't be alone," Lindy said.

Jack felt his heart begin to race, and a rush of troubling scenarios scampered through his mind. How could he slow down his brain, and steady his nerves?

But what if he was attacked? What if Charlie was infested with nanobots?

Lindy kept talking, unaware of Jack's discomfort.

"At first, friends could see I was going through something. But, apparently, I wasn't easy to be around. I had to *one up* everyone with fetching and serving," said Lindy.

Now she was sobbing.

Jack didn't know what to say. He looked at her. She was a mess. Pitiful. Made him want to run. Drove him crazy when girls cried, with red and puffy faces. He had to get out of there.

Abruptly, Jack said he was sorry and left the clinic.

Lindy watched him walk down the street. Then an odd look came over her eyes, like a slot machine hitting the jackpot. Giving a devilish little smile, she picked up her phone.

"Yeah, he totally bought it. Left here completely freaked out," said Lindy.

She pushed up the sleeves on her canary-colored cardigan, revealing Vincent Marcov's initials tattooed on her left arm.

Jack slumped next to the window on the L train. Nanobots again. He started to feel itchy, brushing off imaginary attackers.

Was he losing it? He had to get a grip.

He needed more information. Was there a way to counteract the nanobots? Some, he recalled from the science magazine, had a tiny metal component.

But his worries looped on replay. This was a familiar pattern. He'd obsess about a perceived threat, then grab for a logical explanation, like a trapeze artist flying toward safety.

But now, when Jack thought of Vincent Marcov and all his dirty work, he felt himself light up with fury. This was unfamiliar territory. He was accustomed to fear, yes, but anger? What was happening to him?

Blood rushed to his head, his fists tightened, and he could feel the veins in his neck pulsing. A deep rage detonated in his solar plexus, like a missle leaving the silo.

Not here, not now, not on this train, he told himself, as he struggled to calm down.

Breathe... Breathe, he told himself. Closing his eyes, he held his breath. Then slowly Jack released the air from his lungs. Using his breath to quell the inner storm, he inhaled and exhaled. Finally a space opened in his chest.

He opened his eyes.

Some kids a few train seats away stared at him. His face must be flushed. Jack tried to look normal, raising his eyebrows to clear his expression. They looked away, returning to their conversation. Jack looked out the window.

Later that afternoon

Meanwhile, Mike was dealing with another chapter of teen war games, as he hid in his room. Anyone passing by the open windows at the Farrell house could hear doors slamming and voices screaming. His sister had taken the car without permission, and his parents had had enough.

Mike crouched on the floor on the far side of his bed, trying to lay low. He knew if they found him, he would end up in an argument, and dinner would be miserable. Mike wanted to crawl under his bed. If his sisters only knew about the threat from Marcov, they wouldn't be having these petty fights. Mike had been terrified by Jack's experience, and now felt burdened with the secret.

Other kids thought of him as so relaxed, but underneath he was seething much of the time. And that was *before* learning about the Sophia event. Now, he was a wreck. Secretly, he wished he could be more like Grace because it seemed nothing bothered her.

So Mike would have been surprised to find that several streets over, Grace was dealing with her own set of problems. For the umpteenth time, her mother complained in a deceptively sweet voice that she failed to understand why her daughter wanted to stop ballet lessons.

"Sure, when I was ten I liked the fun black swan costume. But there are more important things going on in the world," said Grace.

Exasperated, her mother left the room.

Watching her mom retreat usually brought Grace a sweet feeling of satisfaction, like a refreshing splash of water. However, most everything seemed insignificant compared to Jack's terrible secret.

The three friends all felt more on edge now that they knew the high stakes game.

CHAPTER SIX

Slick

Saturday morning, Jack followed the coordinates on the next set of numbers from the gold cylinder. A web search showed a sprawling house that a business man had purchased for two point three million dollars. And, apparently, the owner had been convicted of embezzlement, but had weaseled out of serving time.

"I'm going to the library," Jack yelled up the stairwell to his parents.

He felt bad that he was lying again, but following the clues was something he *had* to do.

* * *

Francis Place, Evanston

Trip Grainger toweled off his shoulders after climbing out of the pool. He put on a terrycloth robe and picked up his phone that was vibrating on the table. It was the pro shop at his dad's club.

"OK...Let me get back to you about the tee time." Trip said.

The nineteen-year old ran his fingers through his blond waves and began texting.

A moment later, he entered the house and started up the steps. The housekeeper called after him.

"Sir, will you be here for lunch?" She asked.

"Yeah, there will be three of us. And grill some burgers. It's going to get up to 80 degrees today," Trip said.

Under his breath, he said, "Seems way early for this kind of heat."

A short time later, Jack's bike stopped at a house that matched the web photo. The façade looked like a traffic jam of pillars, stained glass, and arched windows. What an ugly place, he thought.

Parked in the circular drive, a copper-colored Nissan GT-R sat next to a black Range Rover that looked like a rhinoceros on wheels. Several men in overalls raked twigs off the lawn and loaded tarps with tree debris. Jack walked up to the entrance and pressed the bell. A uniformed housekeeper opened the door.

He introduced himself.

"You can wait on the patio. The others will be here soon," she said.

Showing him the way, she asked if he would like something to drink.

"Sure, thank you," he said.

Jack wondered if he had stumbled into a gathering.

In the hallway, Jack passed a glass cabinet filled with trophies. The opposite wall was covered with photos of Grainger posing with various celebrities.

What a showoff, he thought.

The housekeeper led him outside and gestured toward some cushioned chairs. Jack saw an infinity pool with blue glass tiles. A striped cabana stood in the corner, and stacks of terrycloth towels waited for a swimmer.

He thought Grace and Mike would laugh at the pillars and fountain. Then again, they'd like this pool.

The housekeeper returned with a pitcher of iced tea. A few minutes later, a tanned young man wearing aviator sunglasses, a pink polo shirt, and khaki slacks walked down the steps to the patio. He looked perplexed when he saw Jack, but extended his hand, introducing himself.

"I'm Trip Grainger. What can I do you for?"

Trip, with his slicked back blond hairdo, and professionally whitened teeth, gave a disingenuous smile.

Getting to his feet, Jack introduced himself. "Hi, It's nice to meet you. I'm here because your house came up on a Google map, and ...

But before Jack could explain about the coordinates, Trip cut him off.

"Look. The house is off the market. Did your parents send you over? Blanca shouldn't have let you in here," said Trip.

"No, you have the wrong idea. I'm not a realtor. No realtors in my family," said Jack.

"Oh, so a reporter." Trip said in an even more annoyed tone.

"But I'm not a reporter," said Jack.

What a piece of work, Jack thought. This guy reminded him of a used car salesman on TV.

"Out NOW!" Trip said.

Jack had no recourse but to leave, making his way quickly out the front door.

Had he gone to the wrong place? Was this guy under the influence of nanobots? Trip Grainger was an idiot, either way. As he walked back down to the curb, he could hear Trip berating the housekeeper.

What a big waste of time. What was he supposed to do now? Would he get another golden cylinder? How could he continue the quest?

There was a bitter aftertaste in the iced tea. Or maybe he was reacting to being thrown out.

As Jack coasted down Sheridan Road, he thought about the odd people he had met. Margaret Mason and her need for perfection. Lindy Simons who overdid the good works but annoyed others with her incessant fussing. The Graingers, talented in business, but scamming the system.

Maybe the Graingers had been the right place, after all.

Then it occurred to him. He had time this morning. Maybe he would scope out the Masons' cottage again. Watch from the forest's edge. He considered bringing Grace and Mike, but three people would be easier to spot.

Forty minutes later, Jack passed the three evergreens past the lagoon. Getting off his bike, he wanted to find a good spot to observe the house. As he rolled his bike through the forest, he checked his cell phone. There was no service. He must be close.

The smell of smoky embers filled his nose.

Walking around a cluster of tall bushes, he could not believe his eyes.

Jack stood at the edge of a burned-out patch of dirt with a charred heap of rubble. Only the remnants of the chimney and fireplace remained. Had the Masons perished in the fire?

Jack got on his bike and rode as fast as he could. His legs ached as he bore down on the pedals. Like in a bad dream, it seemed the bike was moving in slow motion. The more he pushed forward, the slower the bike moved.

But, eventually, the forest gave way to the sounds of traffic and streets he knew.

Jack wished he could move his family someplace out of Vincent Marcov's range. But where? He ruled out Alaska—not enough sun. Californians put up with earthquakes and fires, and the coast suffered hurricanes. While tornadoes battered the Midwest, the

Southwest and Southeast harbored poisonous snakes...and it was all getting worse. The climate hammered people everywhere. There was no escaping it and nowhere to hide from Dr. Marcov...even way out on the planet Sophia. Each week, Jack heard reports of more melting ice cliffs.

* * *

That evening at Jack's house, Grace and Mike sprawled on the sectional, tossing one of Charlie's soft toys back and forth. They were finishing off a pizza with pineapple and talking about summer plans. The cheesy slices landed inside Jack like a soft pillow. It felt like old times until Grace popped the bubble.

"So Jack, do you think Vincent Marcov is away on Sophia, or somewhere nearby?" Grace asked.

"Shhh...My parents might hear," said Jack.

"Did you shush me?" asked Grace.

He had hoped for a relaxing night with his friends.

"Did you know there was another attack on the ice shelf this morning," she whispered.

Yes, of course he knew. It had been all over the news.

What a pain. If a thought crossed her mind, she just blurted it out. Absolutely no filter. Didn't consider how other people felt. And, if his parents heard them talking about Marcov, it would be a disaster on so many levels.

"Well, you can't pretend Marcov's not out there. When there's a showdown, just know I want to be there," she said, getting in the last word, as usual.

"Shut up, Grace," whispered Jack.

He pointed to the air vents that carried conversations up to the second floor.

"Why would you bring up Marcov? Can't we have *one* evening?" Mike said in a low voice.

"You just want to stick your head in the sand," said Grace. "It's stupid to ignore the threat," she added.

Jack whispered, "Vincent Marcov is *always* on my mind. Those nanobots mess with the brain, turning functions on and off. Changing people. So they act in ways they wouldn't choose."

After a few minutes, Grace piped up again. "Just tell me when and where," she said.

"Enough!" The boys said, tossing toys and pillows at her.

But unruffled by the rebuff, Grace went on. "So, Mike. You all ready for a showdown?" Grace asked.

Fuming now, Mike got up to leave.

"You don't get it, Grace. This is not some Wonder Woman fantasy in your head. You need to grow up." Mike fumed.

Then he turned and left the house.

"Happy now?" Jack asked.

"Yes, actually, I am. Mike needs to wake up," she said.

"Well, you want him to *wake* up. And he wants you to *grow* up. I want you *both* to *shut up!*"

And with that, Jack went upstairs, leaving Grace to let herself out.

As he heard the front door close, Jack passed his parent's bedroom. All was quiet, and the lights were out. But it had been a close call.

* * *

That same night, two hundred miles above the earth, Marcov's satellite sliced off another ice cliff. Shuddering for a moment, it dropped below the water's surface. Popping up, the sheet of ice floated south.

While news outlets covered these strikes, governments around the globe scrambled to fortify the top of the world with an iron dome. It was hoped this technology could block the attacks; however, the construction would take time.

CHAPTER SEVEN

Achilles' Heel vs Kryptonite... Lake Geneva, Wisconsin

From the terrace, a teenage girl stared across the water. A small book of poetry rested in her lap as she reflected on the beautiful phrases. Strains of cello music drifted in the air, muted by the mist not yet cooked off by the sun. The screen door opened, and a woman wearing a turban and a silk caftan stepped out. She sighed deeply, taking in the view.

"Esme, dear, would you like to pick up some glazes for your ceramics?" she asked the girl.

"That would be awesome. I need shades that pick up the colors in the water," said Esme.

"Capturing light, motion, and color variations remains an elusive aspiration," said the aunt, twirling a tendril of red hair that had escaped from her Gucci headgear.

"I'm so lucky to have you Aunt Lutetia. You just *get* me," said Esme.

A mournful look crossed the aunt's face, knowing well the artist's way could be difficult.

Aunt and niece sat in silence, taking in the sky and water.

* * *

Evanston, Illinois

After the fight with Mike and Grace, Jack woke with a headache.

Their long friendship seemed to be falling apart. Maybe they were all just too different. Grace drove him nuts much of the time, and Mike could be so checked out and oblivious. While Grace had said she wanted to help, she could be difficult. Was it too much to ask that she not discuss Marcov where his parents might over-hear? Sharing his secret with his friends had been risky, and maybe foolish, after the close call the previous night.

Jack wondered how he would continue his quest, as he hadn't gotten another cylinder at the Graingers. The three golden cylinders sat in his open drawer. He was about to cover them up, when, to his amazement, a fresh set of numbers appeared on the middle one.

He leaped up, and quickly entered the new coordinates in his laptop. The pin landed on a house in Lake Geneva, the home of a local artist, according to the web.

If he had his driver's license, he could ride up there in a couple of hours.

Maybe Mike could get the car? He picked up his phone.

His friend seemed hesitant at first after the blow up the night before. But Mike wasn't one to hold a grudge. And, really, it had been Grace who started the whole thing.

By ten a.m., the guys were headed north to Lake Geneva. They listened to music, and forty minutes later, they passed the Welcome to Wisconsin sign.

When they reached the resort town, they stopped at a gift shop where the salesgirl greeted them. After looking around, Jack bought some snacks and a toy for Charlie. While the owner rang up the sale, Jack asked for directions to the artist's house.

"Oh, I know her. Prepare yourself. Lutetia is quite a colorful character," said the shop owner, rolling her eyes.

Jack felt some relief that at least this individual was known in the town.

Mike dropped him off at the address and told Jack to text when he was ready. Meanwhile, he planned to walk around the downtown section.

Jack stood and looked at the fieldstone house perched on a bluff. A magnolia tree seemed ready to bloom, even though it was only April. Jack climbed the steps and made his way across the porch.

Hoping someone was home, he knocked.

After a few moments, a girl about eighteen years old opened the door.

"Yes...um. Hello?" She looked distracted, and maybe a little sad.

Jack introduced himself, and showed her the cylinder, explaining the coordinates. The girl's aunt joined her in the doorway.

"Aunt Lutetia, it looks like the gold cylinder you found the other day," the girl said.

"You did?" Jack asked.

"How wonderful!" said the aunt, clapping her hands in delight.

The aunt introduced herself as Lutetia Langdon, and her niece, Esme. They invited him inside, and he followed them down a hallway. The girl was dressed in an oversized mohair sweater and a flowing pleated skirt. She gestured for him to sit near the fire.

Jack looked around. Wooden beams crossed the span of the ceiling, and tribal rugs covered the floors. Everything looked hand-crafted in subtle shades of earth tones. Silk pillows sat propped on a mid-century sofa. He saw a copy of *The Boy Who Drew Cats* on the table.

Jack noticed Esme had a far-away quality in her gaze, and that she looked high maintenance. But, he reasoned, at least she didn't look bossy, like Grace.

Lutetia settled in an oversized chair. Fishing an antique chain out of her bodice, she produced a gold cylinder.

"I found this trinket *so* interesting. Last week the piece was resting at the bottom of my koi pond. Can you imagine that?" Lutetia fluttered.

She opened the clasp, and pulled the gold piece off her chain and handed it to Jack. He felt a shiver as her talon-like fingernails scraped his palm.

"It's yours, dear. When the universe speaks, we must listen," she said.

He explained that he had been following the number sequences, on a kind of a quest. "To get some answers and ...."

But Lutetia interrupted him.

"Oh, I just *LOVE* a quest! You see I define myself as a seeker. Following what I believe is an authentic path." Lutetia sighed.

"SO much more interesting than living a conventional life," she added.

Esme excused herself. Jack could hear the clink of glassware in an adjoining room. The girl returned shortly, balancing a tray with a pitcher of sun tea and tumblers filled with ice.

Lutetia poured a glass for Jack. Her chandelier earrings and bracelets jangled with her movements. Jack also noticed an exotic fragrance. Sensing his reaction, she shared, "It's a Cartier perfume. I *must* give you a sample for your mother," said Lutetia as she reached over and opened a drawer that was filled with unusual containers. Choosing a red lacquered vial, she floated out of the room. "I'll be back in a moment," she called over her shoulder.

Esme smiled and Jack could see the family resemblance. Aunt and niece presented with the same ethereal quality, as if they breathed a different, more refined air.

Lutetia bustled in, carrying a tiny funnel and a round bottle filled with amber liquid. Carefully, she poured perfume into the vial. Sliding the small container into a velvet pouch, she handed it to Jack.

"Your mother will *love* this scent… so, *so* special…just takes you away to the island of Rhodes," said Lutetia.

Jack thanked her. Then he steered the conversation back to his mission. "So… There's a rogue scientist …"

Lutetia immediately cut him off. "Oh, that rascal Vincent Marcov. Again!!"

Her face darkened as she grabbed his arm.

"One of the dangers of a seeker's life is that, off a conventional path, it can be difficult figuring out good and evil. Can you believe I used to date that guy?" Lutetia glared.

Jack recoiled. But the woman seemed not to notice. She rattled on, warning him about the importance of staying away from bad people.

"Vincent was so full of himself, vain, and downright mean. The man was incapable of passing a mirror without preening and checking his hair. The relationship was brief. After I discovered potion granules in my tea, I poured the drink down the drain. Vincent was furious when I refused his special tea and wouldn't answer his calls. He was relentless, finally sending a dozen black roses. The hideous bouquet was infested with these tiny black bugs. And there was a note, condemning me and my darling niece to feeling dissatisfaction with *anything* ordinary. As a result, we remain drawn to all things *special*. Aren't we, my dear?" Lutetia lamented.

"So true. Only art, literature, and music hold any interest for me. Other subjects remain too dry *and boring*," said Esme.

"I'm afraid those bugs were nanobots. You should get checked out by a doctor. Other people I've met had this same thing happen," said Jack.

"That's *very* upsetting. Actually, we *did* go to the doctor, but he assumed we were exaggerating. Being hysterical, hypochondriacal," said Lutetia.

Jack could see how the woman might not be taken seriously. Too intense, and way too dramatic.

But Lutetia switched topics, maybe to manage her anxiety about the threat. Because now she was raving about a new opera production at the Lyric.

Had he heard the story of Orpheus and his love, Eurydice, trapped in the underworld?

Jack did not. But he had a pretty good idea that he was about to find out.

After a recap of the opera, Lutetia, admitted that she actually *relished* the inner pain as it "fed her art."

"Can't say as I've ever been to the opera," Jack said, hoping to put the brakes on this emotional tsunami.

"Oh, but you *must*. This season offers some *glorious* performances. We wouldn't miss them for *anything*. I have a pied-à-terre in Chicago so we can enjoy *every single* performance," said Lutetia.

"A pied what?" asked Jack.

"It's French slang for an apartment," said Esme. She bit her lip.

Was she *laughing* at him?

Maybe Esme only looked uneasy, sensing her aunt's ramblings now were going off the rails. Jack returned to the topic of the rogue scientist. "Marcov has hurt a lot of people." he said.

"I wonder *what* I can tell you about him?" Lutetia pondered.

Then her eyes brightened.

"I know! Vincent absolutely *detests* art. Let me show you an *amazing* piece that he hated... actually broke out in hives," said Lutetia.

Escorting Jack out to her studio, she led the way as they passed by paintings, half-finished canvases, and mosaics. But by far, the most arresting item in the room was a sculpture, a brass chair with cast human arms.

"Woah!" Jack said.

Pleased with Jack's reaction, Lutetia explained about the piece.

"It's part of a series. A marvelous example of modern sculpture. New, yet somehow old. It's titled *Shift & Shadow*, about the individual's journey toward authenticity."

Jack could see this sculpture belonged in a museum. He felt drawn to touch one of the brass arms to see if it was warm. The work seemed to embody the shift he felt when his fear turned into anger. Wasn't great art supposed to move you in a deep way?

Jack looked at his watch, said his friend was waiting for him,. He thanked them for their time.

Lutetia showed him to the front door.

They closed the door, counted to ten, and turned to each other and high fived.

"Now *that* was fun. Excellent performance, my dear," said the aunt.

"What a *stupid* boy," said Esme.

"Not *that* stupid. He seemed to grasp the importance of the sculpture. Could be dangerous," said Lutetia.

" I could barely stop myself from adding some potion to his iced tea," said Esme with a dark gleam in her eyes.

"No, no, dear. Vincent insisted we only *scare* the boy. Apparently, *fear* remains Jack's Achilles' Heel. My Vincent *requires* this victim for himself," Lutetia said.

Then the two co-conspirators entered a small enclave under the stairs. A votive candle flickered under a portrait of Cronus... the god who had devoured his own children. The deity provided the ideal patron for Marcov's mission to destroy the planet for future generations.

Pulling black veils over their heads, Lutetia and Esme muttered some incantations. When the planet's climate flipped, this capricious duo knew they would be among the lucky ones.

Mike and Jack shared some French fries on a bench. After the intensity of the visit, he was grateful to see his friend. Mike was *so* normal. He'd take grounded any day. Art was great, but to live with it, day in and day out, was way too much.

However, Jack had to admit the power he'd seen in that sculpture would stay with him.

On the ride home, Jack filed away the information that Marcov detested art. Apparently, it was like his Kryptonite. Then he settled in the car, taking in the cool breeze coming through the window.

Two hours later, Mike's car rolled up the Abernaults' driveway.

Grace was sitting on his front steps.

It seemed he couldn't get even twenty-four hours without her. Grace was intense. Like those artists. While they existed in a world of high culture, Grace lived to rule. Different things set them off. But, as for being around them, a little went a long way.

"What's up?" he asked, irritably, still annoyed about the previous night.

"I need to show you guys something," Grace said.

"I'm tired. Can it wait?" said Jack.

"No, it can't wait. And I sent you a bunch of texts…which you ignored," said Grace.

"Had my phone off," said Jack.

He had turned off the device, feeling Grace needed a time out.

Jack saw his parents approaching.

He pulled Grace's arm, signaling that the three of them take a walk.

When they were out of earshot, Jack warned them about not talking where his parents might hear.

"OK, OK," said Grace.

"Look, Mike, sorry I attacked you, but we are in big trouble," said Grace.

"Sometimes aggression only make things worse," said Mike.

"Well, another huge portion of the Arctic fell into the sea. Watch this polar bear trying to keep his head above the water. It's horrible," Grace said.

She handed him her phone with the video.

They watched the struggling animal fighting for his life.

"That's not all," she said.

Jack and Mike looked at her phone. A video showed a view of the Arctic. A menacing voice gave the grim forecast, as the entire icecap disappeared into the sea. An hourglass appeared and the sand began to fall, faster and faster.

"Won't be long now," said the voice, followed by maniacal laughter.

"Like we need a reminder," said Jack.

"We've got to find that scientist and destroy his headquarters," she said.

"Woah...you want to take out his place?" asked Mike.

"Hold on, Grace," said Jack.

However, the attacks were mounting; the burned-out remains of the Mason's house, the brain altering nanobots, the laser satellites, the terrible climate news, and now polar bears drowning.

Jack paused, knowing they needed to exercise care.

"Before we think about taking out his place, we would need a *really* good plan," said Jack.

"That polar bear is going to *be us* if we don't do something," she said.

Mike looked grim.

"We do have to act. But with a plan. And at the right time," said Jack, always a fan of a good defense.

The idea of a confrontation with Marcov felt like an icy shirt, right out of the freezer, landing on him.

Mike intervened. "I could set up a list of options if we find his place. You know, the pros and cons," said Mike.

Leave it to Mike to offer something sensible that might slow down Grace.

Jack turned to Grace.

"I'm working on the quest... and on the old book. But, you're right, we *should* work out a plan." said Jack.

Grace seemed ready to press on, but Mike cut her off. "I'll start tonight," Mike said.

Jack was grateful that Mike was willing to support him. Grace was another story. She challenged him in ways that made him uncomfortable, even if he admired her courage.

That evening Jack stared at the ceiling. The large blank square always seemed to clear his thoughts and reset his mind.

Then he thought of the cloth bag with the vial from Lutetia. He grabbed the pouch and found his mom reading a psychology journal. Jack handed her the perfume, telling her it was a free sample from the mall.

His mom dabbed some drops on her wrists, and sniffed.

"This is incredible. We'll have to get your aunt a bottle for her birthday. What's this called?"

She squinted at the label, translating from the French. "*Kiss of the Dragon.* Uh, *no...* Catherine would take offense. This will be my new scent. Although it's a bit heavy for springtime," said his mom.

Jack knew his Aunt Catherine *was* kind of a dragon.

Grace was a dragon, as well. Dragons were a pain, but they could be exciting.

At the high school on Monday, the three friends watched the clock's minute hand slowly lurch forward on the homeroom wall. The teacher's voice droned on. Times like this were pure torture, maddening, agonizing. The planet was failing, but the adults seemed focused on meaningless stuff, like cleaning your room, and taking out the garbage. All of it seemed useless, if there would be no air to breathe or water to drink.

Finally, the bell shrilled, and the class headed out. The friends found a picnic table and began listing ways to take down the scientist. Mike's ideas all had to do with some form of cyber attack, but Grace seemed determined for a direct assault.

Jack recognized her recklessness, and he put the brakes on any desire he had to impress her. He would listen to all her schemes, but, for now, he would stick with the quest. While it was hard to imagine how meeting these odd individuals could save anybody, Jack needed to trust the Council.

Grace, sensing she had hit a wall with these guys, changed the subject to something else that was bothering her.

Apparently, she and her very proper mother were battling again over clothes.

"So, I opened my drawer and there sits a pink cashmere sweater. Can you believe it?" Grace said.

Mike and Jack *could* believe it. Grace's mom had waged a losing battle over clothes for the past decade. They knew Grace would have viewed this innocent pink item as a hand grenade nestled among her black T-shirts. And, there was no denying her mother could be relentless. A *steel magnolia*, born and bred in South Carolina. A dragon dressed in pearls and pastel cashmere.

Grace, as everyone knew, shopped at army surplus for camouflage. And, occasionally she picked up items at vintage shops for black pieces.

"The *nerve* of your mother," Jack said, his eyes sparkling.

And on the topic of annoying family members, Mike proceeded to update his friends on his younger sister who had ruined a sweater belonging to the older one.

"You're a regular Cinderella, with two ugly sisters," said Grace.

"So true," Mike said, shaking his head in agreement.

Jack could see that Mike and Grace were bonding over a sweater theme this afternoon. It almost felt like old times.

On the way home, Jack got to thinking about how Grace loved to live in the eye of the storm. It seemed she packed a funnel cloud in her bag that she pulled out if things got too calm. He could see how the ongoing battle with her mother carried over into all her relationships.

Then he thought about his friends' home situations. Crazy siblings would have driven him nuts, and Grace's mom could be super intrusive. Then he recalled how his own mom had hovered over him until Charlie came along. And, he did have a dad who nagged him about his grades. Before COVID, Jack had enjoyed a kind of *benign neglect*. But his dad was back at it, hounding him about homework and quizzes.

Jack also knew his friends didn't worry like he did. However, if he thought about it, they did *other* stuff. Grace could be *out there*, impulsive and explosive. And Mike often seemed oblivious, missing important things going on around him. The guy just buried himself in his computer.

When Jack opened his front door, he found his little brother playing in the living room. The baby looked up and flashed a huge toothy smile. It was then Jack saw the item in Charlie's chubby hands. It was an oversized **nanobot!**

Jack grabbed the thing with a towel, and ran outside to the curb. Stomping it, towel and all, he kicked it down the sewer drain. The thought occurred to him that Marcov could have filled the thing with tiny nanobots, like a devilish Trojan horse.

He knew he should tell his parents. But then they would figure it out that he hadn't stopped the quest. Overwhelmed that he had brought this danger to their door, a kind of paralysis took over.

CHAPTER EIGHT

Lincoln Park

T he following Friday...

The older man took in the breeze coming through his balcony doors. He heard the sound of rustling leaves as he looked out over Lincoln Park. Joggers loped around the lagoon, and moms dressed in yoga pants pushed strollers past the blossoming trees. Dr. Bernaski loved this view from his condominium, built in the 1920's. It never got old.

Then he retired to his armchair so he could catch the morning news. He paid special attention to the humidity, which he saw as Chicago's only flaw. Today, he learned, the air would be on the dry side. His phone vibrated on the table, alerting him to a delivery in the lobby.

Dr. Bernaski showered and dressed for work, pulling on a fresh shirt and seersucker jacket. Then he descended in the brass cage elevator to the lobby. The doorman handed him a small brown package from behind the marble counter, along with his usual morning greeting.

The doctor noticed the label on the box, scrawled with fancy silver colored ink.

Dropping it in his satchel, he took off on his morning walk to work. The crowd on the sidewalk was filled with people hurrying to their jobs. Kids, in less of a rush, slowly meandered toward the local public school down the block.

Twenty minutes later, the security guard at the Newberry Library held open the heavy glass door for the director. Nodding at the young man, Dr. Bernaski pinned on his name tag and made his way up to his office. Then he remembered the box, pulling it out of his bag. He opened the package with a letter opener, and read the note. Then he picked up his phone and pressed a speed dial contact.

After a brief exchange, the voice on the line told him to stick to the plan.

"So just the one extra ingredient? And the harrowing tale?" said Bernaski.

* * *

Vincent Marcov put down his phone. Why couldn't these idiots follow his directions? They kept questioning the wisdom of turning over the gold tubes to the kid. Didn't they understand that he *required* this cat and mouse game. Letting the kid chase his tail all over the place was fun.

Of course, Marcov preferred to work alone, but he recognized that sometimes he required some assistance. There was no question in his mind that he would prevail over the Council's efforts to stop him, as he had *always* done in the past.

These days he was busy plotting his next environmental disaster. Sitting at his desk with a giant painting of the Titan Cronus hanging on the opposite wall, Marcov stared into the eyes of his patron, this destroyer of future generations.

Although Marcov hated art, he was drawn to this single image. Vincent wondered if Cronus had been bullied on the playground of Mount Othrys. Afterall, the Titan had twenty-three siblings. Lots of opportunities for betrayals there, he thought.

Then Marcov got back to work.

What to do next? His list included DNA tampering and earthquake from fracking. A pandemic had already happened, he thought, now wishing he had thought of it first. He considered the logistics of each disaster. While the ultimate goal remained destruction of the polar ice cap, he enjoyed these sideshows while the ice melted.

The recent breakthrough in atomic fusion had been a potential setback; however, Marcov now had saboteurs in place to block the generator technology that fusion required. So Vincent felt he still held all the cards.

* * *

After school that same day Jack checked the coordinates on Lutetia's cylinder, and he was relieved to see a place he knew, a Chicago landmark library.

Jack boarded the number seven bus, finding a seat near the back. A spring shower began to hit the bus window, making the buildings and utility poles dance in watery shapes. As he looked through the glass, Jack wondered what he would learn this afternoon.

Then Jack thought of the baby holding the nanobot. Haunted by this memory, he tried to ball up the image into a remote part of his mind. Sometimes, he pinched his arm, until the pain blocked out the scene. Other times, he reasoned, he hadn't actually *seen* any small black-like bugs. However, Jack was terrified that Marcov might have hurt Charlie, and that the fiend knew where they lived.

Jack stepped off the bus and found the rain had slowed to a sprinkle. He pulled up the hood on his anorak. A chill hung in the air. Water splashed on his head, dumped from leaves heavy with rain. Jack dodged puddles and arrived at the library building on Walton Street.

A security guard asked for his credentials.

Jack showed his school ID and the guard waved him inside. Towering over his head, a vaulted ceiling displayed old world maps. The main hall impressed a visitor that scholars were at work. Jack's shoes squeaked on the terrazzo floors as he made his way to a marble counter. Before he could ask for information, a man greeted him.

"Follow me, please," said an elderly man.

Jack noticed the gold pin, identifying him as the library director. The man led him into an office separated from the library stacks by an imposing glass wall. The director gestured for Jack to sit in a leather armchair. He shuffled around his desk, introducing himself as Doctor Bernaski.

"So, tell me, young man, how can I help you this afternoon?"

Jack showed the gold cylinder with the Newberry Library's coordinates, setting it on the desk.

"These numbers give the location coordinates for this library," Jack said.

"Hmmm…interesting," said the director. Then the man placed a similar cylinder beside Jack's. "I've been expecting you," said Dr. Bernaski.

Jack met his eyes.

"This was delivered this morning with a note informing me of a special visitor, a green-eyed teenager. I assumed it was from my sister. She's always sending me gifts and adding little riddles," said Bernaski.

"Well, I don't think I know your sister," said Jack.

"So this is something all together different," said Bernaski.

It was then Dr. Bernaski told Jack that the Newberry held a special collection. Usually, these artifacts were kept away from the public because they required interpretation. Dr. Bernaski added he wanted to call in a consultant.

"Sure, if you think it will help. And, I have three more cylinders at home," said Jack.

The man picked up the phone and he turned away in his chair, so Jack failed to hear all of the conversation. He did catch the name *Dr. Vincent Marcov*.

Jack felt his stomach roil at the mention of Marcov, unconsciously letting out a groan.

Dr. Bernaski finished his call, and then told Jack he should return on Wednesday at four o'clock if he wished to proceed. And he told him to bring the other cylinders.

"Do you know Vincent Marcov?" Jack asked.

"Not now. We will have time to talk on Wednesday," and it seemed clear that the director was dismissing him for now.

"It's only that I heard you say his name," said Jack.

"Wednesday, come back on Wednesday," said Bernaski.

"OK, I'll be back," said Jack.

At a grill on Clarke Street, Jack ordered a sandwich for takeout. Then he sat at the bus stop, eating the grilled cheese, and thinking that delays were frustrating. He hated having to wait till Wednesday. Patience and *process*. So annoying.

And had the game changed? This Bernaski guy wanted to see *all* the golden cylinders, it seemed. What was that about?

The northbound bus pulled up, with a splash of water. Jack settled in a seat, and he watched the neighborhoods pass by the windows. It wasn't long before the sign for Evanston appeared. Jack relaxed as the sharp glare of the city shifted into the restful light of the suburbs. A cathedral of elms canopied the road, and the bus passed sprawling homes and expansive lawns. Jack noticed the temperature let down a few degrees.

* * *

A few days later, Jack returned to the Newberry. At four o'clock, Dr. Elizabeth McGloin from the University of Chicago, walked briskly into the library office. She was dressed like a scholar out of central casting, in a tailored linen suit. A tribal beaded necklace broke the severity of her outfit. Doctor Bernaski introduced Jack and they all examined the now five golden cylinders.

Dr. McGloin looked at the golden tubes.

"These items must possess an interesting provenance." Seeing confusion on Jack's face, "I mean to say that I believe they have a special origin," she said.

"You could say that." Jack said.

"I've been collaborating with the chemistry department for a number of years. My area of expertise lies in ancient artifacts and texts. Some of the old documents and items I've run across contain formulas for, dare I say…potions." She said.

"Really?" Jack asked.

But he was thinking, here we go, more crazy town.

Dr. McGloin continued, her voice now strained in a higher pitch.

"This is cutting edge work, and I admit, *very* controversial. Modern scientists generally reject these old formulas as wishful thinking. However, there is a wisdom in the alchemy of ancient scholars who mixed materials in their primitive labs. Most of their efforts, of course, were attempts to create gold out of base metals. But a few of these formulas have proven quite effective as medicines. Others reduce the effects of pollution in the Amazon. And one mixture brings out special qualities in golden objects."

"Wow," Jack said.

But he was thinking, she might have degrees, and might dress the part, but this made no sense. He thought after all the strange occurrences on this quest, nothing would have surprised him. But this information *sounded* bizarre. Alchemy? Potions?

Then he recalled the Council had advised him to keep an open mind. Sometimes, he knew, he had the habit of pushing aside information that challenged his beliefs, or that frightened him. He recalled the Council's letter had instructed him to listen with his heart, head, and gut intuition. It seemed the time was right to go with the flow.

Dr. McGloin opened her bag and brought out a vial with an amber colored liquid. Wiping off the desk with a tissue, she set the vial down.

"I think this formula may reveal the true essence of the golden tubes if we sprinkle some over them. Keep in mind, taking a calculated risk is a necessary part of an experiment. Playing the odds appears in many traditions as far back as Plato. Trailblazers tend to operate at the growth edge in any field of study," she told Jack. "In science, we mold the intuition into a hypothesis. So, in effect, we toss a dice, hoping to produce an 80% significant result."

Jack understood the scientific method, just not the potion stuff.

"Also, collaboration is the way to go. Knowledge and wisdom aren't the same. Wisdom tends to arrive when pride that you have all the answers steps back. Only then can you receive input from others. Sometimes the path is more of a relay race. You do all you can, but others may take a project across the finish line," she said.

"What if the liquid corrodes the metal?" Jack asked.

"It's a risk. But remember, you sought us out," said Bernaski.

Then the library director brought out a vial filled with clear liquid.

"This ingredient will serve as a neutralizer if it seems the metal is disintegrating," said Bernaski.

Dr. McGloin looked surprised at his suggestion to use an additive.

Jack jotted down the new coordinate numbers in case they were ruined in the process. Then he took a deep breath, and he looked into the eyes of Dr. Bernaski. He was hard to read.

But Dr. McGloin, she was different. This was a gut feeling for Jack, an intuition really. So, independent of her degrees, decades of experience, and crazy sounding theories, somehow, he trusted her.

"OK, *do* it," Jack said.

Dr. McGloin opened the vial, and a powerful smell filled the office. The odor was pungent, stinging Jack's nostrils. She swirled the vial, tipping it, as a brown liquid fell from the lip and coated the cylinders. For a moment, it seemed the metal was disintegrating, sizzling before their eyes.

"Seems too much," said Dr. Bernaski, and he poured the clear liquid to stop the process.

They watched and waited. The surfaces frothed and the liquid evaporated. Then a puff of smoke burst into a tiny golden cloud. When the mist cleared only one cylinder remained. The new longer golden tube now was pierced with holes, the engraved numbers preserved.

Jack noticed Dr. Bernaski showed an odd hint of dismay.

The three stared at the tube, now narrower and longer.

"Is that a flute...or a kind of whistle?" asked Jack.

Heat was still coming off the golden surface.

The two doctors began speculating. Bernaski pulled out a mythology book, searching the index for "flute." The story of Pan calling his sheep was the first passage he read. Then Dr. McGloin related stories about flutes, horns, and whistles that marshaled the wind to create special sounds. Hebrew scripture described how a horn had brought down the walls of Jericho. Mozart's *Magic Flute* opera told of the instrument's ability to turn sorrow into joy. Apparently, scores of cultures spun stories about the power of a flute. Even Einstein had written about how everything vibrated at different frequencies, emanating a unique sound.

Dr. McGloin turned to Jack, and asked, "So are you going to try it?"

"Me?" asked Jack.

"That's why we are all here, dear," she said.

Jack put the golden cylinder to his lips and blew, but the whistle only produced a soft whooshing tone. However, moments later, startling them, the large window in the office filled with thousands of butterflies, beating their wings on the glass. The three stared at the phenomenon. Clearly, the golden instrument had unique properties.

"It's like a dog whistle, but for butterflies," said Jack.

After the butterflies flew off, Jack broached the topic of the rogue scientist.

"So, have you actually met Dr. Marcov?" he asked.

"Unfortunately, yes. At a conference years ago, we shared a panel on climate in the Amazon. Marcov had us hoodwinked, playing the part of a concerned academic," said Bernaski.

"And we still encounter his interference when those nanobots attack a researcher," said Dr. McGloin.

"One never knows when and how he attacks," warned Dr. Bernaski.

Dr. McGloin seemed uncomfortable with this focus on the fiend and returned to the topic of research.

"You do realize that the solution to climate change requires more than green technologies. How we *see* our fellow humans is the key to sustainability and to our survival as a species," said McGloin.

Dr. McGloin and Bernaski shared how the rogue scientist had blocked their grant funding, creating an unproductive competition. Researchers found themselves working against each other, hoarding new data, and ultimately wasting time and money.

At five o'clock, Jack rose to leave. He folded the whistle in a tissue and turned to leave the library.

But Doctor McGloin stopped him, touching his arm.

"Be careful. Are you aware that Dr. Marcov has mastered the ability to become invisible for short periods of time? He leaves a sulfurous smell in his wake." She said.

"That's how he has evaded capture by the authorities," added Bernaski.

A shiver went up Jack's spine as he recalled the whiff of smoke on his first visit to Morningside.

Did he smell it now?

But he brushed this off as the power of suggestion.

That evening Dr. Bernaski arrived at the entrance to his condominium building.

The doorman greeted him, handing him an envelope. On the elevator ride up to his place, Bernaski opened the mail and smiled at the large donation to the Newberry signed by Vocram Corporation.

He hoped Dr. McGloin would never find out.

CHAPTER NINE

The Visitation

That night Jack went to bed early. He was not feeling well. Maybe breathing that potion had brought on an allergic reaction? All he wanted now was to curl up in a ball. His joints ached, and he felt feverish. To make matters worse, he could hear the TV nightly news reporting more attacks in the Arctic.

A cool patch of cotton pillowcase gave him a moment of relief until heat from his forehead made him turn the pillow again. A glass of water sat inches away on the nightstand, but he was too weak to reach for it. At some point, he passed out.

Around midnight, Jack heard a noise. Standing beside his bed, a dark shape stooped over him. Sharp features, birdlike eyes, and wearing a sagging cardigan, the figure leaned in and planted a menacing wet kiss on his forehead.

Paralyzed, Jack smelled foul breath with a hint of a lemon drop.

Dr. Marcov grinned, his dark beady eyes glowing. Then he gripped the boy's jaw, and Jack felt swabbing inside his mouth from an insistent hand.

Jack choked. Then he screamed. Smoky fumes filled the room as the figure evaporated.

The bedroom door flew open, and his parents rushed to his side. Jack was sitting up in bed, a terrified look in his eyes. His mom assumed he was having a nightmare, and his dad applied a cool washcloth to his brow. Jack's heart rate began to settle, and when some ibuprofen kicked in, he fell back to sleep.

His mother watched Jack's face relax, but she sensed something was very wrong.

In the morning, with his temperature normal, Jack assumed a spiking fever had brought on a night terror.

But his mother insisted that he stay home from school. Missing classes at this point was not going to make a big difference as his grades were already in free fall. Jack ate some oatmeal, but soon he felt tired again. It was laundry day, so he went upstairs, pulling the bedding on the floor.

A bolt of fear hit him, because on the sheets, Jack found the remains of a lemon drop.

A melting sensation hit the back of his knees. That had been no nightmare...but a **visitation!**

Dr Marcov had been here, in his room!

Jack ran to the bathroom, retching up the oatmeal. Turning on the faucet, he tried to spit away his disgust with mouthwash.

He heard a ringing phone.

Grace's name appeared on his phone's display. Jack paused for a moment and then picked up the call.

"Uh...Grace...Now's not a good time...Can I call you back?"

"I'll see you at first period," she said.

"I'm sick. Not going to school," his voice cracked.

"What's going on? You sound weird," she said.

He drew in a deep breath, closing his eyes, trying to sound normal. "Just that you woke me up," he lied.

"Well, good thing I did. You sound kind of freaked out," Grace said.

"Yeah, umm, OK, then." he said.

"Well, get some rest. Talk later?" Grace said.

"OK, bye."

Jack's dad entered.

"I'm working at home today. Your mother tells me you should get some rest," said his dad.

Jack just couldn't tell him. How Marcov had come into their home. *Again.*

But he also couldn't stay in that room… in that bed.

"Maybe I'll nap on the sofa," said Jack.

He slept most of the day, exhausted, and checked out.

In the next room, his dad worked, tapping away on his laptop. He was preparing another letter to the Pentagon about scheduling an appointment. So far, all his efforts had failed in finding someone with power to tell about the family secret.

* * *

A week passed. A flurry of end of the school year activities kept Jack on the move.

After dinner one evening, Grace called. She insisted that he had to come over right away. Jack welcomed a break from calculus, and from thoughts of Marcov's night time visit.

He turned the corner on Normandy Place and saw Grace on her front lawn, sitting on a blanket. Jack knew her presence outside was a sign she was avoiding her mother.

Now he regretted his decision to ride over here. Getting drawn into her family drama was not something he needed just now.

"I can't stay long. Promised my dad I'd help him with Charlie," Jack said, planning for a quick exit.

She patted the spot next to her.

"I love sitting outside before the mosquitoes take over. Do you realize we only have a few more bug free weeks?" Grace said, brushing her curls off her face.

What was she up to, now? She moved in close one week, then picked a fight the next. Grace seemed to have two settings, making him crazy or luring him in.

Jack sat down, not next to her, but deliberately across from her.

"So, Grace, what's going on?" Jack asked.

"Thought it would be nice to catch up, without Mike around, *every* second," said Grace.

"OK, but I thought you two ironed out your problems," said Jack.

"Oh, we have. But I wanted to ask if you had plans to go to the Spring Formal? If not, I'd like you to take me," Grace lowered her eyes.

Jack had just taken a swig from his water bottle. Now he sputtered, snorting at the idea. Grace consistently had made a big show out of mocking these traditional events.

Then he saw she *wasn't* kidding.

"OK, what's the *real* story here?" Jack asked.

"Well…you see…my Mom is trying to fix me up with the son of our former neighbor *and*… I was kind of hoping to have an excuse. It's not that this kid is awful, or anything. But I don't want to get involved in a big mess, with everybody, in the end, mad and hurt," Grace said.

"Since when did you start concerning yourself with how other people feel?" Jack said.

"Now, that's just harsh. If you don't want to go, I can always ask Mike," said Grace.

Grace shoved him playfully.

Jack flushed. Confused, annoyed, but wanting her, all at once.

"*Well*, guess I could help you out," he said, pushing down his excitement.

Grace's mom called for her.

They rose, and Jack got on his bike. On the ride home, he felt his heart soar. In spite of all her craziness, he could feel hope filling him like a giant party balloon.

CHAPTER TEN

The Mirror

Harold walked his dog around the block, passing the book-store. The window display showcased his favorite author's new book. He would come back later and buy it before the copies ran out.

The dog pulled on the leash, but Harold steered the animal around the metal sewer covers. Only last week, the news reported a dog had been hurt by an electrical shock from one of these metal plates. He was taking no chances.

Rounding the corner, Harold approached his contemporary brick house with iron grills over the windows. Entering the code, he opened the door and released the dog from the leash. The animal made a beeline to his stainless-steel bowl. Harold sat down to catch up on the news. He was not about to miss a severe weather notification or any other threat, for that matter.

* * *

Jack tried to study. But the memory of the cotton swab scraping his mouth made it difficult to focus. He got up again and brushed his teeth. Taking this step seemed to calm him.

Jack also found keeping a routine settled his nerves. This morning he planned to visit the next spot on his quest, and then he would study in the afternoon.

Jack pulled out the gold whistle and entered the coordinates on his map. Right away he recognized the house that could have been mistaken for a small office building. Often, over the years, he had passed this brick block of a structure on his way to the library.

A short time later, Jack parked his bike behind a metal fence on Sherman Avenue. Walking up to the house with the iron grills, he heard a dog bark. He rang the doorbell, noticing a decal from a security company. The door opened a crack, and a boy, looking wary, peered out at him.

"Hello?" The boy said tentatively.

Jack stepped back, introducing himself.

"Hey, I know you from soccer." Relief flooded the boy's voice.

Harold removed the chain, opening the door.

Jack was surprised that this was the kid from his team. Jack asked if he could talk to him for a few minutes.

Before the boy could respond, a massive German Shepard bounded into the hall, skidding on the tile floor as the boy called sharply for him to *Halt!*

Ordering the dog behind a gate, the boy glared at the animal. The dog lowered his tail, and retreated. Jack entered the hall, following the kid to the back of the house. Jack recalled the boy's name was Harold. He remembered at a soccer practice the coach once had called him Harry. And Harold had corrected him, saying he was named after his father. For sure, this kid could be serious, and sometimes talked more like an adult. However, Jack also knew he played well, and always helped pick up equipment after the practices.

Jack showed him the number coordinates on the whistle. The boy studied it carefully, and Jack recognized fear in his eyes.

Harold's breathing accelerated and Jack feared the kid might have an asthma attack. Harold pulled out an inhaler, took a deep draft, until his shoulders settled.

"My dad won't be happy when he hears what brought you here. We try to keep a low profile. You see, we moved to Evanston to get away…from…"

"Let me guess…Vincent Marcov," said Jack.

As if the villain could hear, Harold responded in a whisper.

"How did you know?" Harold's eyes widened.

"I've heard other stories. Can you tell me what happened?" Jack asked.

"Well, I guess it would be OK. Because I know you from school and all," said Harold.

He sighed, like he was ready to jump off a cliff.

"My dad worked at a lab. Marcov also was on the staff, but he went by the name Vocram. Turns out the guy was sabotaging projects. That is until he was discovered. When all the trouble hit the fan, we left town to get away. Marcov *terrified* my dad." Harold said.

Jack sensed that he and Harold were alike, wanting to avoid trouble. At school, they were not the show ponies, but the behind-the-scenes kind of kids. They liked certainty and safety, and honored their commitments.

Jack sensed there was something Harold wasn't telling him.

"Did Dr. Marcov use any nanobots?" asked Jack.

Color drained from Harold's face. "How did you know?" Harold asked, his face ashen.

"He's done that to other people," said Jack.

"I'm trying to find out where Marcov lives. Do you have any ideas?" Jack asked.

"No, we want to steer clear of him. The nanobots crawling up into our nostrils was horrible. Afterwards, my dad and I began to notice we were acting weird, telling lies, acting paranoid, and zoning out. Luckily, we had access to an experimental blood treatment that seemed to clear the effects," said Harold.

Jack wondered now if he was having a panic attack. After all, he had those symptoms.

He had to get out of there, but what could he say?

"When all this is over, we should hang out." Jack said quickly, moving toward the door to escape.

* * *

Meanwhile, in a laboratory deep within his compound, Dr. Vincent Marcov had finished programming the satellite for another polar attack. It was time to work on Jack's DNA from the cotton swab. The cells sat in a Petri dish, ready for a fatal virus, tailor-made for Jack.

Marcov glared at the two photos pinned on his wall, one of Joseph Spencer and one of Jack Abernault. The symmetry of eliminating both of them with a virus felt satisfying.

"One down and one to go," he said, sipping his wine.

* * *

The next morning the *Chicago Sun Times* headline announced the iron dome over the ice cap was complete. Finally, there was some good news.

* * *

Friday night, Jack sat in a brand-new electric Volvo wagon as his dad pulled up in front of Grace's house. The Abernaults finally had replaced the dusty brown minivan, and his mom now drove a new Prius. The cars were the first major purchases from the Spencer estate. Jack dreamed of getting his own car. He couldn't believe his parents still hadn't relented about his license, but they were sticking to their guns.

Jack made his way up Grace's front walk, pushing down his excitement about the upcoming evening. He reached up to ring the doorbell; however, Grace opened the door and abruptly pulled the bouquet of flowers from his hands.

"Go put these in some water," she said, pushing the flowers at her mother.

But Grace's dad stepped in. "Not so fast, Missy. We need a photo," he said.

"OK, but make it quick," said Grace.

Jack was accustomed to this girl's need to control the playbook. But why couldn't she spare a minute for her parents? He took her hand, steering her for a picture.

Both parents aimed their phones.

"One more near the evergreens," said her dad.

The couple moved into position. Jack smiled, Grace, not so much.

"Thanks," he said, waving to the parents as Grace pulled him toward the car.

Once they settled in the back seat Jack asked her, "What's the big rush?"

"They're making *such* a big deal out of this to annoy me," said Grace.

Then her tone brightened. "Hi, Mr. Abernault, sorry to keep you waiting," said Grace.

"Good evening, Grace," he said.

Then he waved up at her parents who stood arm in arm, beaming that their daughter would be attending her first dance... conforming for once.

"Look," Grace said, extending her hands.

Her fingertips, more like talons, glistened with deep red nail polish.

Jack cringed.

"Yikes, that looks like blood," said Jack.

Grace shoved him.

"This color was the compromise. I wanted black polish, and *mother* wanted pink. She was paying, so the manicurist suggested this shade, *Vampire Vixen*," Grace said.

Jack's dad sputtered in the driver's seat. Then he cleared his throat, resuming his role as disinterested chauffeur.

Jack was not about to let this Vampire Vixen moment pass.

"OK…You do know you're *never* going to live this one down," Jack said with delight.

He felt his heart relaxing in his chest. He had worried this car ride might be awkward with his dad at the steering wheel. They must be the only sixteen year olds who needed a ride to this event. But tonight Grace made it easy.

Her dress was black, of course, but cut away at the shoulders.

"By the way, you look great," he said with admiration.

"You look OK yourself," she said, meeting his eyes. "New tie?"

"Oh, this is all new, I assure you. My mom hauled me over to Old Orchard last week," he said. Jack brushed some petals off his sport jacket's sleeve.

"Thanks, by the way, for the bouquet. I imagine my mother is busy pressing a few of the blossoms in her scrapbook as we speak," said Grace.

Jack took her hand. It felt warm.

The car rolled up to the high school, and they thanked Mr. Abernault, who told them to text when they were ready to leave.

"OK, *Vampire Vixen*, Are you ready for this?" Jack's eyes twinkled.

"Keep that up, and you *will* get a big bite on the neck," she said.

"Oh, I'm counting on it," he said, pulling her up the walk.

The gym looked awesome, transformed into a French village by the decoration committee.

"Our next song, *Coucher du Soleil,* is dedicated to our exchange student from France."

Jack led Grace to the dance floor and pulled her in close. They moved, rocking gently to the music.

The next song blasted into the gym with hypnotic drumbeats.

After several more dances, the music stopped.

"We're going to take a break now, so get yourself some food. See you in fifteen," said the deejay.

Jack and Grace moved over to one of the food stations serving French fries and sauces.

"These are amazing. Try the peri-peri dip," Grace said, popping one into Jack's mouth.

Mike suddenly appeared with his date.

"Hey, buddy," said Mike.

"Hey, Mike ..." Jack said, trying to conceal his annoyance at the interruption.

"Hi, Ellie," said Grace.

"Jack, we need to meet tomorrow. I found some interesting stuff to show you about you know what," said Mike.

"Sure," Jack said, feeling disappointment that the mood had shifted. For tonight, at least, he wanted to block thoughts of Vincent Marcov.

Grace and Ellie turned to make their way to the rest room. Mike started in on the computer talk, but Jack barely listened as he was watching Grace's hips slide through the crowd.

Soon the deejay resumed, and the couples swarmed the dance floor. The evening passed, and the closeness Jack had felt earlier seemed lost. At eleven thirty, the lights blinked to signal the event was winding down. Jack pulled out his phone to text his dad, but Grace caught his arm.

"Not so fast, buddy," she said.

She took his hand, dragging him willingly into the hall. Around a corner, he pulled her in.

They kissed next to the lockers, until footsteps approached.

Over Jack's shoulders, Grace saw her math teacher, hands on hips.

"Ahem," the teacher interrupted.

"Well, *well*...*Grace*," the teacher's tone indicating that she was not surprised to see her.

"Time to move along, dear," the woman said.

"Sure thing," Jack said, sheepishly.

But, Grace, unwilling to cede any ground, responded coolly.

"Ahhhh, yes...Ms. Pagano. *So* nice to see you this evening. What a *fetching* ensemble," she said.

Ms. Pagano actually let out a laugh at Grace's chutzpah.

Pulling out his phone, Jack texted his dad, and nudged Grace toward the exit.

A little while later, Jack walked Grace up to her door. And hoping his dad wasn't watching, he leaned in and kissed her.

CHAPTER ELEVEN

Party Girl

T he music filled the hall as Daisy bounced her hips to the beat of the rhythm. She loved leading this Zumba class, clapping her hands above her head. The group followed along, dressed in their candy-colored yoga pants. After the class, Daisy toweled off her forehead and sent her ladies off to do their errands. Grabbing a bottle of water, she drank it down.

The seventeen year old was enjoying her summer internship at the Evanston Park District. While her parents kept reminding her that a college degree in recreational management entailed more than dancing and games, Daisy wanted to enjoy her time in high school. She popped a candy in her mouth, and then she prepared for the next session.

* * *

The month of June finally had arrived, and Jack wanted to put the school year behind him. Final exams had been rough, with his grades slipping to new lows. There was talk of dropping him down an academic level, but he couldn't seem to care, except for another delay with the driver's license. At least his dad's harping about his grades, and how he should be studying, maybe would stop for the summer.

He had juggled a mountain of trouble, from Charlie and the nanobot to Marcov's nighttime visit. And, COVID brain still impacted his ability to focus. Jack felt he was stumbling out of Spring, like a soldier on his hands and knees escaping the battlefield.

Jack slept until ten o'clock, and when he finally sat up, he felt rested for the first time in weeks. After a bowl of cereal, he checked the gold whistle's numbers and found the pin on the map. Was that place the local fieldhouse on Noyes Street?

Hopping on his bike, he rode three blocks, cruising under the elevated station. The fieldhouse hosted the neighborhood sport camps and crafts, so Jack knew it well.

He leaned his bike in the rack, like he'd done hundreds of times, and walked past the tall nineteenth century windows. This old Noyes Street School, built back in 1892 by architect Daniel Burnham, now also served the arts community. And his grandmother still recalled a Halloween Haunted House set up here in 1955. Jack appreciated these family connections, anchoring his roots to Evanston's history. Charlie would begin classes in a few years, following the tradition.

Jack entered the building, his shoes squeaking on the waxed floors. He turned into the office where he saw a girl bouncing a ball on her knee. She looked up, flashing him a big smile. Sparkling rhinestone letters on her sunflower yellow shirt claimed that *Girls Just Want to Have Fun*! A giant air conditioner thrummed, red ribbons blowing in celebration mode.

"Hey," said Jack.

"If you need to register for a game? Sign-up sheet is on the counter," she said.

"No, thanks... I think I need to talk to you," said Jack.

"Sure," she said brightly, motioning him over to a round table in the corner.

Jack introduced himself, and the girl said her name was Daisy.

Thinking she looked familiar, Jack couldn't place her at first. Then it dawned on him. Wasn't she a cheerleader? He was standing in the presence of high school royalty.

Football was the highlight of autumn weekends in Evanston. Jack remembered Daisy, perched atop the Homecoming float, and throwing smiles like she was tossing gold coins to the crowd.

Jack looked at Daisy's kindergarten colored outfit. It seemed to match the girl's upbeat attitude.

Pulling out the golden whistle, Jack set it on the table.

"Wow that's cool," said Daisy.

But Jack began telling her about Vincent Marcov.

Daisy's face went ashen. "No. No. No. Not HIM Again," she said.

"What happened?" asked Jack.

"My dad worked in a lab downtown, and one day he forgot to enter a file from one of the researchers. But it turned out the delay saved the project, because apparently, the scientist's real intention was to mess up the data with a flood of errors. The guilty guy went by an alias, but we found out it was Vincent Marcov. Later, he programmed some nanobots to tinker with our brains." Daisy explained.

"That's awful. What happened then?" asked Jack.

"Soon my dad and I noticed a whirring sound in our heads that brought on *terrible* headaches. Luckily, the pain has stopped. But now, I have trouble settling down to work. And I struggle with food, wanting to eat sweets all the time. Our dental bills are through the roof. And, if that's not bad enough, I started playing a videogame that I can't stop. If something is good, I only want more. I take binging to a whole new level," said Daisy.

"I've heard other people tell stories about how Vincent Marcov used nanobots.... the whirring, the headaches, and the behavior changes. It sounds bad," said Jack.

Then Daisy picked up the gold whistle and, like magic, they noticed a new series of digits appear on the surface. Her eyes widened as she held up the golden whistle to the light.

"Wow, that's some awesome technology! Is it heat sensitive?" Daisy asked.

"Not that I know of. But there *are* smart phones, so maybe it's a smart whistle," said Jack.

"The engraved numbers provide latitude and longitude coordinates for locations. You're my seventh visit," said Jack.

He got up to leave, pocketing the whistle.

"Some people still have crippling headaches from the nanobots. It's a serious medical condition," Jack said.

He was surprised he had been so blunt. But it seemed this girl, with her sunny disposition, would not be too disturbed.

And he was right. Daisy took this troubling information and flipped it into a positive interpretation.

"I guess we were lucky," Daisy said.

As soon as Jack left the building, Daisy began texting. In a moment, she got a response.

Nice work scaring the kid. Stay tuned for more news from the Arctic.

Daisy smiled, it always was fun to be in the *In Crowd*.

Jack cruised back under the L tracks. It occurred to him that Daisy lived in a bubble of fun even though sometimes she wanted to be more serious.

After he got home, he went for a run and then spent the afternoon at the lakeshore with Mike and Grace. He recalled other summers at this beach as they ate their sandwiches. Jack squinted as he looked up at the old lighthouse looming above him. The landmark had a rich history. During the Civil War, the Union army had buried the Austrian crystal light in the sand. The North couldn't have the strategic lighthouse falling into the hands of the

Confederacy. Jack thought of his own battle. Somehow, the lighthouse's survival in 1865 filled him with hope.

He rolled over. Heat filled his pores, and he heard the sound of gulls squabbling over food scraps. Roasting on the sand, he breathed in the waxy scent of sunblock.

Late that afternoon, he texted his friends to see if they wanted to come over for Chinese food. At five thirty, with the group around the dining room table, his mother walked in from the pantry. She held an armful of serving bowls and cloth napkins, planning a proper meal. However, the white cartons of food were already making their way around the table strewn with paper plates.

Jack's dad saw his wife's disappointment. "Hey, fewer dishes to wash. Come sit down," he said.

"OK, then," she said, setting the bowls down on the sideboard.

"At least use these napkins," she said, handing them out.

"My mom does the *same* thing. Proper this and proper that," Grace said.

"I think parents want to be sure that you learn some manners," said Jack's mom.

"You guys mean well, I know," the girl said.

"Well, thanks, Grace. I'm happy you approve," said Jack's mom.

"Sure," said Grace.

"No worries, dear," said Ms. Abernault, settling the topic.

"This food is great! Where's it from?" asked Mike.

"Pine Yard," said Jack.

Even Charlie liked the rice, but, soon bored, he started throwing food off his tray.

Mike quipped that his sisters were a pain, but at least they didn't hurl food around.

Grace, teasing the baby, tossed some crunchy noodles back at him.

However, Charlie burst into tears, not knowing what to make of this unexpected assault.

"Oops, my bad," said Grace.

Jack's mom plucked Charlie out of the high chair to soothe him.

"Sometimes I go too far," said Grace, stroking her curls.

"Charlie's pretty tough. He's OK," said Jack.

But the baby glowered at Grace, his arms wrapped around his mother's neck.

Grace pulled out a balloon, blew it up, and tossed it up in the air. Dazzled, Charlie stopped crying and smiled, reaching to bat the balloon.

"See, he's a trouper." said his dad proudly.

The group finished dinner and settled in the family room.

Jack volunteered to take out the garbage, and Grace hopped up.

"I'll help you," said Grace.

"Of *course* you will." Mike couldn't resist.

Jack threw Charlie's bean bag at him, and then left the room with Grace.

The two hauled the garbage bags into the bins next to the garage, and then proceeded to kiss.

"We need to go," said Grace.

"I know," he said, and then pulled her in again for another kiss.

Then, after smoothing her hair, Jack led her back into the house.

Jack's mom was preparing the baby for bed, but Charlie lit up at the sight of Grace.

"Uh oh," said his mom. "Now he's going to want to play."

Grabbing his rabbit, she picked up Charlie, and headed for the stairs. The little guy strongly protested, wanting Grace and her balloon.

"OK...how about Grace reads Charlie a story to settle him down," said Jack's mom.

Grace hopped up.

"That's only fair, as I riled him up," said Grace.

Jack taunted her.

"Yup, you need to fix this. We're going to have some dessert while you get a taste of bedtime routine gone south," said Jack.

"Hah, *Hah*. This is going to be fun," said Grace, as they disappeared upstairs.

The rest of them finished the apple crisp.

An hour later, they could still hear Grace's voice reading book after book after book.

* * *

The next morning, Jack's phone dinged. When he saw the display with University of Chicago, his insides froze. He picked up the call.

"Jack, good, I'm glad to speak directly. This is Dr. McGloin."

"Oh, hi. What's going on?" Jack asked.

"I got a troubling message this morning. I'm going to forward it to you. It includes a video that's quite disturbing, to say in the least," said McGloin.

"Let me guess. Arctic ice cap, polar bears, and an hourglass?" Jack said.

Just saying the words aloud made his insides contract.

"My friend Grace got that message," Jack said.

"Well, I'm sure you're aware that this summer's weather has been much warmer than usual. And, another thing, Dr. Bernaski isn't returning my calls. I don't know what to think," said Dr. McGloin.

Jack felt himself float out of his body. Could Bernaski be working for Vincent Marcov? He remembered how sick he had been after his visit to the library.

"Jack, are you there?" McGloin asked.

"Uh, yes. It's hard to know who to trust," said Jack.

"It's *very* disturbing. I found out that the Newberry received a donation of ten million dollars. That's a huge temptation for a non-profit organization," said McGloin.

Before Jack could respond, the phone went dead. He hit redial, but an automated message said the line was out of order. Jack heard another click. Cell service in the city had been spotty due to the heat wave.

He hoped it wasn't something more sinister.

CHAPTER TWELVE

Tattoo Girl

The blender growled, pulverizing the kale protein drink. Then Tanya Stokes drank directly out of the appliance pitcher. She smirked as she recalled her mother's horrified look when she witnessed this habit of hers.

"Tanya Louise! *Really*. Pour that into a proper glass," said the woman.

And Tanya would respond with a long, steady glare.

And that would be the end of it, with her mom shaking her head in total disbelief.

But, in recent years, her mother had given up on the etiquette tips. And Tanya had always felt closer to her dad and brothers, as they were more straightforward. She couldn't take her mother's longing for the good old days, when young ladies wore dresses. Her mother had grown up in South Carolina, where feminine roles were tightly defined and etiquette was considered high art.

Tanya splashed water on her face and headed off to the L stop at Wilson Avenue. Finding a seat in the back of the car, she watched the blank-faced commuters file into the gritty train. Most people found the noise level unnerving. However, Tanya loved the screeching sounds as the train lurched around bends, threatening apartment buildings built way too close to the tracks. The shrieking noise of metal on metal resonated with Tanya's steeliness.

A crackly voice from the conductor announced the Wells stop. Tanya hopped off, skipping down the steps to the street. Flipping up her hood, she smirked, thinking of her mother's objection that she spent so much time down here. But the gym had been in her father's family for three generations. She knew her mother worried for her safety, but nobody messed with Tanya. She felt totally at ease walking in this area, as it felt tough, like her.

Tanya entered the gym, and threw her hoodie behind the counter where it slipped to the floor...and where she left it. She flipped on the fluorescent ceiling fixtures, filling the space with a flush of harsh light.

Soon the regulars would be showing up expecting a fresh tank on the water cooler. She hoisted the refill, turning it until she heard the click. Pulling out a jump rope, she began her work out routine, raising her heart rate for the grueling session on the Everlast bag.

* * *

Fifteen miles north in Evanston, Jack checked the coordinates on the whistle. When he entered the numbers, the location pin dropped on a gym in a seedy section near downtown. Boxers trained there for the Golden Gloves Boxing Tournament according to a web article.

Jack pulled out some masking tape and secured the whistle on the underside of his bottom dresser drawer. After the suspicious actions of Bernaski, Jack felt he needed to take extra precautions. And, of course, he didn't want his mom finding it.

Jack grabbed his wallet and called to his mom.

"I'm going to take a run, then see Mike."

"OK, tell Mike hi for me," said his mom.

He left for the Noyes Street L station and took the train down to Wells Street. He found a rundown block, with vacant store fronts and grimy windows. Old newspapers blew down the sidewalk. A homeless man slouched under a blanket, looking dazed and toothless.

This didn't look promising and he wondered if he'd meet some bouncer type guy. Sweat popped on his temples. The day was heating up to be a sizzler. A cloud of ashes blew up from the gutter catching him off guard. The grime tasted like cinders and cheap cigarettes.

Jack reached the gym, pulling open the door. A blast of frosty air hit him, sending goosebumps up his arms. Immediately, a girl blocked his way. "Hey, today is closed to the public...members only," she said.

Should he turn around, he wondered, but he'd come all this way. "I'm not here to box. Do you have a minute?" asked Jack.

"Don't make me punch you," she said.

When Jack looked surprised, she smirked.

"Only kidding," but then delivered a substantial jab in his side.

"AAGHH"...let out Jack. A sting burned his ribs.

"Tanya... Tanya Stokes," she said, introducing herself with a grin.

"You OK?" she asked.

"Yeah," Jack managed.

"This is my dad's gym," she said.

"Can you talk? Just five minutes?" asked Jack.

"Sure, I guess," said Tanya.

She stepped aside to let him in the door. Tanya folded her arms across her chest, they were covered with tattoos of reptiles. An oniony smell wafted off her shirt. Behind her, boxers pummeled punching bags, and for an instant Jack imagined they were hammering away at beef carcasses with their bare fists. The once white walls oozed a grittiness that he could almost taste. Smells of the gym left him with a queasy feeling, and his side stung from Tanya's jab.

"I'm training for a big match. So I can't talk long," said Tanya.

Jack told her that map coordinates with her gym's location had brought him to the gym.

"Show me?" asked Tanya.

"Uh, can't. Left it at home," he said.

Then he asked the girl if he could have a towel as he was freezing.

"Yeah, thermostat is broken. Hope the repair guy can make it today. The boxers don't mind, but you have to keep moving," Tanya said.

She handed him two big towels and he wrapped them over his shoulders. She also kicked a rubber wedge under the heavy door to let in some warmer air.

A blast of Chicago summer pushed back the icy gym air. Jack shivered from the shock of the heat after the chill from the out-of-control air conditioner.

Jack asked if the name Vincent Marcov meant anything.

Tanya slammed her fists together.

"That weasel . . !" She said.

"I've heard some bad stuff," said Jack.

"Marcov heard about our gym and sent some guys over to train as his security detail. Right away, these bums ignored the rules. So, my dad canceled their gym memberships and banned his goons from our place. Marcov was furious."

Tanya took a swig of water from her bottle.

"The day after all the fuss, a pizza was delivered, and when we opened the box, these tiny bug-like things ran up our noses. Right away, my dad and I had splitting headaches that must have lasted a week. We went to the doctor, but nothing came up on the scans. We thought it might be COVID, but our tests were negative. I think the doctors chalked up our symptoms to boxer brain syndrome. But we *knew* Marcov had done this. After the infested pizza, I noticed I felt more aggressive...more revved up. Since then, I've had a bunch of run-ins with the cops."

"I've met a number of people who had the same thing happen. It always goes, first Marcov, next nanobots, then headaches or worse," said Jack.

Then the tough girl said it was time for her next boxing session.

Jack left the gym, his ribs still smarting. He headed back to the elevated station.

Back in the gym, Tanya Stokes felt an iron grip on her neck. She turned and found Vincent Marcov.

"So did you insert the nanobot?" he asked in a raspy voice.

"All done. Jabbed it in when I punched his side."

"Knew I could depend on you, my young pugilist," Marcov said.

"Timing couldn't be better. The kid was due for a second dose," he said.

As Jack rode home on the L train, he thought about how Tanya Stokes could end up in big trouble if she didn't get that temper under control. When he got home, he lifted his shirt and looked in the mirror. A patch of deep red swelling showed on his ribs, so he taped on a cold pack to ease the pain. Then he checked the whistle. New numbers glistened on the surface that Jack committed to memory. Then he returned the gold item to its hiding place.

That evening, Grace called. She was angry. There had been a setback with the web searches on security systems likely used by Marcov. Jack held the phone away from his ear, not needing the speaker feature. In her loud and demanding voice, she insisted that he come over. He told her his side was swollen. Why couldn't she understand that he didn't feel all that great?

But, apparently, she and Mike had spent the whole day cataloguing security systems on the market. They were making progress, even narrowing down the designs best suited to protect a laboratory. But, then the computer had crashed, and they had lost all the information. An electrical power surge, followed by rolling outages, had occurred over Northern Illinois due to the heat wave.

Just then the lights went out in the Abernault house. Jack looked through the window and saw no streetlights, the neighboring houses reduced to dark shapes.

Still on the phone, Jack walked out his front door, assuring Grace that they would figure it out. He ended the call. Soon he was riding his bike through the darkened streets. Headlights from a few passing cars illuminated the road. Suddenly, it occurred to Jack that Grace reminded him of Tanya Stokes…like sisters from another mother. The blast-furnace-like anger was the common denominator.

Jack arrived on his friend's porch and knocked.

After a moment, Grace's mom opened the door.

"Your friend is in the kitchen," said Grace's mom. Her face looked serious.

Jack noted her unusual tone as he made his way down the hall. What was going on?

The kitchen was lit with candles, the heat, stifling. Around the table sat her dad, and Grace's uncle, the police detective. The room felt like a pressure cooker. Grace's eyes glared, and she sat slumped with her arms crossed over her chest.

Jack met her gaze.

"Hi," Jack said tentatively.

"You can save the pleasantries. Sit," said Grace's dad sternly.

Ouch. His words felt like a swarm of bees, ready to dive bomb.

Apparently, Grace's dad had overheard her phone call about the security system searches, and her uncle just happened to be over. This was bad. Very bad. What if his parents heard about this?

Hadn't he warned Grace to watch out where and how she spoke about their secret?

Mike arrived, and when he read the room, it seemed clear he felt ambushed.

"I can come back later. Looks like you're all in the middle of something," said Mike.

He started to back away. However, Grace's dad, glared at him, blocking the door.

"Sit yourself down here Mike," as he forcefully pulled out a chair, insisting the boy, *park his backside* next to Jack. The uncle's law enforcement badge glistened from the detective's belt.

Then the adults accused them of hacking. Hadn't Grace been caught red handed? The kitchen felt intense. Skin glistened with sweat. Jack's shirt felt like a wet canvas tent had collapsed on him, and the pain in his side intensified. His temples pulsed, feeling like two demons were taking turns with red hot pokers.

"Mike, your dad would be pretty upset that you're tempting fate. Computers are for school work, period. How much clearer can we make it?" Grace's dad lectured.

Jack sat stunned.

Why had Grace been so careless to make that phone call about security systems where she might be overheard? If his parents heard he had been investigating Marcov, he'd be dead meat.

The adults, glaring now, were expecting a response.

Jack felt something like a capsule open in his head, and suddenly found words tumbling out of his mouth. "Oh no, this is just a misunderstanding. Grace was only helping me with my robotics project for the state competition. There's no hacking involved. See, I'm looking into a way to enhance my robot's defensive capabilities. It's not against the rules or anything…and there's absolutely no hacking involved. None." Jack assured the adults.

The fact that the lie slipped so smoothly from his lips, shocked Jack. Sweat rolled down his face. He hoped the adults chalked it up to the oppressive heat in the room.

Relief flooded the faces of Grace's parents. They really had no clue about coding and robotics. To them, Jack's explanation sounded plausible. After all, Jack was the careful one, the one who followed the rules. Now, it seemed, the parents wondered if they had jumped the gun, making assumptions and premature accusations.

"*See!*" Grace, said, shifting from defense to offense, her comfort zone. "I *told* you this was nothing. Why do you *always* think the worst?" Grace piled on.

Mike sat there frozen in his chair, attempting to be invisible and possibly imagining how he could beam up to someplace safe… or at least someplace cool.

Then Grace's mom intervened, breaking the tension in the room.

"Well, we were concerned that you might get in trouble. You all have such bright futures. It would be a shame to jeopardize that," said Grace's mom.

Jack knew this motherly tone drove Grace nuts. At these times, her mother's southern drawl seemed exaggerated.

The detective stood up.

"I've got to get back to work, but I don't want to hear about anything like this again. Are we clear?" said the detective.

The teenagers nodded.

Just then the appliances groaned. Lights flickered on. The TV began talking, and, most welcome of all, a blast of cool air flowed from the vents.

Sighing relief, Jack stole a look at the face of Grace's uncle.

Jack could tell the detective wasn't buying his explanation. The uncle was not as gullible as the parents. He had seen just too much on the job. His expression was clear that he knew his niece was a spitfire. And he likely sensed that Jack had served up a steaming plate of BS.

A half hour later, the friends sat on swings at the park. Mike congratulated Jack on his quick explanation. However, after his initial relief at escaping that kitchen, Jack worried. If *his* parents got wind of their hunt for Marcov, Jack knew there was more than his driver's license at stake. Not only would they feel betrayed, but they would be livid that he was putting the family at risk.

And, now, Grace's family was in the mix, and he suspected that detective knew the truth. It bothered him that he and his friends were edging closer to breaking the law. However, a little bit of him, still, was pleased that he had rescued Grace from that kitchen.

Grace, however, did not see it that way. She didn't need a rescue. The showdown around the table seemed only a tiny blip in the flow of her day. She had moved on.

"We have to get that security system figured out," said Grace.

Jack tried to take her hand, but she pulled it away, apparently, in no mood for closeness. She still had a pile of anger to unload, and now she seemed to direct it toward fueling the mission.

Grace's cavalier attitude about the confrontation amazed Jack. Mike, on the other hand, dialed down his feelings, and it was clear he was busy pushing the unpleasantness away, smoothing over any ripples of distress. Mike's goal would be avoiding the possibility that *his* dad might hear about this incident.

Jack marveled how his friends clearly did not have his scruples. He *always* felt guilty. And when he wasn't feeling guilty, he worried about it. Worry seemed to be his default setting. And now his headache was getting worse and his side was throbbing.

Jack's phone dinged with a text. He touched the play icon, and the dreaded hourglass video began to play, showing a noose tightening on the planet. The clip highlighted the baking hot weather, fires in California, and coastal flooding. Marcov mocked the powers in Washington D.C. who acted like the proverbial frog swimming contentedly in the warm pot as the temperature climbed to the boiling point.

Heavy hearted, the kids rode their bikes through the quiet streets of Evanston.

That night, a nightmarish scene slithered into Jack's restless sleep. Trapped inside a hourglass with Charlie, Jack pounded frantically. The frightened eyes of his little brother looked up at him. The baby's curls disappearing under the sand was the last thing Jack saw.

CHAPTER THIRTEEN

Namaste

Winnifred Weaver pulled up her eye mask. This morning she regretted staying up too late, binging on *House Hunters International*. Someday she hoped to see the world, however, these days it took real effort just to make it downstairs to the communal kitchen.

It was her turn to prepare the oatmeal for the house residents. Why couldn't they just have toast? Why the big deal about a hot breakfast? If she had her choice, she'd snack on cashews if she got hungry. Her frustration grew at the thought of hauling out the big pot, waiting for the water to boil…but only momentarily. Because, as always, she lowered her irritation by focusing on something pleasant. Maybe that afternoon, she would catch the next three episodes of *House Hunters*. She pictured herself, draped over the long sectional, enjoying a chai tea latte, covered in a fluffy blanket. Within minutes Winnifred dozed off, sending up a series of soft snores, as she drifted away to an exotic beach in the Seychelles.

* * *

That morning Jack awoke early. He pulled out the bottom drawer and took the whistle from the underside. Checking the coordinates to be sure he had memorized correctly, he entered them on a map search. The pin dropped on an ashram up in the hills near Galena and the Mississippi River. Jack returned the whistle to its place, and slid the drawer back in the bureau.

From his parent's bedroom, he heard loud voices.

What was going on? This couldn't be good.

His parents didn't usually argue. So he moved into the hall to listen. But the floor creaked under his feet. His parents stopped talking.

Jack turned and went down to the kitchen. He poured some cereal in a bowl and then went back to his room. He heard his mom's voice, and she was upset. It was something about Charlie's doctor visit.

A shot of fear hit Jack. What if his brother was *not* OK? He didn't want to hear it.

Jack had to get away.

What would his parents do if they knew the truth?

He decided to go to Galena. Do one thing right. He checked his wallet for cash and the bus schedule on his phone. He started walking to the bus station.

Jack arrived just in time, jumping aboard. He settled in a seat next to the window, and texted his parents that he would be out all day with Mike. A minute later, they responded, clearly not happy that he had taken off. Then he texted Mike to cover for him.

Jack brushed tears away with the back of his hand. Something was wrong with his brother.

Then Jack had a thought. Everybody lied, didn't they?

He doubted telling his parent's the truth about Charlie and the nanobot would have made a difference. He shouldn't feel bad. It wasn't *his* fault. They should get a nanny if they couldn't watch the baby. A tiny voice deep inside protested, but this new, stronger voice silenced the doubts.

Jack stared out the window. Ugly storefronts made the city looked like an endless maze of cheap strip malls. A jack hammer started up. The arms of a beefy construction worker brutalized the cement. The drill's noise was ear-splitting, reverberating in Jack's skull. Hell must be filled with jack hammers, he thought.

Why wasn't the bus moving? And how had he left the house without his sunglasses? His headache flamed.

After creeping along for what seemed forever, the bus finally sped up once they passed the turn off for the airport. The day was heating up and the sun beat down, cooking the bus's metal roof. Jack moved across the aisle, seeking a cooler spot. The air conditioner cranked out musty fumes that fogged the windows on the bus. After several hours, prairies gave way to bluffs and the Mississippi River. Jack's bus turned into the depot in Galena.

He stepped down on to the hot pavement, moving away to escape the smell of diesel. A shaft of sun hit his face. Up the hill, he saw a row of brick buildings built over a hundred years ago. Jack ordered a car service, and ten minutes later, an old jalopy pulled up with a Lyft placard in the window. He got in, noticing the worn car seat gave off a tangle of smells. When they arrived at the destination, the driver asked if Jack wanted him to wait. Jack shook his head and got out.

The homestead sat on a hill, surrounded by tall pine trees. Young people tossed a frisbee in front of a wrap-around porch. One of the kids directed Jack to the entrance, and he headed up toward the house, feeling unsteady from the ride across Illinois.

Jack wished he had stopped in town for a sandwich. He took in some deep breaths, trying to bring up his energy. If he didn't learn something today, that uncomfortable bus ride would have been for nothing.

Jack went up the steps and saw a brass plate with the official Illinois seal hung on the brick wall next to the door. He knocked, and a teenage girl greeted him. She showed him into a spacious room with tie dyed hangings. In the corner, a fan turned and wobbled on its stand, humming out tepid air.

"I'm Winnifred Weaver, the hostess at our ashram...Well, this week, anyway.

Our next meditation class is going to be at two this afternoon. You're welcome to join us then," she said.

"I'm actually not here for the meditation group. I took the bus from Chicago because I'm following some directions," he said.

Then he explained the map coordinates.

"Have you ever heard of Dr. Vincent Marcov?" he asked.

Winnifred's eyes fluttered back and she fell to the floor.

Jack called for help, and a boy rushed in with a bottle of water.

"Do you need a doctor?" Jack asked as the girl opened her eyes.

Winnifred shook her head. After more water and an apple slice, the color returned to her cheeks.

"Sorry. Didn't mean to upset you. Maybe we can talk another time, on the phone?" Jack said.

But Winnifred shook her head, insisting that he stay.

"Hearing his name again was a shock," she said.

Winnifred's voice quivered as she began to tell how Dr. Marcov caused a disaster that left her an orphan.

"Our ashram here was founded when that environmental disaster killed our parents. It was in all the newspapers," said the girl.

"Oh, yeah. I remember my parents talking about this. Everyone was shocked because the town was so far west of Chicago, away from industry," said Jack.

Winnifred began to cry.

She took another sip of water and began her story.

"I was ten years old when we moved to a new house. At first, we were happy to have the space, a big backyard, with a pretty stream. But soon the neighbors up and down the street in my subdivision began to sicken with strange cancers. It seemed everybody had breathing problems. My dad got a weird lump on his leg, and my mother needed an inhaler to get through the day. It wasn't long before the Environmental Protection Agency found a cluster of cancers. Soon my neighborhood was crawling with scientists in hazardous material suits," said Winnifred.

"*That* must have been frightening," said Jack.

"They discovered a laboratory a mile from us with safety violations for a toxic chemical valve. This company poisoned the air and water. Finally, the place was shut down, but not before my parents died," said Winnifred.

"I'm so sorry," Jack said.

"In the end, the social workers brought us survivors to Galena. Everyone was kind, and under the circumstances, we felt fortunate. The police found that the Vocram Lab was owned by Marcov. It's his name spelled backward," she said.

"No wonder you fainted when I said his name," Jack said.

"Marcov disappeared before the trial. The cops looked everywhere, but he seemed to have vanished. Then a package arrived here that was filled with these mechanical bugs. By the time we saw the note from him, it was too late. We were all suffering from terrible headaches. So, while it's peaceful here, we can't seem to get any projects completed. We just put them off," said the girl.

It occurred to Jack that the intensity of his own headaches had increased. He had assumed this was more long haul COVID symptoms. But then there was his growing tendency to lie.

Jack noticed that Winnifred spoke without inflection, rolling out the facts in a monotone voice, almost on automatic pilot.

"So terrible with so many dead," Jack said.

He explained how other people had told a similar story. The nanobots, then the headaches, sometimes a whirring sound, and the personality changes. All this occurred after an encounter with Vincent Marcov.

But the news that nanobots could kill was devastating. He thought of Charlie.

Winnifred took a sip of iced tea, and her face suddenly brightened. Reaching in her pocket, she pulled out a handful of sparkling crystals. Winnifred explained that these colorful rocks could help defeat Marcov.

Jack didn't know quite how to respond. After all, he believed in science, certainly not in the power of crystals, seeing these glassy stones as an abdication of personal power. However, they gave comfort to some people. And, no one could deny, they were beautiful. So, Jack thanked her, accepting the bag of stones. Then he left the ashram, telling Winnifred that he would let her know if there were any developments.

Jack called for a Lyft, and a driver arrived. Once the car reached the highway, he checked to see if there was anyone following him. The visit had rattled him.

Jack leaned back in the seat, trying to calm himself.

Maybe he should see a doctor? Get checked out. Then the terrible thought hit him. Did Charlie suffer headaches?

Jack dreaded learning the truth about the baby's medical tests. On the bus ride back to Chicago, Jack felt a tsunami of trouble heading his way. The skyline rose in the distance, and dark menacing clouds hung over the city.

Jack opened the front door at nine p.m. and found his agitated parents standing in the living room.

"I'm sorry I left like that," Jack said, too tired to get into it with his parents.

But his parents didn't seem to register what he was saying. They looked broken. He could see his mom had been crying.

"We need to tell you something," said his dad.

Jack's heart constricted.

"What's happened?" Jack asked.

"Charlie's lab work and brain scan came back. There's damage… from a nanobot," said his dad.

Jack closed his eyes; the words took his breath away.

"Charlie hadn't been sleeping. And there was the falling issue, so we had him checked out," said his dad.

Jack dropped into the sofa.

"I should have refused the inheritance. Not gotten us involved," Jack said.

"You couldn't have known. None of us could have known," said his mom.

"Can the nanobot be removed?" asked Jack.

"Apparently, the device passed out of his body after it weakened his muscle tone," said his mom.

"Law enforcement will have to deal with Vincent Marcov," said Mr. Abernault.

"What can be done for Charlie?" Jack asked.

"All we can do is start some physical therapy. Time will tell. There's little research on this type of brain damage," said his dad.

Consumed with guilt, Jack felt he had failed his brother, and his family.

There was no question that he must stop the quest now.

A little part of him was relieved. This was his off ramp. No one could blame him for stepping back when they heard about Charlie…not even the Council.

Jack went to his room. He felt empty. He took the whistle from its hiding place, noticing the numbers had not changed. It was as if the whistle sat silenced.

* * *

For the next few days, Jack walked around in a fog. When Grace called, he didn't pick up.

He tried to ignore the news and avoided his friends. A week passed, and then all of them left town on family vacations—Mike to the Ozarks, and Grace to Minnesota. The Abernault family spent July and August in Charlevoix, Michigan, with his grandparents. His parents took leaves of absences from work to spend more time with Charlie, hoping the change of scenery might help with his rehabilitation.

Mike learned about Charlie's condition, and he understood why Jack was stepping back from the hunt for Marcov. Mike said he would try to bring Grace around, try to get her to understand, but she was fuming that he had abandoned the mission.

* * *

September arrived and the Abernaults returned to Evanston, and the family resumed their routine. Jack's headaches had subsided, and he hoped he was recovering from his long haul COVID issues.

One good thing to come from the summer was the long conversations with his grandmother, Mimi. The septuagenarian had taken up breathwork, and Jack learned several techniques, experiencing some of the benefits.

Charlie, tanned from all the time at the beach, had loved digging in the sand with his grandma. The toddler seemed more content, although there was a clumsiness when he moved. Every time Jack saw the child topple over, he felt a piece of his heart shrivel.

Jack dreaded going back to school. Mike said a rumor was circulating that Morningside had been promised to another relative, and that Jack should not be the estate's owner.

Mike had countered the gossip by saying the crazy story came from someone envious of Jack's inheritance.

That first week back at school, however, Jack imagined kids staring and whispering. Grace acted icy when they bumped into each other in the hall. Jack felt terrible. And he needed to get his grades back up.

When the first math quiz was announced, Jack settled on a new trick—cheating. He told himself it would be stupid not to help himself out. Lots of kids did it. Wasn't it all part of the game? A faint voice inside him protested, but Jack cranked up the volume on the music pulsing through his earbuds.

At the end of that first week of school, Jack breathed a little easier. Making lists and checking off tasks seemed to help manage the stress. Jack also helped Charlie with his physical therapy exercises. He sensed his parents worried about his isolation, because, other than Mike, he preferred to be alone.

In mid-September, Jack received a text from his school counselor. Apparently, some visitors from Chicago's corporate community planned to visit the high school's robotic lab. The principal wanted him to give them a tour.

Jack entered the main office after his last period, and his counselor introduced him to three businessmen. Tanned and manicured, they wore expensive suits and shoes, and looked like mannequins who had broken out of a Michigan Avenue window display.

"Jack, it's nice to meet you. We understand you're assembling a robot for the state competition. We're always interested in up and coming engineers," the man said.

"I'm happy to show you the lab," Jack said, feeling a flush of pride.

For the next forty-five minutes, he showed the visitors around the computer lab, explaining the interface with his robot.

"Very impressive. Jack. We would like to offer you an apprenticeship. Now you would need to talk it over with your parents and get back to us," said the man.

"That's amazing. Is it focused on robots?" Jack asked.

"Yes, and other cutting-edge technology. It would involve spending a week at a conference center in Minnesota," the man said.

At this point the principal intervened.

"You would get extra credit, of course, boosting your math, and science grades. It's really a wonderful opportunity. I've called your parents to let them know the details."

"Sounds great," Jack said.

Jack walked them to the parking lot, as they continued to discuss their projects.

Parked at the curb sat a black Maserati that looked like a high tech shark. The principal held the door open and gestured for Jack to get in the car. The vehicle was equipped with features not yet on the market. The CEOs had arranged a special ride for Jack as a thank you for the tour. The principal got behind the wheel.

"Jack can drive," said the CEO, frowning at the principal.

"Oh, he doesn't have his drivers license yet," said the principal.

They look surprised, and Jack's face flushed.

How embarrassing. What a loser. What sixteen year old didn't have his driver's license?

The men turned to leave.

Despite his humiliation, Jack couldn't help but be dazzled by the vehicle, and he got in the passenger side. After clicking the seat belts, they glided into traffic. The dashboard had options for humidity, heated seats, and automatic adjustable cruise control. When the car pulled up in front of Jack's house, several neighbors, out for a walk, stopped to see who was in the flashy coupe. Evanston residents were accustomed to seeing understated family cars.

That night Jack brought up the apprenticeship with his parents. They seemed inclined to let him go. After all, Jack had dropped out of school clubs and avoided most of his friends. Even Grace hadn't been around. His parents worried about his isolation, thinking the trauma with the space kids was weighing on him.

His dad said that given Jack's poor showing second semester of sophomore year, this apprenticeship would be a good idea. Focusing on robots, and spending a week away sounded promising.

Jack felt the zing, hearing about his *poor showing*. His dad couldn't resist taking a shot.

"Well, it's up to you," said his dad.

"I'll think about it," said Jack.

He didn't want to give in too easily.

In the old days, he knew, learning something new would have been the draw, but now it was all about the credit, all about appearances.

Later that evening, Jack checked the apprenticeship website and found the sponsor actually was connected to a big oil company. The CEOs had withheld that bit of information.

Jack considered this troubling information, but decided he could feign ignorance about the sponsor if anyone found out. This betrayal of his values went against *everything* he professed about renewable energy. Six months ago, the oil company connection alone would have been a deal breaker.

But he was different now. Jack opened his laptop and emailed his acceptance.

* * *

Several weeks later, his mother hovered as he packed his suitcase for the conference.

"You know it's going to be cold. Pack some sweaters and warm socks. They have a winter that lasts from September to May," said his mom.

"Wonder how the melting ice cap has changed Minnesota. The polar vortex sometimes dips so low that Illinois is colder than the North Pole," Jack said.

"The satellite attacks on the Arctic Shelf definitely are making all this worse," she said.

"I feel bad I've abandoned my promise to the Council," said Jack.

"I know. But really, you were tricked, kidnapped in that glass cube," she said.

"And your dad still hasn't found a way to deal with the authorities. Everything is *classified this*, and *national security that*. The Council needs to find someone with top scientific credentials in the military. Our family has suffered enough. Charlie was sacrificed," and she started to cry.

Jack wrapped his arms around his mother.

"It'll be all right, Mom," he said.

But he didn't believe it.

* * *

The next morning, Jack boarded the train headed for Minneapolis. He looked through the thick plated glass, and saw his little brother in his dad's arms. Charlie was the last thing he saw as the train slid out of the station.

After twenty minutes rocking gently through the city, Jack let his mind wander. Trees with yellowing leaves streaked past. Then farms flew by, and a spattering of cows ignored the train's passing.

Jack closed his eyes, sighing. He was glad to get away from the dreaded school hallways with the kids and the rumors. But he couldn't deny that he missed Grace.

Then he thought of Mike. His friend would have been disgusted at the big oil connection. And didn't Mike always complain when kids cheated on tests? Their unfair advantage made the grading curves more difficult for the honest students.

Several hours later, Jack's train pulled into the Minneapolis Union Depot. Icy air hit his face as he climbed down to the station platform. It felt like winter, and Jack put on his wool coat. He scanned the crowd at the terminal.

As expected, a young man in a black cap and uniform held a sign with *Abernault*. A scheduled car was part of the plan. Jack settled in the vehicle and texted his parents that he had arrived in Minnesota.

The driver handed him a box lunch and told him they had a three-hour drive to the conference center. Sitting in the limousine, he thought about the CEOs and imagined how he would feel wearing custom suits and expensive watches. Some kids at his school came from families with country club memberships, and who went on exotic vacations. Their parents generally worked in finance or the corporate world.

Now, with the Morningside inheritance, he had that kind of money. Jack considered how it would feel driving a ridiculously expensive car. What would it be like picking up Grace for a date in a Lamborghini? This fantasy took off in his head like a silver tipped Lear jet climbing into the clouds. This thought was followed quickly by a stab in his heart as he knew Grace was furious with him. Although he couldn't deny that he had disappointed her, failing his promise to the Council's mission. And maybe he felt that he didn't deserve love. He felt awful.

Maybe having some food would help. Jack ate a sandwich and drank the juice bottle, but it only left a sour taste in his mouth.

His life was a wreck. The girl, the mission, all gone. He looked out the car window, noticing the weather turning ugly. The sky shifted as the sun slid ominously behind dark clouds, the kind one sees in the dead of winter. Snow flurries began to swirl, and the wind picked up. Giant pine trees leaned into the highway. Drowsy from the travel and the darkening scene, Jack's eyes closed, and he fell into a deep sleep.

* * *

Jack awoke, shivering in pitch blackness.

His socks and coat missing, he was on his back. He struggled to his feet, staggering a few steps until he felt a wall of dirt. He seemed to be standing in a deep pit.

What was going on?

He screamed for help, but the darkness swallowed his voice.

Had the car veered off the road into a ditch? Or was this some kind of insane initiation? Nothing made sense. Bitter cold gripped his body. Howling wind rushed overhead.

Had Marcov taken him? Was the Council seeking revenge for breaking his promise? Had he been drugged? That juice had not agreed with him.

He could not see his hand in front of his eyes. It seemed he was abandoned, and freezing. Would his parents miss him? Would his last text keep them from worrying?

His throat felt lined with razors, as he tried to swallow. It hurt too much to scream. His mind began to play tricks on him. What was crawling on his legs? Could it be nanobots? Frantically he tried to brush off whatever was attacking him. The creeping sensation ceased, but maybe his skin was too cold to register the bots.

Jack had to do something. He had read a book once about a prisoner in solitary confinement who had kept his sanity by organizing his thoughts. Jack focused on memories of his family.

Willing himself to recall his earliest recollection in life, Jack conjured up the scene of a fire in the house across the street. He must have been three years old. The memory now played out like a movie. Blaring sirens had awakened him from a nap. He recalled how scared he had been, watching the long red trucks pull up to the curb. Flames from the house where his friend lived burst from an upstairs window. He heard cries for help. Then, it seemed out of nowhere, these wonderful big figures in shiny black coats carried his friend Nathan out of the burning house.

Clinging to his mother, Jack remembered seeing the mask and tubes pulled over the little boy's face. Hours later, the fire was out, and, thankfully, everyone had survived. Nathan had come home the following week from the hospital. The Abernaults had brought over a casserole for the family. Jack could still feel the sense of his friend's bruised hand in his.

This event marked a turning point in Jack's development. It had created a lasting impression of what a hero could do. After that fire, little Jack announced he planned to be a firefighter when he grew up. But the trauma of that incident also left him with the understanding that the world could be an exceedingly dangerous place.

Now, in this dark hole, Jack drew in a breath, recalling Nathan's rescue. The actions of those firefighters, imprinted in his young mind, burned a lasting impression of courage and loyalty. Every year after, during Evanston's Fourth of July Parade, his heart skipped a beat when the venerable hook and ladder truck slowly rolled past. Jack understood these were the *special ones* who rushed into trouble, protecting others from harm.

As the years passed, however, he discovered science and math, and let go of the notion of becoming a firefighter. What had stayed with him were the core values of loyalty and service. Honoring tradition, following a path under the direction of teachers and mentors, felt right to Jack. Even the rules of math, and now engineering, fit his need for structure. They also seemed a path for making a contribution of some kind. This feeling of responsibility created a rudder that had guided him. All that was true, up until recently, when he had begun to lie, to cheat, and to rationalize his actions.

Darkness had followed him into their home, and it had landed on the most vulnerable. Jack had been a rotten big brother. He deserved to be in this pit. He had put Charlie at risk and given in to the temptations from the CEOs. His commitment to green energy had collapsed like a house of cards.

He didn't recognize himself anymore. Had he been a victim of nanobots? There were the headaches. He had put off the doctor appointment, afraid to know the truth.

He worried that the people he'd met on the quest couldn't be trusted. Definitely, not the Masons, not Trip Grainger, not Bernaski. Maybe they'd all made stuff up? But why?

Who *could* he trust? Not even himself, he thought bitterly.

Jack thought of Mike, peaceful and gentle, always ready to smooth over any trouble. And Grace, outspoken and bossy, seemed even now to reach across the miles. Despite the fact they were no longer together, he sensed her presence. Most of his life he had depended on these two friends. It had only been in the past year that Jack had been more apt to keep his own council, fearing Grace's judgment. He wondered what they were doing right now. He tried to imagine their faces, but he was fading fast. Lightheadedness overtook him. His head cradled in the dirt, he passed out.

It must have been hours later, he stirred. A glimmer of awareness flickered in his mind. He had to decide. Give in to the cold and the signals his body was sending. Or take charge of his situation. The face of Joseph Spencer now appeared.

Jack marshalled his will and began to sit straight-backed, with legs crossed. Willing himself to focus, a technique he had learned at the karate dojo, he sat. First, he told himself, get in touch with a felt sense in the body. Second, find an image that fits the bodily tightness, and lastly, come up with a word that catches the essence of the image and physical sense. Working this sequence, he moved his awareness from sense, to picture, and to word, over, and over, and over again. And it was working. At each stage, he felt a release, along with a deeper breath. The tightness in his chest shifted a bit. He had learned this focusing technique might not solve his problem, but he'd carry the burden in a easier way.

Jack saw the *wheel of fortune* in his mind, turning around, up and down, pausing a moment in the best place and then spinning down into the worst. Moving his feelings from the highs and lows on the circumference of this circle, he moved his attention to the center, to the hub of stillness.

He breathed in the moment.

From this centeredness, he would will himself into this experience for whatever came. Jack now switched into a meditation pose, seeking a place beyond his attachments, under his fear, and even beyond his hope for rescue.

He drew in a deep breath.

Then softly, Jack's chest released.

He was free.

At that moment, a flood gate of lights blasted into the hole.

Jack awoke, finding himself still in the car heading north to the conference center. His head was pounding, and his throat raw. Had it all been a terrible nightmare?

He fell back into the car seat, his forehead burning up.

By the time he arrived at the conference center near the Boundary Waters, he was running a high fever. The worried director called a doctor, who insisted they arrange to have a corporate jet fly Jack back to Chicago. Too sick to argue, he had no choice but to board the plane on the private airstrip.

Hours later, in his room at home, Jack sat on the edge of his bed. As he pulled off his socks, a shot of terror hit him as he noticed one of his socks, covered in dried mud, was on inside out!

CHAPTER FOURTEEN

The *Anamchara Text*

Diagnosed with a severe bout of strep, Jack languished in bed for days, watching TV and eating soup. Each day was like the next, until one afternoon Grace came to visit.

Jack felt his heart jump when her voice came up the stairwell. He sat up, plumping his pillow behind his back. Grace poked her head in the door.

"Hey...sleepy boy. How you doing?" Grace asked.

"Grace, hey, come on in. Doing better. But the medicine wears me out. All I do is sleep," he said.

She handed him a peace offering, a black knit cap.

"My mom knitted it for you. But I picked the color," she said.

"Thanks, it's great. I should be back at school next week, at least for half days," said Jack.

"We all miss you. I miss you," said Grace.

"It's going to be hard catching up on work," said Jack.

"Don't think about that. You need to rest up. That's the most important thing," she said.

"I've never felt this wiped out, with the strep on top of the COVID," said Jack.

"You do look pale," said Grace.

She hadn't stayed long, but the visit had mended their relationship. The pain of their separation had drained from him in those few minutes.

The glow lasted for the rest of the afternoon; however, as evening approached, Jack's mood darkened. Now that he had started to recover physically, memory of the pit haunted him. When he tried to push the experience off as a feverous hallucination, the dried mud on the sock offered contradicting evidence.

But what exactly had happened?

Confused and conflicted, Jack felt like a *fight club* had taken up residence in his chest. From the four corners of this boxing ring the contenders glared. In corner #1, his need for self-preservation, in corner #2, the promise to the Council, in corner # 3, his family's safety, and in the last corner, the Earth's survival. These warring forces felt like vicious dogs tearing him apart.

The next morning, after some breakfast, he felt stronger. But then his thoughts turned to Grace. Did she blame him for abandoning the quest? He figured she knew about Charlie's diagnosis.

Jack pulled out the items from Sophia. It seemed even the gold whistle was content to sit dormant. No new numbers had appeared on the engraved surface. He taped it under his drawer.

The following week, Jack returned to school with a plan for an early dismissal. This shortened day worked for the first week back. The following week Jack felt stronger, and he resumed his full day of classes.

Grace had been patient to let him recover. But now that he was better, she couldn't resist bringing up the topic of taking out Marcov's headquarters. She laid out her argument, but Jack stood firm despite his low energy, and Mike backed him up.

"What part of *no* don't you get?" Jack stared Grace down.

But Grace shot back. "No, *you* don't get it. The best defense is an escalated offense. *Art of War*, Sun Tzu."

"Sun Who?" asked Mike.

"Don't pretend you don't know who I'm talking about. Look, I get it that Charlie has taken a terrible hit. But if you think that backing down will stop Marcov, you really are bat crap crazy. Power is the only language he speaks. Time to double down, not back away. That monster will only ratchet up the attacks," Grace said.

"Have you seen Charlie wobble as he tries to walk?" asked Jack.

Hearing his friend's voice crack, Mike said, "We love Charlie, too, you know. We're here for you."

"Some of us, more than others," said Grace, taking a shot at Mike's reticence.

"Enough. Stop," said Jack.

But Grace, of course, did not stop.

"Look, Jack, the best way to shield Charlie is not to ignore the reality. If we can figure out which security system Marcov installed, we can do this. Don't we *always* say people give up too easily? If we stick to the course, we can protect your family, *and* maybe save the polar bears. Somehow Marcov's satellite lasers are evading the Iron Dome. Marcov doesn't even bother to send threatening texts anymore. He thinks he's won."

Mike spoke up.

"Here's a thought. Grace and I keep looking for likely security systems. Meanwhile, Jack can learn what's written in that *Anamchara Text*. You didn't promise your parents you wouldn't look at it. Right?" Mike said.

Technically, Mike was correct. While his parents had asked him to stop the quest, nothing had been said about the text.

And anyway, what harm could come from reading a book?

"OK, I see what you're saying. That could work," said Jack.

So after school the next afternoon, Jack prepared to look at the book.

But first he would do some Navy Seal deep breathing: inhale for four counts, hold breath for four counts, release air for four counts, lungs empty for four counts, and then repeat. After four sets of this sequence, he felt stronger and more centered.

Jack went to the kitchen and stood in the opened refrigerator, looking for sandwich makings.

Plate in hand, he took his food, moving carefully up the stairs, passing Charlie's door. Sitting on his bed, he ate his sandwich, brushing the crumbs off his spread. Then he opened his drawer and pulled out the *Anamchara Text*.

Weird how the book weighed next to nothing. His mother would freak if she discovered what he was up to.

But he had to do this.

Jack opened the book. The page stared back at him, challenging him to break the code. Reading the lines was slow going, and made his eyes feel like they were plodding through mud. Some of the letters looked Arabic, graceful like a waterfowl leaning over the edge of a pond. But how was he supposed to figure out the meaning with so much of the print gone? He rolled over on his back, feeling defeated.

He stared at the ceiling, his eyes scanning the empty surface.

Then he recalled the words from the Council's letter.

Listen with your heart, with your head, and with your gut.

He repeated the words...*with my heart, with my head, and with my gut.*

Jack sat up and flipped the book's pages to the diagram with the star-encircled symbol. With fresh eyes, his mind began to put something together, like a puzzle dancing into place.

It dawned on him that he had made *nine* visits, and there were *nine* points around this circle. Turning to his notes, words now popped off the page, *anger, pride, deceit, envy, avarice, fear, gluttony, lust,* and *sloth*… nine points, nine visits, nine flaws.

This couldn't be a coincidence.

Resting back on his pillow, he thought about the people he had met on his visits. Margaret Mason nagged and bristled with *anger.* While he could admire her striving for perfection, she seemed to go overboard.

Jack sensed a key turning in his mind, opening a lock that guarded the secret of the coded diagram. He began to write down his thoughts.

Lindy Simons made him recoil with her neediness and self-denial. Did her compulsion to serve others and one up everyone with her helping come from *pride*? She was kind, but it was too much.

Trip Grainger used people and relationships like pawns in a game. The Graingers operated in a transactional way. They gave to get, finding shortcuts to trump their competition. The shady behavior relied on *deceit.* They were successful, but to what ends? They craved recognition.

Jack sat up. A scaffold of understanding was building in his mind.

Lutetia and Esme set themselves apart by rejecting anything *ordinary.* The *by-pass* into art required constant comparisons, the stuff of *envy.*

Dr. Bernaski hoarded data, stockpiling information. *Avarice?*

However, Dr. McGloin's work restoring the Amazon showed something better. The truth about these behavior styles seemed more *dynamic than static.*

Then there was Harold, on alert for threats, searching for safety and certainty. Jack could relate, as he also anticipated worst case scenarios, a wheel of worry spinning in his head.

Daisy and her appetite for *more* seemed on a *gluttonous* path. She focused on plans for novel entertainment, filling her calendar with activities and fun. Happy and full of joy, Daisy overdid it.

Tanya Simons, on the other hand, *lusted* for power, punching her way through life. Anger fueled her as she sought to control the people and situations in her environment.

Winnifred admitted she could be lazy. She seemed to push down tremendous anger, so the effects of her trauma came out in sneaky ways, like being late, or incompetent. Could her low key approach be considered *slothful?* She controlled any unpleasantness by dialing down her awareness.

Jack thought he'd made a breakthrough.

But there still was a problem. Where on the circle, in which position, did each of the nine people fit?

Well, there remained two problems really, because he also didn't know what the connecting lines meant in the diagram. They looked like a tangled spider web.

Just then, Charlie began to howl. Jack jumped off his bed. A moment later, he lifted the baby out of the crib. The damp curls and warm little body smelled of sweet baby sweat. With Charlie's arms circling his neck, he carried the little guy down to the kitchen. Jack sat him in the high chair and maneuvered the tray in place till he heard the click. Then he poured a bowl of cracker octagons, adding some cheese cubes to the tray. Charlie kicked his legs, pointing to his cup.

"You want milk. I'm moving as fast as I can," said Jack.

Grabbing the milk, he filled Charlie's favorite blue cup.

His mother called down the hall.

"I have to run some errands. Can you watch Charlie? I'll be back in a few hours."

"Sure. No problem," said Jack.

His mother picked up her car keys, and he heard the door close.

Watching his brother chomp on the snack, Jack considered the anger, fear, and anxiety he'd felt during the nine visits.

He looked at the notes he'd scribbled. Tanya Stokes, Winnifred Weaver, and Margaret Mason operated out of an angry gut center. Tanya exploded with anger. Winnifred dialed down her rage, controlling it by "forgetting" her anger. While Margret Mason released her anger and frustration with a steady barrage of criticism. Jack recalled how talking to these three people had made him notice his own anger, in his gut.

He poured more milk for Charlie. While he waited for the next refill, Jack considered how anxious he had felt with Lindy Simons, Trip Grainger, and Lutetia Langdon. It seemed all three sought relationships, but each used a different tactic.

Lindy needed to be needed and served people. Being alone was difficult for her.

Trip Grainger, on the other hand, sought recognition from others and was driven to impress people. Failure was not an option and maintaining a top position was key.

Lutetia needed to feel special, and was drawn to creativity as a way to avoid ordinary elements of life. Her relationships were drama filled, like a bad play.

Dr. Bernaski, Harold, and Daisy operated out of fear. Their need for certainty was managed with hoarding, worrying, or planning.

The professor managed fear by gathering information.

Harold attempted to get out ahead of his fear by scanning for danger, and by preparing for trouble.

Daisy avoided fear by escaping into fun and by planning for the future.

But the question of who fit where on the diagram remained.

Charlie now was fussing.

"Buh-ee. BUH-EE!" he demanded.

Jack loped up the stairs to find the bunny.

He looked in the usual places, crib, floor, toy box...but no bunny. He checked his room. Sometimes, Charlie wandered in there.

The treasured rabbit sat slumped next to his bed. Jack scooped it up.

Then something caught his eye.

The gold whistle was perched on top of the nightstand, next to the lamp. He knew he had left it taped under the drawer so his parents wouldn't find it. Jack picked it up and saw a new engraving etched on the surface of the gold:

Mason 1:00 p.m. it read.

What *could* that mean?

Then a sudden flash of understanding!

He could barely control his fingers as he texted his friends.

A half hour later, Mike and Grace sat around the Abernaults' kitchen table, while Jack explained his theory about the body centers (head, heart, and gut), and the three core emotions: anger and the need for control, anxiety and the need for connection, and fear and the need for certainty.

"The problem is we don't know who fits where on the diagram," said Mike.

"We do now," said Jack, setting the golden whistle on the table.

They stared at the new engraving.

"This clue puts Margaret Mason in the one o'clock position on the circumference of the circle. Now we have the orientation. I'll add the other people in the order I met them," said Jack.

"Grab some index cards. We can map this out on the round table," said Mike.

Jack got a text from his mom asking if he could babysit for another few hours. His parents wanted to go out for dinner.

"Great! We have extra time now," said Jack.

And it seemed Charlie was content to sit on Grace's lap, hugging his bunny while the teens worked.

They added names, numbers, and attributes around the edge of the table, in the order of the visits.

"This works for the nine types, and the three body centers. But each type has *two* lines connecting them to other types. What does *that* mean?"

Picking up the *Anamchara Text*, Jack flipped through the pages, scanning for diagrams.

"The lines maybe could be **vectors**. You know, directional arrows. That would explain a path," said Jack.

"You mean a way to *balance* a personality?" asked Grace.

"Except each point is connected with *two* lines," said Mike.

"Maybe these points on the circle are more like *comfort zone*s," said Grace.

"And the connected points maybe add more resources for a personality," said Jack.

They turned pages in the *Anamchara Text* and cobbled together a list of points and attributes.

Nine Patterns

1. The Perfectionist... Values goodness... "I am right"... overdone becomes anger
2. The Giver... Values love... "I am kind"... overdone becomes pride
3. The Performer... Values effectiveness... "I am successful"... overdone becomes deceit
4. The Artist... Values beauty and creativity... "I am special"... overdone becomes envy

5. The Observer... Values knowledge... "I am wise"...
   overdone becomes avarice
6. The Loyal Skeptic... Values faithfulness... "I am loyal"...
   overdone becomes fear
7. The Epicure... Values joy... "I am happy"... overdone
   becomes gluttony
8. The Boss... Values power... "I am powerful"...overdone
   becomes lust
9. The Mediator... Values peace... "I am peaceful"...
   overdone becomes sloth

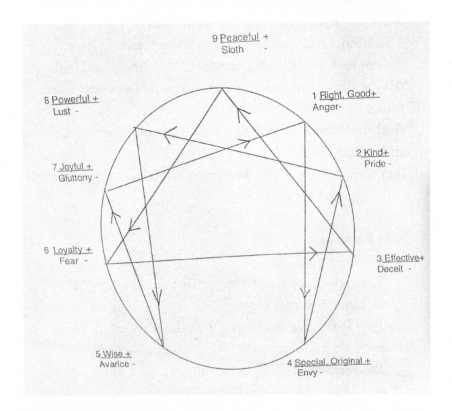

Although the paper was crumpled, this was coming together, showing a path through the diagram's web, and releasing the

mysteries in the text. No longer an enigmatic star design, the code was broken. Jack felt excited.

"But, I don't think a type could *ever* contain your total identity," said Mike.

"Like I read somewhere, the map is not the territory," said Grace.

"Yeah, but this map offers a good first step. You need to know your particular starting point, what sliver of reality you overvalue," said Jack.

"Maybe shows us our blind spot, the stuff we hide from ourselves," said Mike.

Jack and Grace stared at him. Underneath Mike's calm nature rested a deep pool of understanding, like an old soul.

"So guys, I see myself at point 8, but the lines connect to 2 and 5. Think if I took on some of Lindy Simon's sweetness, would it tone down my feistiness?" asked Grace.

"Uh, couldn't hurt. Although we wouldn't know what to do if you started wearing pink and baking us cookies," said Jack.

"I could do with some cookies," said Mike.

"Uh...but I guess I shouldn't use this for taking shots at Grace," said Jack.

"*Yeah*," said Grace.

"And you bake your *own* cookies, buddy." Grace smiled at Mike.

"We need to look within ourselves, not to type *other* people," said Grace.

Then she considered the other line connected to point 8.

"The 5 gift is wisdom so maybe I would wait before I act?" asked Grace.

"Then I have kindness features from point 2, and prudence from point 5. I'd be pretty much perfect," said Grace, smiling.

Jack spoke up. "Point 6 looks familiar to me, and calming down like Winnifred at point 9 would interrupt my focus on worst case scenarios. So when I do the deep breathing it energizes my gut center. This allows me to act with courage like at point 3. I think the three body centers are important. I know I depend mostly on my head, my thinking capacity. But I'm often out of touch with my gut. However, when I deep breathe, my gut energizes." said Jack.

"But you need to avoid the negative parts of 6, 3, and 9, like I need to avoid the negative qualities at 8, 2, and 5," said Grace.

Mike said he must be at point 9, and conceded that getting energized at point 3 would motivate him. But he needed to avoid the negative fear at point 6.

"Wonder if a meditation group would help us," said Jack. He recalled his grandmother Mimi with her breath and meditation practice. The family had all noticed that Mimi had seemed more centered this visit, less apt to offer unsolicited advice.

"That's a *great* idea," said Grace.

"OK, here's a thought. Imagine the nine points as types of boats. The number one type acts as a border patrol craft, the number two serves as a hospital ship, and the three type is an impressive yacht. The four type skims through life as an elegant sailboat. The five type acts as a research vessel. The six type works as a tugboat, the seven type, a fun cruise ship, and the eight type is a battleship. The nine type is a pontoon boat, floating on the lake." said Mike.

"Yeah, that's a nice way to look at the surface image of the types. But those nine boats show only the strengths. We should look at the nine flaws, or to use your boat metaphor, the nine different rudders that hide under the gifts, steering off into unproductive routes, and eventually sinking the boats," said Jack.

"We should check this out with an expert. We can't ask Jack's mom, even though she's a psychologist. Your mom would flip out that we're doing this. Could we call your grandfather, Mike?" Grace asked.

Mike's grandfather was a respected Jungian analyst, and Mike trusted him. Jack and Grace remembered all the cool mythology books that Mike had shown them, gifts from this grandpa.

Mike found his number and called on FaceTime. A moment later the septuagenarian was listening thoughtfully while the three teens explained the personality map laid out on the table. When they showed him the diagram, the elderly man's face brightened.

"I want to look at something. This reminds me of an unpublished paper. I'll call you back," said Mike's grandfather.

The three heated up a frozen pizza while they waited.

About forty minutes later, he called back. A smiling Grandpa Joseph appeared on the screen.

"I found it. This paper, *The Tangled Wing*, describes how people get tripped up in different ways. The author was the director of a school in Paris in the 1920s. All sorts of people attended his salon, from avant-garde writers to a Russian ballerina. Some of the notes ended up in the Yale Library. I recall I was quite taken by the ideas based on a nine-pointed star, like the one you showed me."

"The theory goes that a young child adopts a personal world view that colors how they proceed in life. It's as if, around the age of seven, a child stands in front of nine doors, and walks through one. Now behind that door are three more doors, and so on, and so on. The result is a limited view of the self and of the world. And during teenage years and young adulthood there is a tendency to overwork this one particular style. The *Anamchara Text* sounds like these enneagram writings."

"And new data on *neural integration* supports this view. As a behavior, thought, or feeling is repeated, a neural pathway deepens, making an actual groove, which results in habitual patterns."

"The nine paths are motivational styles. For instance, a young child, scolded for a mistake, decides to never let that happen again.

As a result, they overvalue not making mistakes, and become per-fectionistic. They overuse one rigid pattern of functioning."

"You have described the nine life strategies in your explana-tions this afternoon. The enneagram describes clusters of thoughts, feelings and behaviors. While we are all unique, it's easy to get lost without a map of some kind. The lines on the diagram show the flow in the patterns of personality. So qualities at these connected points offer valuable resources, but also the less resourceful pitfalls."

"We are told to 'be good,' but often that requires different paths for people with different impulses. It helps to be aware of your particular path so you can make adjustments."

"The goal is to stay present in the moment, and to respond appropriately, and not constricted by a bias of your type or point. While I do think that rigid patterns soften as people age, as life ex-periences tend to sand down the false facades, learning this system could save people lots of pain and wasted time."

"I should mention that I recall this wisdom came with a warning. An individual could get stuck, feeling their type justi-fied the way they thought, felt, and behaved. But the whole point was to become aware of one's imbalance, and to move out of the comfort zone."

Mike was taking notes. Grace looked thoughtful. Jack felt validated.

The map made sense to someone they trusted, someone with cre-dentials. This was a *discernment*, a term used in the *Anamchara Text*.

At ten o'clock, Grace and Mike went home, and Jack went to bed.

However, three hours later Jack still was awake, tossing and turning. His excitement about breaking the book's code, and the encouraging words of Mike's grandpa, had been replaced now by a painful self-evaluation.

He had to make some changes, and the task felt overwhelming. He knew he'd made progress since his confession in the pit. He thought about how the Council had told him to spread the lessons in the *Anamchara Text*. He was the messenger. He'd never be perfect. But he could *do the next right thing.*

The thought that a sizable number of people would need to take these lessons to heart seemed overwhelming. How was that supposed to happen? Seemed impossible. The digital clock glowed three a.m. before Jack finally fell asleep.

The alarm clock's buzzer sounded the next morning. A dull haze camped between his temples, and Jack's insides refused to rally. Finally, he managed to make it down the stairs where he found his dad in the kitchen.

"Rough night?" asked Dad.

"Couldn't get to sleep," said Jack.

"Grace and Mike came over for a while?" asked Dad, looking at the dirty glasses in the sink.

"Yeah," said Jack. Then he rested his head on the counter between his arms.

"Let me make you some eggs," his dad said.

"Thanks. My body feels like I'm jet lagged," said Jack.

"Go take a shower while I fix breakfast," said Dad.

After his shower, Jack dressed and ate scrambled eggs. He felt glued back together.

"Thanks, Dad," said Jack.

"I live to serve," said his dad, grinning.

Jack met Grace and Mike before first period. They talked about the night before and Jack shared that some things were bothering him.

"It's hard to admit this stuff," said Jack.

"Yeah," said Grace. "I barely slept."

"Me, too," said Mike. "The description of the #9 made me feel like a butterfly pinned to a board. Sometimes I get frozen in a routine that pulls my energy down."

"OK, but remember our pattern is only a sliver of our true self, even if the map nails the parts that could use some fixing," said Jack.

"I think I fight too much," said Grace. "Maybe I'm really afraid to look weak, scared that I'll lose control," she added.

The three were quiet.

All these insights were eye opening; however, Jack knew two big issues remained. How would they get the word out about the personality map? And what would happen when his parents found out he had lied to them, gone on the quest and learned the knowledge in the text? His relationship with his parents would be shredded. They would feel betrayed and would blame him for Charlie's disability.

But Jack knew he had to go forward. The stakes were too high.

Jack reasoned that the danger his parents feared *already* had happened. Marcov would reach them one way or another. Sooner with a nanobot or virus, or later with a collapsed environment.

Jack knew he *had* to act.

"Let's teach this *people map* to everyone we know. If they find it helpful, they'll pass it on. We can say we learned it from an old book that was found in the university library stacks," said Jack.

"*Ding!*" Grace's phone notified her of a message.

The idea registered simultaneously with the three friends. The way to get the word out was obvious:

social media

Their fingers got busy.

It wasn't long before the enneagram was the hot topic around school. Mike, Jack, and Grace taught the nine patterns to an afterschool club. Soon, everyone wanted to learn more about how people saw the world from different perspectives. First, they learned about the *gift* at each point, then about the needed shift.

Grace started a blog, and Mike managed an Instagram account. Then they asked the school social worker to start a meditation group. At the first session, the counselor explained a simple breathing technique, and how a pattern of inhaling and exhaling would help one to *sit in the moment.* She added some guided imagery and a centering experience. When the social worker finished, Jack noticed his heart felt more open. Grace's eyes glistened with tears.

A week passed, and all seemed to be going well, until the inevitable showdown with Jack's parents.

When they discovered that Jack had continued with his quest, and had deciphered the *Anamchara Text*, they were livid. And they were absolutely furious that Jack had told Mike and Grace about Sophia and Marcov. His mom did not speak to him for a week. His dad felt Jack was playing with fire, and with something so dangerous that only the government should handle. Although they didn't say it, it was clear they blamed him for putting Charlie and the family at risk.

Jack winced when they yelled, but he knew that part of growing up was taking the heat from parents when you knew you were right.

While the Abernaults' home brimmed with tension over the broken trust, kids in the town started changing. Teachers noticed their classes seemed easier to manage. When the bell rang, the students settled into their seats without the usual ruckus. Then there was the class participation from formerly quiet students. And the kids who normally dominated the discussions were more apt to listen and to share the air time. History and English classes took on a new energy.

During lunch period, the kids started a sign-up sheet to discuss the enneagram. Many kids could not identify their pattern, but listening to the conversations helped them eliminate some possibilities. Other kids found that while they had a predominant type, they also resonated with several types.

Some resonated with three types...one in the gut, one in the head, and one of the heart centers. Many kids noticed they used two body centers, but needed to bring up the awareness and resources from the third center. Jack shared how he relied on his head center, leaned on his heart center, and mostly ignored the gut center. Paying attention to this tendency helped him gain a better balance through the breath work.

One girl shared that she was comfortable with her thinking and feeling capacities. However, she often felt like she was a "pushover." By working with her gut center, she found a new grounded quality, so she didn't feel washed away by a flood of emotions.

Kids commented that listening to these insights gave them new vocabulary to describe their experiences and motivations.

Mike came up with a great idea, creating motivational posters for each type. If a kid was confident they knew their point/pattern, having a few cues on the wall could help prompt the needed shift.

For the type/point one, the poster served as a reminder to "lighten up"' and to relax the need for perfection.

The type/point two poster suggested the helper step back and try self care, with some independent activity or creative pursuit.

The type/point three poster encouraged the driven teenager to volunteer their talents for the benefit of the group.

The type/point four poster advised the creative kid to make a list, and to get organized. Learn to appreciate and respect the simple, ordinary aspects of life.

The type/point five poster encouraged action, and taking knowledge into the wider community.

The type/point six poster reassured a fearful kid to trust the process. Breathe into the gut, and embrace an inner authority. Notice the way you look for things to worry about, or how you seek to follow others. Come to understand and accept there is only certainty in the present moment.

The type/point seven poster reminded the upbeat kid to resist seeking *more,* in favor of learning restraint and reflection.

The type/point eight poster suggested the boss type protect the vulnerable. Learn to speak from an open heart.

And the type/point nine poster, geared for a laid back personality, suggested movement. Becoming energized and effective was the goal.

These posters served as hacks, showing the first steps one needed to make. The posters soon sold out, so Mike printed more. Breathwork and meditation sessions boosted the impact of the insights learned from the enneagram patterns.

It wasn't long before the school administration noticed that bullying incidences were down. Hallways and locker rooms, former hotbeds of trouble, now seemed more mellow.

The Student Council, wanting to make the school environment more welcoming, surveyed the student body. It seemed the teenagers wanted to make more of an impact on the wider community.

One suggestion was a preschool/daycare program staffed by teachers and students. Teens would help the four year olds with crafts and playground skills.

Other kids raised money for special outdoor equipment designed by Cas Holman. Apparently, as children assembled the large pieces, there was opportunity for creativity and cooperation. And when a design failed, the kids developed their resilience and language skills reworking a structure.

Green projects also appeared on the bulletin boards at school. Kids picked up trash on the way to school and altered old clothes. Using the sewing machines at the local library, the teens breathed new life into bell bottomed jeans and denim jackets.

The shift in Evanston could be felt even around the family dinner table. As one parent put it, "My fourteen year old is not sulking around, or burying his head in his phone. No, he's making other people happy, even his sister! At first I suspected he was smoking something, but it was this personality lesson he'd come across at school."

Even dinner at the Farrells' now approached a pleasurable experience. Mike saw a change of heart happening with his sisters, as they now shared their belongings and clothes.

Grace began to see her brothers in a new light. And even Snickers the cat began coming around Grace's ankles after years of steering clear of her. Overall, Grace felt less judgmental, appreciating the differences in other people.

At a high school faculty meeting, the question arose, *What in the world was going on?* When the kids were asked about the big shift, they described the personality lessons in the enneagram.

Facebook pages of Evanston parents lit up with stories about how their kids were suddenly cleaning their rooms, helping out with younger siblings, even volunteering on Saturday morning. A *GoFundMe* page for removing plastic from the ocean was set up at the junior high.

Kids still talked back sometimes, and came home late, but these things happened less frequently. In the school halls, there was a change in the air that you could feel. It felt lighter, friendlier.

One afternoon, a neighbor stopped Jack's mom in the grocery store and thanked her for her son's work. The woman related how her daughter had sworn off drugs as a result of learning more about herself. The girl had explained to her astonished parents how she now realized that she had looked for ways to be oppositional, and that she wanted to change.

Jack's mom told her husband about the encounter, and how the woman had tears of gratitude in her eyes. It seemed their son seemed to be having a real impact in the culture, just as the letter from Spencer's lawyers had predicted.

Mr. Abernault had a similar experience when a neighbor mentioned that her kid seemed more tuned in to her inner life. The teen had been caught up with social media and unrealistic body images. Now she was off the platforms, spending time with friends, and volunteering.

One of these families had an aunt in Montecito, California. A well-known talk show host happened to live on the same cul de sac. Over cocktails on a neighbor's patio, the television celebrity heard about the unusual phenomenon taking place with the teenagers in Illinois.

The following month Grace and Mike sat with the Abernaults watching the television broadcast when Jack and Dr. McGloin were interviewed about the lessons in the *Anamchara Text*.

Jack's parents eventually had come around after a few weeks of tension. So now, Charlie sat on his mom's lap while his parents sat dumbfounded as they watched Jack on the television screen.

The TV host began the interview.

"Thank you for joining us. Today we are going to be talking to a young man, Jack Abernault, and Dr. Elizabeth McGloin from the University of Chicago," said the host.

Then she gave a brief description of the enneagram patterns.

"So, I understand this material came from an ancient text. Is that correct?" She asked.

"Yes, we translated this *Anamchara Text* that was sitting in the college archives," said Dr. McGloin.

"And Jack, you helped figure out the personality puzzle by chance? You were researching a school assignment?" The host asked.

"Yeah, I happened to be in the building. I overheard Dr. McGloin discussing the enneagon diagram. I recognized it from my paper about Pythagoras." Jack said.

Then the interviewer said, "Even *I* remember Pythagoras from my high school math class. So I understand, Dr. McGloin, you believe these insights if implemented could help solve climate issues? How can that be? That seems quite a leap," the host asked.

Dr. McGloin explained.

"Well, I've been researching why green technologies haven't caught on. It turns out that the problem lies *within* people. Change the people, change the policies. The enneagram, in the *Anamchara Text*, shows nine gifts, each with its own blind spot. Everyone has one. The teaching explains how to recognize the pattern and then how to make a shift in a specific way. With this new clarity, people change their priorities. Green choices become a viable option. What begins within the person moves out into the world. The result is that we can turn back the tide on climate. Of course, we must act fast," the professor said.

"What a wonderful coincidence that you two met. And I understand that the National Institutes of Health and the Department of Energy are funding the nine patterns of personality podcasts," said the host.

"Yes, it's a collaboration that you helped set up for us," said Dr. McGloin.

"Well, I was happy to make a few phone calls," said the host.

"So, Jack, I hope you got an A on that project," the host asked.

"Yes, ma'am, I did." Jack smiled into the camera, knowing Grace and Mike would be howling.

"Oh, my gosh. He's *such* a good liar," said Grace, throwing a potato chip at the TV.

"He couldn't very well talk about aliens and a flying glass cube," said Mike.

CHAPTER FIFTEEN

All Vehicles, Big and Small

After the national broadcast, Jack and his friends presented the personality map to the entire high school. The opening talk was going well; however, one girl asked if the enneagram was stereotyping, putting people in boxes. She sounded irritated.

Jack responded. "You see, the thing is, you're already in a box. We all are. This model offers a way to get out of the box."

"Hmm, I'll have to think about it," the girl said, and sat down.

Suddenly, the auditorium went dark. A loud buzzing filled the room. The students called out in distress. Jack reached for his phone, turning on his flashlight feature.

"OK everybody, stay calm. Use your phone flashlights, and we'll see what's going on," he said.

Then he went to investigate.

Jack moved out into the dark hall.

He heard running.

He spun around to see a figure moving fast. The person somehow looked familiar, but he couldn't quite place him. Jack took off after him.

Mike joined in the chase, but they lost the guy when he disappeared near the gym. The boys stopped to listen, but they couldn't hear or see anyone. It seemed the person had gotten away.

Jack and Mike turned back to find someone to fix the lights.

But as they passed an exit, Jack saw a copper-colored sports car peel out of the parking lot. The car triggered something that he couldn't seem to put together.

Just then the building custodian rounded the corner.

"Someone called the office about the lights," the man said.

The loud buzzing continued.

The boys followed the man into the storeroom that housed the metal boxes wired for each bank of lights.

Flipping the switches, the custodian smiled.

"Someone must be playing a prank on you all today."

Suddenly, the significance of the buzzing registered with Jack.

Without a word, he reached up and set off the fire alarm.

"What the hell! What are you doing?" The custodian said.

"We *have* to evacuate the school," Jack said.

Running back into the auditorium, Jack passed students streaming for the exits.

Minutes later, a thin stream of sirens grew to a loud wail. Six fire trucks pulled up in front of the building. The bulky doors opened, and firefighters jumped out wearing their shiny helmets. Jack waved down one of them.

"Don't go in there without hazmat suits," Jack warned.

"You have to stand back," said the firefighter.

"You don't understand. I think someone released nanobots," said Jack.

"Nano what?" The firefighter asked.

"Nanobots. Mechanical bug like things," said Jack. "I can hear the buzzing."

But the buzzing had stopped.

"Are you the one who pulled the fire alarm?" asked the firefighter.

"Yes, so the kids could get away from the nanobots," said Jack. His speech was pressured.

The fireman's expression shifted then, as something seemed to dawn on him.

Signaling the EMT, he said quietly into his body microphone, "I think we may have a 10-96."

The principal walked over and spoke with the firefighter.

Jack overheard his name.

"He's been under a great deal of pressure. A good kid, but his grades have dropped," said the principal.

"Look, he's walking away," the chief said, watching Jack move toward the street.

Jack approached a group of kids, standing at the curb.

"Anybody have a headache?" asked Jack.

Several sophomores raised their hands.

Now the EMTs were coming for him with a stretcher.

Three men surrounded him, urging him to sit on the stretcher.

"These kids have headaches. Because they've been *attacked* with nanobots," protested Jack, as the men laid hands on his shoulders.

"Sit down here a minute and tell me about it," said the EMT in a soothing voice.

An EMT covered Jack's shoulders with a foil blanket.

Did they think he was crazy?

He was blurting out words, not making any sense. "Tinkers with the brain. Call the hospital," Jack said urgently.

He sounded deranged.

"And I *don't* need a blanket," he said, pushing it off his shoulders.

But his body was trembling.

By then, many students were complaining they didn't feel well. Several more ambulances pulled up. More kids were taken to the hospital.

Jack looked up to see a number of firefighters coming out of the auditorium. They were hauling sensors.

"Nothing in there. They're all imagining their symptoms. Power of suggestion," said a firefighter.

The EMT pulled the straps over Jack's chest.

"*Something's* in there," he said, begging them to look again.

They ignored him, rolling his gurney toward the ambulance, set on his hospitalization.

Mike saw Jack's predicament and phoned his dad for help. Mr. Farrell called the police chief, demanding they take Jack's warning seriously, or there would be legal repercussions. Well known in the community, this attorney was not to be ignored.

The fire chief's cell rang. It was the hospital.

"This is Dr. LaPata. Chief of Radiology. We found high tech nanobots on the first brain scan. All the kids from that auditorium need to be examined."

After a short conversation, the fire chief ended the call.

"The kid was right. They found nanobots," called out the fire chief to the police captain.

"And I *still* don't know what a nanobot is! Just how am I supposed to find them?" asked the police chief.

Jack called out from the back of an ambulance, just before the EMT closed the door.

"Nanobots might have a metallic component. The construction site at the corner over there has an industrial magnet. Use that to sweep the school," yelled Jack.

The firefighters looked at him and huddled. After a moment, four of the men rushed off to the construction site.

Jack rested his head on the pillow.

An hour later, the firefighters exited the school. Shaking their heads in disbelief, they had captured over a thousand nanobots. The things looked like spider mites, barely visible to the eye.

Just then, four black SUVs screeched to the curb. The doors flung open and a dozen FBI agents walked at a fast clip toward the police chief. The guy in charge wore a jacket with *Bernstein* on the back. After flipping his badge, he took custody of the containers with the nanobots.

Jack left for the hospital, where he would undergo the long overdue brain scan.

What had begun as a day of lessons from the *Anamchara Text* had turned into the largest terror attack in Illinois history. However, that was *not* the story reported to the public.

The local television news that night led with a story about an electrical mishap at the high school. According to the news anchor, the cooling system had malfunctioned, leaving some students hospitalized.

Agent Bernstein had seen to it there was no mention of nanobots. Surgeons had implanted miniscule filters to catch the tiny bots. Scores of nondisclosure paperwork had been signed that day at the hospital. The FBI had suppressed the facts, because if the truth got out, there would be panic.

* * *

That evening, Vincent Marcov paced in his compound, fuming that his attack on the school had been thwarted.

First, Jack's interview on national television, with that meddling Elizabeth McGloin, had infuriated him. Now lessons from the ancient text were taking place right under his nose. It had to be the Council's work.

The powerful teachings were spreading like wildfire. A more enlightened population surely would lead to green policies. Marcov was too close to knocking out the polar ice cap. Too close to finishing the virus for Jack. And too close to his triumphant voyage to Sophia.

Before the day was out, the rogue scientist accepted delivery of a giant 3D printer. Marcov read the instructions, and after several hours, added the last component. Firing up the massive copy machine, he fed in the data and watched as the contraption built a large satellite out of liquid titanium paste. The printer head hummed, moving side to side as the scientist watched. Two hours later, the first satellite bumped off the platform. Excited with the quality of the craft, he reloaded the machine's tank.

Vincent Marcov knew it was time to go big. But where would he find a place large enough for his satellites? That afternoon he bought a ten-thousand-acre tract of Canadian land for his base of operations. The fleet of satellites would be manufactured there, bringing him one step closer to obliterating the top of the world.

CHAPTER SIXTEEN

Debriefing

The following afternoon, two FBI agents appeared at the Abernaults' door. Soon it became evident that Jack was a prime suspect in the school attack.

After all, hadn't he been the one who reported the nanobots?

"So we understand your son has been ill. That he's been under a lot of stress. We also know he received a lot of attention after his television interview," said the agent.

Mr. Abernault's face darkened as he choked back his anger.

"Are you kidding? My son *saved* the kids yesterday. And now you come here and imply he had something to do with that attack?" Jack's dad said.

"Well, it's just that, sometimes, kids want to play the hero. Maybe need the attention," said the agent.

"Let me explain," Jack said.

"Don't say *one* word. We need a lawyer here," said Mr. Abernault, his eyes glaring at the agents.

The doorbell rang.

Jack's mom returned a moment later. Behind her, filling the door, stood the FBI agent in charge the previous day.

Jack's mom introduced him as Agent Bernstein.

The large man addressed the other officers.

"I'll take over here. Agent Walker, Agent Reilly. You're needed in the office."

After the two agents left, Bernstein turned to the family.

"Sorry about that. Lots going on today. I assure you that Jack is *not* a suspect. Anything but."

The Abernaults looked relieved. Jack slumped on the sofa. Letting out a deep sigh he closed his eyes.

"Can I get you some coffee?" asked his mom.

"That would be great. Thanks," said the agent.

Bernstein turned to Jack.

"How are you doing today? I understand the doctor found traces of a previous nanobot," said Bernstein.

"WHAT?" said the Abernaults all at once.

"This is the first we're hearing about this," said Jack's dad.

Jack stared at the agent.

So, he *had* been infected. The bots *had* kept him from telling his parents about Charlie holding the nanobot. And had caused his cheating on tests?

But then he thought. *No*, if he was honest with himself, and although lying had been easier, deep inside, he knew he'd had a choice.

"Sorry to drop that information on you like that. The radiologist just finalized the results of your scan," said Bernstein.

"Apparently, your system now is clear of the nanobots. The damage was minor," said the agent.

"And *you* know all this, before *we* find out?" asked Jack's dad.

But Jack cut him off. "Actually, that explains some things," Jack said.

His parents looked uneasy, maybe wondering what else Jack had been hiding. They assumed any issues their son was experiencing came from his COVID infection.

"Tell me everything. Start from the beginning. OK if I record this?" Bernstein looked at them.

Jack nodded, looking at his dad, who shrugged his shoulders. Clearly, he still was processing the privacy breach of Jack's medical record.

But Jack knew he had to trust someone, so he told how the lights had gone out. And that he had seen this guy running and then driving off in a copper-colored sports car. He explained the guy looked familiar.

"I suddenly had this overwhelming feeling that nanobots had been released. There'd been a loud buzzing sound," said Jack.

Jack's mom returned with the coffee, and Bernstein took a sip.

"Nice, Thanks," said the agent. "I happen to have some background on nanobot attacks."

"So, we don't need a lawyer here?" asked Mr. Abernault.

"No, but what I'm going to share is classified. For reasons that will become apparent, your family is cleared to hear this information. However, you'll need to check with me if someone else needs to know. National security overrides everything, even medical privacy regulations," said the agent.

And with that, he pulled out some confidentiality papers for the three of them to sign.

Relieved that Jack wasn't in trouble, Mr. Abernault carefully read the documents. Then they all added their signatures.

Bernstein gathered up the papers, sliding them into a folder.

Then, the agent began to talk.

"OK. Where to start? Several months before you met Joseph Spencer, he hired a private investigator who pulled Jack's DNA from a paper cup at his soccer practice. You see, it seems when your mother submitted her DNA to that genealogy database, Spencer was alerted that a match for him might be found in your family.

The private detective's work and the DNA confirmed what he suspected," said Bernstein.

"Apparently, Jack, you shared a rare string of chromosomes with him, a certain maternal haplogroup, K2B1a. This blood line remains unusual, even within your extended family. While the gene has popped up on all the continents, the sequence seems connected to green eyes and to a talent for problem solving. The migration route of this gene cluster was studied by *National Geographic*. This blood line traveled from Africa to Southeast Asia. There's a bloom of the haplogroup in the center of China, then west along the Silk Road, back into the Rhine Valley. From there, it disperses, down into Africa, and north to Finland. Seven percent of Ireland's population contains this sequence. But you and Spencer have some additional mutations."

"Whaaaat!" said Jack.

"Spencer orchestrated your meeting at the family reunion, even ordering your favorite apple pie for the buffet. You see, he did his homework," said Bernstein.

Was he a pawn in some bizarre genome conspiracy? Jack wondered.

"Using DNA off a paper cup? Is that even legal?" asked his dad.

"Well, you see, by this time, Spencer was desperate. He had been receiving death threats, and he feared he might not have long to live. Wanting to prepare for the worst, he needed to find a relative with his special string of chromosomes to pass on his legacy," said Bernstein.

While the agent talked, Jack's mind was scrolling through his memory of the family reunion. Now that he thought about it, Spencer had steered the conversation, eliciting Jack's interest in solving mechanical problems. The elderly man also said something about how, even as a boy, he had been more serious than other kids his age, thinking about his future role in life.

Jack felt a rush of sadness, but also anger. The connection to Spencer was a tainted blessing, just like he had feared. Spencer had put him and his family in danger.

On the other hand, Jack couldn't deny it connected him to a larger scheme.

Bernstein continued, adding that the federal government had worked with Joseph Spencer's company for decades on reducing carbon emissions. And on a regular basis, they had encountered Vincent Marcov's sabotage. Jack now recalled that Harold, Winnifred, and Dr. McGloin all had referred to Marcov's criminal record.

Bernstein shared that Marcov's felonies spanned decades, escalating over the years to serious environmental attacks. The fugitive had stacked up hundreds of convictions from courts in the United States and the European Union. Unfortunately, the agent admitted, Marcov always evaded capture, remaining one step ahead of law enforcement. Various agencies had staged all kinds of traps without success.

"Either he vanishes into thin air, or he repels SWAT teams with a microwave defense system. He has houses all over the world," said the agent.

"That is terrifying," said Jack's mom.

"How could Spencer put our son into the middle of all this?" asked Mr. Abernault.

"There seemed no other way. Spencer knew he was running out of time," said the agent.

Jack figured that someone like Spencer who ran with the *big dogs* probably had a comfort level with bending the rules.

Now Jack wanted to unburden himself from all the secrets he had been keeping. He wouldn't be like Spencer, drawing in unsuspecting folks.

So Jack told the agent everything…all about Max and Izzy, the Council, and Sophia.

The agent sat back, sighing.

"I *was* aware of the space/time portal. The Sophian children must be part of the Ghost Fleet," said Bernstein.

"The *what?*" asked Mr. Abernault.

"Ghost Fleet refers to alien visits from an advanced civilization. This information is highly classified, as you can imagine the panic that would result if this news got out."

Now it was clear why Jack's dad had been foiled at every turn when he tried to report the Sophian trip to the government. They already knew all about it!

Jack thought about the rogue scientist. It sounded like it wouldn't be long now before things would come to a head. But when it came to the planet's survival, Jack felt he'd always be playing catch up. He was no match for the rogue scientist. Maybe he'd have a stroke of luck here and there. A hint of intuition. Help from Max and Izzy. But, Marcov led an army of minions, nanobots and satellites. He could even disappear on demand. It seemed hopeless.

CHAPTER SEVENTEEN

Vincent Marcov

S quawking crows awoke Vincent Marcov the next day. He rolled off the sofa, bumping his head on the table. After his plan for the attack at the high school was shut down, all he could think about was revenge.

But Vincent also knew he had narrowly escaped this time. When the squad car with the flashing lights rounded the corner near the high school, Marcov had disappeared into thin air. All he required was a moment to perform a special focusing technique. But he had almost been caught off guard as he'd been checking his phone.

His ability to vanish relied on an ancient meditation practice he had mastered at a Himalayan monastery. When he had learned only two monks knew this technique, Marcov had shoved them off a cliff. Then he had hightailed it out of the country.

Marcov descended the steps in his compound that evening. The rogue scientist felt he did his best work at night. Gearing up for a retaliatory strike, his thoughts turned to grievances from long ago…faces of children, sneering on a playground.

And then the worst memory, the sting of betrayal by his only brother. The brother he loved, the one who deserted him, leaving him alone within a ring of bullies. Something inside him cracked that day, leaving a festering wound, and sending him on a path of revenge. That was the day he vowed never to be a victim again.

He was an old man now. But he hadn't forgotten. Now they would all pay. He would destroy all the playgrounds, all the children's faces, all the children's children, the entire planet.

Marcov eyed his lab's refrigerator where the glass vials waited, filled with an almost ready dose. He loved the symmetry of taking out both Joseph Spencer and Jack Abernault with a virus. He relished the stalking, toying with his prey. He could take out Jack at any time. But, he fashioned himself a kind of a theater director, producing a performance. His cast of actors included the Masons and Bernaski, instructed to terrify Jack with stories of treachery and nanobots. Marcov knew just how to turn the screws, targeting Jack's most obvious vulnerability... the boy's unfailing tendency to worry.

At this point, the virus only required some minor tweaking. He had ordered some test tubes that would arrive tomorrow for the final step. Marcov would time the youth's murder after the destruction of the ice cap, so the boy would witness the mayhem. Then the green-eyed bloodline would be finished on earth.

The next morning Vincent Marcov paced in his office, and watched from his window, waiting for the FedEx truck. A crate of glass filaments for the virus should arrive anytime now. However, when he checked the delivery status, a message from customs listed his shipment as *detained due to national security*. Furious, he threw the laptop against the wall.

* * *

Planet Sophia

Up, beyond the clouds, and through the space/time portal, the Council gathered. The news that Marcov was engineering a deadly virus had reached them. They had also learned about Jack's nanobot infection. But the most troubling incident was Jack's ordeal in the Minnesota pit when Marcov's agent had drugged him. The plan had been to weaken the kid's resolve, hoping to recruit Jack into their web of destruction.

However, Marcov hadn't anticipated that the dark hole would serve as a soul-searching experience, or that Izzy and Max would rescue the boy.

The Council now debated about how they might support Jack. The chairman noted that interfering could interrupt his hero's journey, as the path required overcoming adversity.

And there was the issue of unintended consequences. Sometimes well-meaning actions ended up causing collateral damage. So even when the *Anamchara Text* was degraded during the transport to the earth, the Council had not intervened. And their trust in Jack had paid off. Because rather than give up, he had made sense of the book. He also had recruited his friends to help him along the way.

But the stakes were growing. The earth was running out of time. The planet's deteriorating climate and the threat of mass migrations to Sophia worried them all. They didn't know how they could help. So the Council decided, rather than fumble with a clumsy intervention, they would wait. For now, Jack was on his own.

In the corner of the chamber, Izzy sat on his little chair, listening with growing concern. While he didn't yet have voting rights, he knew he needed a plan, even if it meant banishment from the Council's apprenticeship.

After all, that kid, Jack Abernault, was in serious trouble.

* * *

Back in Evanston, the Abernaults slept under a full moon. At five a.m., ear-splitting cries woke the family. Jack heard his mom dash into Charlie's bedroom. He leaped out of bed and rushed across the hall.

A horrible struggle was happening. His terrified mother, Max, and Izzy, were all trying to help the hysterical baby. Over the child's body, a menacing blanket of maroon mist was bearing down, smothering him.

His mother wailed in anguish.

Max and Izzy, climbed frantically on the sides of the crib, pulling and pushing, trying to free the baby from the sticky monster. When they seemed to make some progress, the menacing mist reached up like a claw, grabbing Izzy around the neck and slamming him to the floor.

Max tried to free him, pulling the maroon tentacles off the boy. But the mist glowed orange, burning his hands and blistering his skin.

Izzy's eyes rolled back. He didn't seem to be breathing.

Jack's dad ran in, turned on the lamp, and opened the window.

Repelled by the light, the malevolent mist slithered away into the night air.

Jack lifted Charlie into his mom's arms, while his dad performed CPR on Izzy.

They called 911.

Maniacal laughter reverberated from the tree outside the window. The thing with gleaming fangs coiled in the branches like a giant serpent. Jack's dad shined a bright light and the thing evaporated. A burning smell lingered in the air.

The police and ambulance arrived in minutes. The EMTs pulled an oxygen mask over Izzy's face and he was rolled out on a gurney. Max was treated for burns. Charlie screamed as he was checked out by the paramedics, but somehow the child had escaped harm from the attack.

Max took off in the glass cube, returning later with a medicine-filled case and instructions for those caring for Izzy. Agent

Bernstein oversaw the doctors as they administered the radical treatment. The hospital staff had never seen anything like the special infusion prepared by the Sophian physicians.

Soon Izzy's condition was upgraded. The doctors, amazed at the child's improvement, insisted that the formula undergo analysis. Bernstein agreed, but insisted that everyone sign confidentiality documents. If news got out about alien treatments, there was no telling what would happen.

Izzy had almost died, and Charlie had been attacked. Jack felt numb. After they returned from the hospital, his mother went into the living room and pulled down the old family Bible from the top shelf. In times of crisis, she looked to the wisdom in the book, and gained comfort from the list of ancestors on the family tree written on the first pages. Those who had gone before had survived famine, war, and sickness.

"While we were waiting for the doctor's report, I thought of a passage from Ephesians," said his mom.

Jack took the book, and flipped open the text. He saw the lines of scripture.

Warning about a war, *battling powers and principalities…* negative constellations; *anger, pride, deceit, envy, avarice, fear, gluttony, lust,* and *sloth.*

His mother told him that the poet Dante, back in 1300, had written about these same shadowy complexes that caused so much misery in the world.

Jack could see tears well up in his mother's eyes. They both knew they were in the middle of a battle fought on many levels.

After hearing the heavy weight of that prophesy, Jack went outside and sat on the porch.

He heard footsteps approaching, and he looked up, surprised to see Harold coming up the walk with his German Shephard.

"Are you still trying to find Vincent Marcov?" Harold asked.

"Let's walk?" said Jack.

His parents did not need to hear anymore about the fiend. When they were out of earshot, Jack asked, "So what's going on?"

"I overheard my dad on the phone talking about Marcov. No idea who he was talking to, or why," Harold said.

"Woah, that's weird," said Jack.

"No kidding," said Harold.

"But sometimes he works as a consultant," said Harold.

"For the government?" asked Jack.

Harold looked around, and then whispered, "Maybe."

"After my dad left, I looked at the notepad next to the phone to see if there was an impression. And, like in the movies, I rubbed the side of a pencil over the page. Here's the message," and he handed the paper to Jack.

Jack looked at the note.

building permit #MW1966, 2100 Ridge

"Oh, wow, that address is Evanston City Hall," said Jack.

"I can't go in there alone, but if there's two of us, we *maybe* could get the address and blueprint plans for Marcov's house, given what I overheard," said Harold.

It sounded sort of crazy. But, at this point, with all the threats around them, doing nothing seemed even more risky.

"OK. But we need help. I have two friends," Jack said.

"Like could they create a distraction, or something?" asked Harold.

"Yeah, something like that. Let's see if they can meet us at the park." Jack said.

He texted his friends, and half an hour later, they found Jack and Harold sitting on the bleachers. The German Shephard's ears shot up when the kids approached.

"Nice dog," said Grace.

"I brought doughnuts. Breakfast in the park," said Mike.

"First period starts in forty-five minutes. So talk fast. What's going on?" Mike added.

Jack and Grace looked at Mike with surprise.

"Since when did you turn into the Energizer Bunny?" Grace asked.

"Well, I'm trying to be more point three. You know, motivated," Mike said.

"Well, OK, then," said Grace.

"This is Harold. He has an idea," said Jack.

Then Jack noticed powdered sugar on Grace's leather jacket. But, even more arresting, underneath the lapels, he saw a pink sweater.

Grace quickly zipped up, and Jack resisted making a comment on the unusual color or on the evidence that she clearly had helped herself to the bakery box.

Jack described the plan to find the building permit in City Hall, adding they needed to create a distraction.

"I like it," said Grace.

"Could work," said Mike.

"Tomorrow," Jack said.

Teacher conferences the next day gave the teens the time needed for their caper. So at eleven o'clock, the four teens waited at the bottom of the west side steps of the municipal building. Mike entered the main door first, carrying a bag with soda, and three pizza boxes. He wore the red hat and sweatshirt from a local Italian eatery. Grace waited in a wide brimmed hat and woolen dress coat, borrowed from her mom's closet. With heavy eyeliner and lipstick, she could pass for a young matron. After a few minutes, she started up the steps. Harold and Jack followed, and they all headed for the third floor. Mike turned into the Building and Zoning Office where four office assistants sat focused on their computer screens.

"Hi, Mr. Roberts sent me. He was super pleased with the fast inspections last week. He's treating you all to lunch for passing his permit so quickly," said Mike.

The office assistants looked up and happily moved to the counter to check out the pizza.

"This is great. So nice." The staff picked up paper plates, lining up for slices.

Then Grace rushed in, bumping into Mike who had set the open soda bottle on the counter. Grace screamed as the soda covered her coat. "You clumsy ass! This is a Balenciaga!" She fumed.

The office workers scrambled for paper towels to help her, as Jack and Harold slipped in around the counter.

"*Please* don't report me, I'll get fired for sure. I'm so sorry," wailed Mike.

But Grace only escalated her indignation.

"You *should* be fired. You've ruined my day. I'm supposed to lunch with the hospital board. I can't go looking like an incontinent crazy person."

Meanwhile, Harold and Jack rifled through the file cabinets lined up inside the interior office. With the threat of discovery, Jack opened file drawer after file drawer, his fingers flying through the tabs, trying to locate the permit.

Then, he spied the matching numbers.

Grabbing the document, he photographed the building layout. He had just shut the drawer when he heard the inner office door open.

"What are you doing in here?" a voice snapped.

The boys turned to see a large woman blocking the doorway.

Jack swallowed.

"I'm so sorry. I know we should have asked first. This is going to sound weird, but my grandmother graduated from Marywood

High School back in the 1960s. Her memory is spotty, but sometimes she remembers stuff from long ago. She wanted to see if there were initials still carved in the windowsill. I'm pretty sure this used to be her homeroom based on her description." Jack said.

"It would mean a great deal if I could take a photo to her," Jack added.

The office manager stopped, her eyes softening. She knew the city hall indeed had been a girl's academy back in the day, before it was converted by the City of Evanston.

"You say the 1960s? My aunt went to Marywood, as well. Let's check the windowsill," said the office manager.

They examined the wood, and under layers of varnish, the faint letters A.M. were barely visible.

No one was more surprised than Jack, and he snapped the photo.

Thanking the woman profusely, Jack and Harold backed out of the office.

They passed Grace and Mike, as the mopping up continued. Worried they were running out of time, Mike had flipped open one of the pizza boxes. Gooey cheese was everywhere.

"Please don't call my boss. I'll pay your cleaning bill," said Mike.

But Grace was having none of it, wailing, "Oh, my beautiful coat!"

The four kids entered the halls of the high school, still laughing at the morning escapade.

"At least those office workers got two free pizzas out of our little performance," said Mike.

After school, Jack printed out Marcov's building permit, along with the blueprints.

Although there was no street address, he compared the contours of the property to a map of the area. He found the rogue scientist's compound matched an area on a bluff, known as *No Man's Land*. The permit listed the owner as A. Vocram, the name of the shell company mentioned by Winnifred Weaver.

They finally had Marcov's location.

While Grace was ready to go, Mike seemed paralyzed. Jack worried about all the things that could go wrong. The image of the microwave weapon sent shivers up his spine, knowing what that technology did to a frozen entrée.

CHAPTER EIGHTEEN

More News

D r. Marcov received a promising report from his Canadian facility. The progress with the satellite fleet was ahead of schedule. The rogue scientist decided to spend the day collapsing beehives. After all, bees pollinated crops, and crops fed the nation. A food shortage would add more chaos and he wanted everyone and everything targeted; bees, bats, people, ice, air, and water. All of it.

* * *

That afternoon, Jack returned Charlie's library books in downtown Evanston. As he approached the main square, he was more than a little surprised to find himself staring at a familiar glass cube.

Shoppers were gathered around, speculating the cube must be a new theater project. Jack found a bench and waited until the dinner hour. Eventually, the crowd thinned out. He looked around to check that no one was watching, and opened the sliding panel.

Max and Izzy casually jumped out.

Grousing, the older boy complained. "Man, I thought those shoppers would never go home. That's what I get for letting Izzy practice his parking skills. We were aiming for the lot behind Ryan Stadium."

But Izzy wasn't having it. "You know he was nagging me. Firing off all these instructions. Turn here. Pull up now. Talk about a backseat driver!" Izzy's cheeks were flushed.

Jack figured the boys did not ride around in the cube for any old reason. He asked what was up.

"OK. But first, we're hungry?" Izzy said.

Jack led them over to a food truck parked around the corner. The boys ate a pizza each, wiping sauce off their cheeks with paper napkins.

"So what's going on?" Jack asked.

Izzy whispered in Max's ear. Jack heard urgent words, *You tell him!* and *brother.*

"Uh, so there's something we haven't told you yet." Max said, hesitating.

Jack felt his chest tighten, bracing for bad news.

"What is it? Is Charlie OK? I heard Izzy say *brother.*" Jack asked anxiously.

"No, no. It's not *your* brother that's the problem. But, it's time for you to know the whole truth," said Max.

"What? What whole truth?" Jack said, his heart racing now.

"The thing is, Vincent Marcov is sort of related to you," said Max.

"WHAT! WHAT! NO WAY!"

"See, actually, the rogue scientist and Joseph Spencer were brothers. Vincent Marcov's real name was Walden Spencer, and, as Joseph's closest relative, he felt *he* should have inherited Morningside. Which is odd, when you think about it, because the two hadn't spoken for decades," said Max.

Jack felt the blood drain from his head. This was a nightmare.

Vincent Marcov – Relative.

Jack could not believe his ears.

Max continued.

"The brothers, it seems, were inseparable when they were young, about as close as two kids could be. They spent hours playing outside, climbing trees, and building forts. But when Joseph was eight years old, everything changed. The trouble began on the school playground when someone began to tease Walden about his unusual name. The younger boy looked to Joseph for help, but his brother stood silent. Walden began to cry when he saw his brother look away," said Max.

"Joseph, his dearest friend, didn't seem to care about him. The other kids thought it was funny that his brother wasn't going to help. They taunted Walden all the more, calling him Waldo the Weirdo. The tormenting continued and Joseph walked away, leaving Walden sobbing in a circle of sneering kids," said Izzy.

"Later, Joseph said he was sorry, but his brother wouldn't listen. The parents tried to intervene, however Walden seemed to grow a thick shell. The humiliation of the betrayal had wounded him to the core," Max said.

Walden began playing tricks on his brother. In the beginning, the pranks were harmless, but as the boys got older, he put Joseph in real danger. The family went to counseling, and things seemed to improve for a while. Then there would be a setback.

Walden began to run with a bad crowd. As the years passed the police were involved when Walden set some fires. Finally, a judge sentenced Walden to a state facility, said Max.

"Walden hated the place, and blamed his brother. A darkness seemed to take over his character. Years passed and they seldom saw each other. Joseph earned a university scholarship, while Walden dropped out of school. Walden changed his name to Vincent Marcov, and began to study science," Max said.

"Why the name *Vincent Marcov*?" asked Jack.

"Walden always liked to draw, and he created a character in a graphic novel that sounded like a dangerous criminal." said Max.

"So you can see why Marcov would have it out for you, as you remind him of Joseph with your green eyes, and now as the heir to Morningside. But most of all it's your close relationship with Charlie. The way you take care of him. It's a trigger for re-living his own brother's betrayal. He sees Charlie as your Achilles' heel," Max said.

Jack stared at a pile of dead leaves.

This terrible family history, brother betraying brother, had struck again. Joseph hadn't protected Walden, just as he hadn't looked out for Charlie.

Izzy was staring at him. The boy had read his thoughts, and a tear rolled down the child's cheek.

Izzy now knew his darkest secret, about Charlie holding the oversized nanobot. However, the little boy from Sophia took Jack's hand, giving it an understanding squeeze. The touch felt like forgiveness.

Jack choked back his tears.

Suddenly, a high-pitched beeping sound rose from the cube's surface.

"Oh no, that signal means the cube needs a recharge. We're stuck here for twenty-four hours," said Max.

And it was clear he was prepared to sleep in the cube, right in the middle of Evanston, on a frigid October night.

"Come home with me. Stay in the guestroom. You guys can come to school with me tomorrow. We can say you're my cousins from Portland. And you finally can meet Mike and Grace," said Jack.

Izzy looked hopefully at his brother.

"OK, sure," said Max. And he started walking.

"You can't leave the cube here," Jack said.

"Sure, we can," said Max.

And with that, Max slapped an official looking Apple Store decal on the glass cube.

"Hah, it looks totally like a pop-up kiosk," said Jack.

"Where do you think Steve Jobs got all those designs?" Max said.

"No way," said Jack.

"*Way*," said Max.

Jack brought the boys inside the house to see his parents. They tossed their jackets on the bench and the boys eyed the pot cooking on the stove.

"Something smells good," said Max.

Even though they had just had pizza, the brothers were ready to eat again.

Jack's parents welcomed the boys, remembering how valiantly they had fought when Charlie was attacked by the strangling mist. The baby gave Max and Izzy a quizzical look, furrowing his brow at the silver and green curls that resembled some of his more flamboyant stuffed animals.

Then Izzy announced he needed to make a formal apology to the family.

"What can you possibly have done, dear?" Jack's mom asked, surprised.

"Well, you see, kids from Sophia play a game. When we visit your planet, we like to go into jewelry boxes and tangle chains. Sometimes we mess with phone cords, really anything long and twisty," said Izzy.

"Well, that explains it. I've spent a lot of time untangling cords and chains over the years," said Jack's mom.

Had these aliens been visiting for decades? Jack was thinking.

"If it's any consolation, we *do* get grounded for doing it," Max said.

Did these visiting aliens always have benign intentions?

Sensing their concern, Izzy said, "Don't worry. It's just Sophians. We're good guys."

"Remember, Sophia is an advanced civilization. They can help us," said Jack.

Jack's mom nodded, and seeming relieved, she resumed getting dinner on the table.

Jack helped his parents set out the dishes and flatware. In the other room, they overheard the brothers' peculiar interactions with Charlie. The boys communicated in that strange language, their chatter sounding like a festive chicken coop, with the clicks and chirps. On an earlier visit, Max had explained that their speech progressively matched the native tongue as they acclimated to Earth. But sometimes, young children preferred hearing Sophian.

The doorbell rang. It was Mike and Grace.

His friends had rushed over when they heard who was coming to dinner.

"So this is Grace," said Max.

"And you are Max," said Grace.

Izzy shook Mike's hand.

Grace whispered to Jack that they looked cool, like a K-pop band.

Mike kept staring at the boys, and Jack could only imagine what his friend was thinking.

Mr. Abernault saw to it that Grace and Mike signed Bernstein's state secret documents, but he knew Jack's friends had kept the Sophian secret for over six months.

As the dishes were passed around the table, something inside Grace wanted to liven things up.

"So, Izzy, when do Sophian kids get their driver's licenses?" Grace asked.

What? Jack thought of *all* the topics in the world, she *would* bring up that tender subject.

"Sophia does not *issue* a license. When we feel we are ready, we drive," said Izzy.

"And, sometimes, what we *feel* is just wrong, so we end up in the *wrong* location" said Max, still annoyed about the landing in downtown Evanston.

Grace looked satisfied that she had stirred things up. Now Jack, Izzy, and Max all had ruffled feathers and were feeling on edge.

Jack's mom, well-versed in all things Grace, was ready with a little confrontation of her own.

"So, dear, I'm wondering why you felt the need to bring up driver's licenses?"

"Uh, uh…I don't know," Grace said, now looking uncomfortable.

"Hmm…maybe a dose of point two might be helpful," said Mike.

Grace blushed.

"You're right. It wasn't kind of me to say that. I'm sorry," said Grace.

"Your apology is accepted," said Jack.

Max said he was sorry, and Izzy smiled.

Charlie, who also liked to stir things up, began throwing his noodles on the floor.

The remainder of the evening went along peacefully as the Sophian boys showed off some magic tricks.

Later, the visiting brothers were tucked in bed, and the lights dimmed. Through the bedroom door, the Abernaults overheard the boys reciting some form of prayer, and the house settled down.

The next morning Jack awoke early. He looked in on Max and Izzy but the boys were still sleeping. They looked so peaceful, it was hard to imagine that there was so much trouble brewing with the rogue scientist.

Jack thought about Marcov's plan, and he thought about the way the earth was fighting back.

While there had been a breakthrough in atomic fusion energy, the race was on to invent a generator to hook up the electrical grid. It wasn't hard to imagine that Marcov was targeting that crucial technology.

Jack couldn't deny that the teachings about the personality patterns were ushering in a more conscious community. And the Council had been right when they predicted a more aware population would insist on more green policies. Bills were flying through state and federal legislatures, responding to the citizens' demands.

But Jack worried that all this change might be too late.

Later that afternoon, Jack, Grace, and the brothers walked to Fountain Square. However, as they approached the glass vehicle, they saw something was wrong.

A disgruntled crowd had gathered around the cube. Red paint was splashed on the glass, and it was clear someone had tried to break in. A line of yellow police tape had been set up around the structure.

"Uh oh," said Max.

"Do you think they damaged it?" asked Jack.

"Not likely, but this can't be good," said Max.

"Time for some special tactics so we can get out of here. We will say our goodbyes now," said Max.

"What do you mean? Shouldn't you come back with us? I can call Agent Bernstein for help," said Jack.

"No time for that. You'll be fine," said Max.

"What are you going to do?" asked Grace.

Max pulled out a small device. He set some coordinates, and...

One minute later …

Jack and Grace looked around.

What were they doing in downtown Evanston?

Other people looked confused, as well. Yellow crime tape was tangled in the branches of a nearby tree.

"My head hurts. Why are we here?" asked Grace.

"Uh, no clue," said Jack.

They walked back to Jack's house, and his parents asked if Max and Izzy had taken off without any problem.

"They're not here?" said Jack.

Jack's parents shook their heads.

"Max and Izzy left for downtown with you two," said his mom.

Grace's brow furrowed. She seemed to be retracing her steps.

Some vague memory remained.

"My mind feels fuzzy," said Jack.

"Remember the boys said their battery recharged by sapping up hydrogen and trace minerals. Maybe you were exposed to some kind of exhaust," said his dad.

Later that evening after Grace went home, Jack tried to study. But he couldn't focus. There was too much going on…with the climate crisis and Marcov's threat.

Jack wondered what would happen next. He liked certainty, and his life was anything but that. He was trying to keep up with all the challenges and changes, doing the best he knew how.

He asked himself, hadn't he followed the quest? Met all those odd folks?

Defied his parents, and taught the *Anamchara Text*?

But would it be enough?

The news reports on the fragile ice cap were terrifying.

Then the phrase from the Council's letter returned, about his final task. *Neutralize Vincent Marcov.*

A new level of darkness seemed to open up before him.

* * *

And, perhaps it was this final challenge that spurred Jack to return to the place his adventure had begun. So, on the following Saturday, he brought Grace back to Morningside.

The teenagers lifted their bikes off the train at Lake Forest, and ten minutes later they rolled up to the mansion's entrance.

Jack felt Grace was the bright spot in his life, because she radiated courage. He wanted her with him when he explored a section of the estate built into the hillside. The wing was accessed behind a mural of a Persian garden. And they found the entrance without too much trouble and made their way down a stone staircase.

A large chamber with a vaulted ceiling suddenly illuminated with designs. The images seemed to come from a hidden projector triggered by their movements. The two stood mesmerized, as they watched unfolding fractals and intricately shifting snowflakes. Jack recognized Romanesco broccoli, a defrosting action, and other designs from nature. A flush of dahlias appeared above their heads. And no sooner had they witnessed this glorious array than holograms of tropical plants sprang up around them. Grace moved through the vines and blossoms, overcome with the Eden-like phenomenon, swaying her arms like an entranced dancer.

Jack sensed he was standing in the palm of a divine creator, as a tight lump hardened in his throat. Awash in these lifeforms, his eyes brimmed with tears. There seemed a connection to the tree of life, as vines began to sprout from his mouth and hands, his skin turning green.

Grace looked surprised; however, her own skin was turning blue, and her hands glowed.

What was happening to them? The event lasted for some time, but the two felt in no hurry to end the experience.

Soft sounds of wind chimes and silver bells began to fill the air.

Then, almost imperceptibly, a soft light replaced the images and holograms. Jack now saw a ring of cushioned seats around a contemplation pool. Had this space served as the Spencer's chapel?

At peace, the two sat for some time, looking at the the water. Jack sensed his forehead, core, and gut brighten and connect.

* * *

Later the two sat on the train heading south to Evanston. They didn't feel the need to talk, however Jack wondered what this girl was thinking.

The spell broke when Jack's phone rang.

It was Bernstein. He informed Jack they had arrested the owner of the copper-colored Nissan who had released the nano-bots in the school auditorium.

"You're never going to guess who it is," Bernstein said.

But suddenly, Jack *did* know.

"It's Trip Grainger, isn't it?" Jack said.

"How did you know?" asked the agent.

"Just now, when you said *copper-colored Nissan*, it all came back. I remember seeing that car parked in the driveway when I visited the Grainger's house. I knew I'd seen that car someplace," said Jack.

The agent continued, telling him that Trip Grainger and his father turned out to be major players in Marcov's web of collaborators. A laptop in the Graingers' house showed that the Masons, Tanya Stokes, Bernaski, and Lindy Simons also were involved.

"I can fill you in later, but be careful. No telling who we can trust," said the agent.

That the Masons and Tanya Stokes were bad actors did not surprise him. However, Lindy Simons had fooled him with the sweetness routine.

Jack wondered if Bernstein knew about the family relationship between Joseph Spencer and Walden.

"So, I found out that Joseph and Marcov were brothers. Did you know?" asked Jack.

After pausing a moment, Bernstein admitted that this was not new information.

"I was aware of the sibling connection, but we worried your family might be targeted," said the agent.

"I should have been told," said Jack.

"All this devastation due to bullying over Walden's unusual name. It's ironic that Walden was named after Walden Pond, a lake known for the glory of untouched nature. Hard to make sense of this. Although, the FBI profilers claim a trauma like this can result in a victim taking a vow that leads to a life of crime," he said.

Jack thought of the nine types of vows individuals made to protect themselves from hurt. For many, it seemed, the destruction was limited to a constricted life pattern. But for Walden, his need for revenge had put the entire planet at risk.

* * *

The following weekend, Jack and his friends returned to Morningside. Sitting around the fireplace that evening, they talked about the advancements in green technology.

"Speaking of advancements, have you seen Max and Izzy lately? I had a dream about them last night. They gave us an amazing gift, but I can't remember what it was," Grace said.

"Max told me the way to contact him was to point the telescope directly overhead, like a *bat signal*," said Jack.

"Can we try it?" asked Mike.

So they wheeled the telescope out on to the patio and adjusted the lens.

They waited, shivering in the cold.

Then Jack saw a bright star moving like a comet. Could that be the glass cube? The answer came a moment later when the space vehicle settled on the lawn next to the patio, and out slid Max and Izzy on an inflatable ramp.

"Where did you go the other day?" asked Jack.

"Oh that. Emergency maneuvers. We used a frequency alternating disrupter. Our departure won't even show up on security cameras or in anyone's memory," said Max.

"Woah, I keep thinking there's no more surprises from you guys. And then...*Boom,*" said Jack.

"Sorry," said Izzy. "Those people were getting riled up."

"We're starving. Any chance you have leftovers from dinner?" Max asked.

Jack ushered them into the kitchen, and after a few servings of pasta salad and fruit, the boys were ready to talk.

Max reached in his pocket.

"We have something important to give you," said Max as he handed a flash drive to Jack.

"The Council on Sophia feels your people are ready to take the next step. All our formulas, laws, and designs are on this flash drive. Now you will know most of what we know," said Max.

"That's incredible!" said Jack.

"The Council was pleased that the rollout of the enneagram went so well. You didn't get stuck focusing on the personality types, but understood there's a flow to these patterns," said Max. "That's the good news, but there's bad news, as well. I know this will be hard to hear, but Marcov is working on a virus tailored for you Jack," said Max.

"Marcov killed Joseph Spencer with a special virus," said Izzy.

Jack couldn't deny that he had feared something like this after his DNA was swabbed in the middle of the night. Still, it was terrifying to hear Spencer's murder confirmed by the boys.

The already dangerous world was becoming even more treacherous.

Jack called Bernstein, and the agent sent an FBI team to take custody of the flash drive from Sophia.

The hour was late.

The boys returned to the cube and disappeared in the night sky. The teens caught the last train to Evanston.

The next morning, Mike called Jack.

"After hearing all that intense stuff from Max and Izzy, I stayed up all night. Used game theory to figure out Marcov's security system. I'm sure it's a design by the Aniketos and Alexiares Company. They were the Greek gods of defense," Mike said.

"That sounds right. The building permit listed a firm, *A & A*. I figured it was a contractor, but there're lots of companies that begin with *A*," said Jack.

"So all we need to do is to hack into that company's security system," Mike said.

Realizing his friend had been up all night, Jack knew this was not the moment to object.

"Get some sleep. We can meet this afternoon. And, great work," said Jack.

Jack valued logic, and he knew hacking was a bad idea. Mike and Grace tended to use gut intuition, and maybe didn't see the big picture the way he did.

So when the three friends met up after school, Jack hedged, insisting he needed more time.

"What do you mean, *more* time?" said Grace, outraged.

"We have the address, we have the security system. The polar ice cap is melting. It's now or never," she said.

"Don't you think the FBI already tried hacking?" said Jack.

Mike grabbed Grace's hand, suggesting they take a walk. He recognized that when Jack dug in his heels, there was no point in pushing him.

After his friends left, Jack closed his eyes, clearing his mind.

Taking a deep breath, he pushed away all thoughts of Grace's disapproval, worries about Mike's disappointment, and even fears of Vincent Marcov.

It was time to go deeper.

Jack took another breath, and pushed the air down so it filled his lungs.

An image of a waterfall rushing over his mind quieted his thoughts.

However, soon a parade of characters intruded.

The faces of Elinor and Joseph Spencer appeared. Jack let them pass, returning to his breath. Morningside's mural with the engineers flashed in his mind.

He breathed again.

Grace diving in the pool.

He breathed.

Gears ticking inside the glass clocks at Morningside.

Another breath.

The goddesses on the mosaic ceiling at Morningside appeared and passed.

Then, in slow motion, Max and Izzy floating under a pastel blue dome, like Renaissance angels...

Emptiness.

Silence.

Then flashing words, *Keep it simple*.

Suddenly, parked in his mind; the image of his neighbor's dusty plumbing van.

Jack opened his eyes.

That was it...the *plumbing!*

Maybe... *maybe,* it was time to go *old school.*

Grace and Mike walked in the door.

"Hey, I've got an idea. Hear me out," said Jack.

"Marcov's security system likely is aimed at protecting incoming systems... electric, water, gas, cable, but probably not focused on the outgoing system...specifically, the sewer line," said Jack.

"And we know the scientist's compound sits on a bluff over the lake," he added.

"Interesting," said Mike.

"Go on," said Grace.

"We could tunnel through the waste pipe with a remote camera. My robot has the capacity to carry one, and to perform simple tasks, like opening a cabinet. Add a laser gun and we can inflict a ton of damage. Basically, take out his lab if we keep our wits about us. No hacking necessary. Of course, there's still the issue of the microwaves, but it's unlikely the weapon is triggered by the sewer pipes. And we won't be inside the house. This will be a remote-controlled attack." Jack said.

His friends couldn't deny he had made some good points. They decided to sleep on it and meet up in the morning.

That night, Jack flopped around on his bed, unable to settle down. His body coursed with adrenaline. Finally, after midnight, he dropped into a deep sleep, and a dream began to play.

Spoons and forks with arms and legs marched past, like in a movie theater ad for popcorn and drinks. Then kitchen utensils followed in parade fashion, two by two. Finally, the golden whistle appeared, twirling and bowing. In place of the engraved numbers, an array of dancing letters arranged themselves on the golden surface... spelling a word...

HARMONICS

This image, sinking in Jack's sleeping brain, bounced and boomeranged, chiseling the word in a remote corner of his mind.

When Jack awoke the next morning, as hard as he tried, he could not recall the dream. Somehow, though, he sensed that the time was right to attack Marcov's compound.

After school, they finalized the plan, and signaled Max and Izzy to meet at Jack's house. Soon they were rushing around town with a list of items needed for their operation. Max claimed he could bring the laser gun. The following day was Thanksgiving, and they hoped the holiday would serve as a perfect cover for their covert mission.

The next evening, the teenagers bowed out of their family gatherings, claiming they needed a walk after the heavy meal. At 9:00 p.m. they met up with Max and Izzy at the harbor north of town. The area was deserted, as most people were parked in front of their televisions watching holiday specials. Above them, the gorgeous white dome of the Bahai Temple glowed through the bare tree branches.

Dressed head to toe in slick black wetsuits, and looking like well-oiled Doberman Pinschers, they descended the steps to the docks. The bone-chilling November weather whipped around them, but the extra layers they wore protected them from the elements. Max and Izzy looked like giant babies with their moss green and silver curls tucked in their hoods.

At the end of the pier, they boarded a motorized raft like those used by the Coast Guard. Jack did not ask how Max and Izzy had scored the laser gun or the boat, but the stenciled words *Great Lakes Naval Station* provided a clue. Working quickly, they hauled their tools and Jack's robot into the watercraft. Fortunately, the wind off the lake had died down making the waves more manageable.

Growling, the motor roared to life, and they headed north, hugging the shore of Lake Michigan. The boat created a sizable wake as the sleek craft cut through the dark water, sending up cold spray. A curtain of clouds veiled the moonlight as they approached the compound. When they saw the line of trees on the bluff, they knew they were close. Max flipped a switch, turning on a sound-canceling device that masked the roar of the motor.

Soon the dark outline of Vincent Marcov's compound appeared, sending a shiver up Jack's spine. The structure rose above them as the craft approached a wall of stone. Behind this barrier of rock stood a veritable fortress. Shuddering, Jack saw the massive structure, and for a split second, he wondered if this venture amounted to pure folly. Then he saw the scientist's silhouette moving on the second floor of the estate. Seeing the rogue scientist again sent a chill through him, but he pushed down his fear, drawing in a steadying breath.

Jack turned to his crew and signaled the *go* sign. Pulling the raft quickly up on the beach, the five crouched silently until, one by one, all the windows in the mansion darkened. Jack touched the chest pocket of his wetsuit, checking the golden whistle. Then the wind picked up again, and they smelled the stench of the sewer line.

It was showtime. Mike located the sewer pipe jutting out from the rock, above the lapping water. It was illegal to send raw waste into the lake, however, Marcov, of course, ignored the law. Izzy stepped forward with a canister from a Sophia environmental lab. He released a massive shot of a bacteria-neutralizing foam into the pipe, flushing out the sewage. Then Max pulled out a rotor blade, produced from one of Sophia's newly discovered metals. It made short work of drilling, widening the pipe into a tunnel big enough to accommodate Jack's talented little robot.

Next, Jack released a plastic strip that unfurled into the tunnel. They had practiced sending the robot over the sheet, adding treads to increase the traction. Now their preparation paid off as the robot disappeared into the passageway.

A few minutes later, the camera transmitted an image of the compound's basement. They were in. And the little robot got to work. The five kids took turns operating it, sending it down hallways and careening into different rooms. As it traveled, it destroyed everything in sight with a compact laser gun. So far, they saw no sign of the refrigerator holding the virus meant for Jack. Max had outfitted the drill with a white noise apparatus so that the demolition remained almost silent, blending into the sound of crashing waves.

With one more floor to visit, Jack took the controls. In the next room he saw two posters, one of Joseph Spencer and the other of him. The red X over Spencer's image sent a shiver up his spine. He saw the portrait of Cronos' menacing face glistening with malice.

Jack sent a blast from the laser, setting fire to the painting. Then he turned the robot, sending him out into the hall. The monitor now showed a frosted glass door with *LABORATORY* etched into the surface. Jack pivoted the controls and rolled the robot inside. Spinning, to survey the walls, the camera rested on a refrigerator with a biohazard sticker. Jack fired up the laser, training it on the deadly target that housed the virus meant for him.

But then, the image went dark.

In the same instant, the controls in Jack's hand fell slack.

His heart froze.

Suddenly Marcov's booming voice blasted over the roof from an outdoor PA system. **"Got you now! Alexa...turn on the microwave!"**

A giant search beam now rotated wildly around the property, hunting for prey. The kids could hear the electromagnetic radiation weapon powering up with a growing hum.

Trapped, the five kids understood the impossibility of outrunning the microwaves that would cook them in minutes.

But in a flash of inspiration, from somewhere deep in his mind, the word *Harmonic* glowed. Jack pulled out the golden whistle, blowing as hard as he could.

A tremendous whoosh emitted from the instrument...and the kids ran like crazy.

Max summoned the raft by remote control.

They all jumped in the boat, just in time, because a powerful sound wave, a *harmonic*, hit the compound. In seconds, shaking the entire fortress, walls and towers collapsed, crumbling the scientist's lair into a giant heap of rubble.

The force shook the earth, and a massive mountain of water rolled toward the shore.

The raft sped away with the kids leaning into the wind. But outrunning the wave seemed impossible. A huge death wall of water headed directly toward them. No way they could survive. They would perish in the frigid water.

Suddenly, a shaft of light from above appeared, calming the waves around the boat, and holding back the black wall of water.

Max and Izzy shouted, "The Council is helping us!"

They all cheered, and Jack followed the path illuminated in the water from the column of light.

After what seemed like forever gripping the steering wheel, Jack saw the gleaming alabaster dome of the Bahai Temple. Moments later the boat pulled up alongside the dock. Climbing out of the rocking raft, the kids fell over themselves onto the pier, rolling with amazement at their success.

The miraculous beam from above did a final circle in the dark sky, like a salute, and disappeared.

Jack felt tears of gratitude.

The Council had finally intervened!

They were lucky to be alive. Jack marveled how, at that last instant, the word HARMONIC in neon color, had flashed in his mind.

Without the whistle sending out the massive vibration, the microwave would have pulverized them.

Then the massive wall of water rolling toward them...the terror... then the incredible rescue by the Council. They had survived and the rogue scientist's complex was gone.

Jack wondered, had he just neutralized Vincent Marcov?

* * *

However, the next morning he couldn't dismiss the nagging feeling that the rogue scientist had escaped.

Later that day, his fear was confirmed when a meme appeared on his phone. It showed the last grain of sand dropping in the hourglass and Marcov's maniacal laughing.

It seemed that just before the harmonic hit, the scientist had gone invisible, transporting himself to an abandoned railroad yard. Outsmarted by a teenager, and dressed in a charred cardigan, Marcov berated himself that a harmonic weapon and access through the sewer line had never occurred to him.

Now he vowed to obliterate the green-eyed kid from the face of the earth.

"I *still* have the ice cap. No more futzing around with that lost virus," he muttered to himself.

He pulled out his phone, checked for service bars and connected to his Canadian facility via a dark web link. The screen flickered for a moment and then zoomed into the remote location in Saskatchewan. The hundred individuals, dressed in maroon jumpsuits, saluted their leader.

"As you were," said Dr. Marcov.

The mercenaries looked around at each other, worried about what might come next. Contact at this hour was unusual.

"It's time," Marcov said. "Load the lasers on the entire fleet ASAP," barked Dr. Marcov.

"Sir, yes, sir," the team leader saluted.

For the next two hours Vincent Marcov watched his screen as his minions scrambled in the long hangar.

When the work was complete, the team lined up.

Marcov drew in a deep breath.

He ordered them to open the large doors. A dozen of the team broke ranks and moved to push on the corrugated steel panels. The metal hinges let out a frightful screech and the frigid Canadian air rushed into the hangar. The satellites, lined up on a conveyor belt, slowly began to move out to the launching pads.

Marcov drew in a breath, trying to manage his emotions.

Tears streamed down the craters in his old face.

"They will all *pay* now," he wailed.

With trembling hands, he tapped in the code. In synchronized pairs, his shiny satellites, atop rocket boosters, blasted into the sky.

Flying in formation two hundred miles above the earth, they headed straight for the Arctic Circle.

Immediately, radar defense systems in a dozen countries in the Northern Hemisphere lit up as the rockets registered on military tracking screens. The United States Space Force scrambled to intercept, but the rogue scientist activated thousands of decoys, his fingers moving furiously on his keyboard.

CHAPTER NINETEEN

Armageddon

I n the northern skies, a full-scale war erupted as Marcov's fleet of satellites raced into position. The Navy responded by firing heat-seeking missiles to disrupt the laser attacks. Torpedoes and water drones rode under the waves, seeking out targets that turned out to be decoys. Canada, the United States, and the European Union hoped the reinforced *iron dome* would protect the ice cap.

After hours of intense battle in the air and ocean, the radar screens at the Pentagon began to show Marcov's lasers disappearing with trails of light going dark. The Space Force and Navy Commanders hoped the tide had turned in their favor.

Minutes passed.

Vincent Marcov grinned as he imagined his enemy's confusion. Drawing in a breath of anticipation, he counted, "One Mississippi, Two Mississippi ..." until he reached ten.

Then he pushed a button. Flaps lifted on his satellites. Another tap on the keyboard, and tens of millions of tiny metal darts shot toward the Arctic. The stiletto-sharp blades hit the surface of the ice, hacking off a blast of glassy shards. Gigantic mountains of ice disintegrated into the sea.

Fast, cheap and out of control worked every time, Marcov smirked.

With the polar ice cap disappearing before their eyes, commanders at the Pentagon knew the iron dome was useless. It was clear the earth had lost the battle. When the destruction came, their screens shimmered, the images flickering, overwhelmed by the incoming data.

* * *

After early reports hit the news outlets, many people *still* dismissed the battle as just more conspiracy theories. On the streets of Chicago, London, New York, Sydney, Paris, and Hong Kong, most of the population went on as though everything was normal. People found it hard to imagine the possibility of losing the planet. It was easier to ignore the signs. They figured things must be OK as they saw airplanes flying, people shopping, and traffic lights still working. Maybe the climate issue was just another hype. If there was real danger, surely the government, or *somebody*, could handle it.

That evening, Jack's phone rattled on his nightstand. Seeing it was the FBI agent, a shot of fear hit him as he picked up the call.

"Are you watching TV?" said Bernstein.

"Why? What happened?" asked Jack.

"The polar ice disintegrated a half hour ago. It's over," said the agent, his voice cracking.

"No, **no**. There *must* be something we can do," said Jack.

"Spend time with your family. The president will address the nation soon," said Bernstein.

The line disconnected. Jack put down the phone.

Vincent Marcov had won.

The earth was on life support.

All the work, and all the danger had been for nothing... the damage to Charlie, his family targeted. And still...the planet would shrivel in the heat. New York under forty feet of water, Miami and New Orleans gone. Storms and fires would take out what was left. Crops would fail. Millions of people on the move, hungry, thirsty, trying to escape to higher ground. But there was *no higher ground*, nowhere to hide.

Jack turned on the television and the emergency broadcast channel flashed the message:

Environmental disaster. Stay calm.

Jack raised his phone to call Grace, but the device was dead now. He wondered where his parents were, as they had taken Charlie for a doctor appointment. They should have been home hours ago. Then he heard the distinctive loud pop of an electric transformer.

Jack walked outside and heard people running and shouting in the dark. Neighbors were loading up their cars. Maybe trying to escape to a cabin in the Northwoods?

In a daze, he walked a few blocks toward downtown Evanston, but he saw people fighting over food and plastic water jugs. Broken glass covered the sidewalks, and Jack could hear rocks hitting store windows. Looting and the sound of gunshots in his town? It seemed impossible. Up ahead, a line of flashing lights from emergency vehicles blocked the street. Flames rose from a burned-out police car. Cracks of gunfire were getting closer.

Jack turned back, and as he approached his house, he saw candlelight flickering behind the shades. His parents must have made it home. Pushing open the door, however, he saw Grace sitting alone on the living room rug, hugging her knees.

"Oh my gosh, you're OK," he said.

He wrapped his arms around her.

"I didn't know what to do. I took your house key from under the rock. I couldn't get home. The roads are blocked. I don't even know if my family is OK," said Grace.

"Let me get the battery-powered radio," said Jack.

He returned with the device. But before they could turn it on, loud banging startled them.

"Blow out the candle," he told Grace.

They heard heavy footsteps on the porch. An angry voice called out.

"Hey, get that guy before he makes it to his car."

Jack peeked behind the shade. A gang of tough-looking guys carried crow bars and a flare.

Grace and Jack heard the men go down the steps, and he saw his nextdoor neighbor jump into his car and speed off. The attackers ran off after the car, but it was traveling too fast. The gang, now down the block, turned the corner.

"We better hide. Bring the radio in the back. I'll grab some food and water," said Jack.

"Where do you think Charlie and your parents are?" Grace asked.

"I don't know," said Jack.

So they listened to the radio, but there was only the message to stay calm, while classical music played, an attempt to soothe the lost citizenry.

With the sounds of mayhem all around, Jack and Grace held each other.

There would be no graduations, no prom, no college, no studying science, and no children. All their plans, hopes, and dreams, crushed.

They ate some leftovers, crackers, and cheese, and then curled up in a big quilt.

Were their families even alive?

Hours passed. Still no parents, no Charlie.

Exhausted and defeated, their eyes closed.

* * *

The same evening, on Sophia, Izzy couldn't sleep. Something was wrong. He could *feel* it. Checking the news, he saw the alert about the Earth's polar cap. Even across the vast intergalactic span Izzy sensed Jack's despair. In his mind he could see the boy rolled up under the quilt with Grace. Jack and his family had suffered terrible losses, and for what? The teenager had honored his commitment to the Council, despite his fear and attacks from Marcov.

The worst had happened. The ice cap was gone.

And Vincent Marcov would flee the gasping planet…to Sophia.

The child turned over these facts in his mind.

Now Izzy had turned eight years old the previous week, and as he blew out the candles on his cake, he felt a new sense of independence. Something was shifting inside him. He could feel it.

Max would be mad, of course. And he knew there would be hell to pay, but it was time to act.

Tiptoeing down the hall, he rounded a corner and went up the massive staircase. He counted the rooms as he passed the thresholds in the darkened hallway. One door, two doors, three doors. He took a deep breath, and then pushed open the forbidden door. The one no one had dared to open... not for millennia. The door with the letter *P* carved into the oak.

On a massive bed, slept great, great, great, et cetera, grandfather. Izzy paused a moment.

For all of his eight years, he had been warned—under no condition, was he ever, *ever*, to enter this room.

But Izzy trusted his gut, moving quickly over to the bed, fearing if he thought about this too long, he might back down.

Izzy saw the famous lyre at the bedside. This ancient musical instrument, according to the stories, was used by the old man to illustrate the psychic tension within people. In order to function in harmony, the strings could not be too slack or too tight.

"Psst...Time to get up, Grandpa," Izzy jiggled the bed.

The old man said, "Go away."

Izzy jiggled the bed again. This time with more force.

The old man let out a series of snorts.

Izzy now stood on the bed, jumping as high as he could.

"Hey, Grandpa, wake up!"

"Stop the boat," the old man yelled, disoriented.

Izzy stopped jumping and their eyes met.

Emerald-green irises, hooded under the heavy lids, looked out of a face so wrinkled it looked like a mountain range.

"Who's that now?" asked the ancient figure, as he rolled over to see the child, who had slipped off the bed.

"It's Izzy. We haven't actually met. Well, how could we have? I'm eight years old. I've been told you've been sleeping for millennia. But, right now, *you* have to get up. There's an emergency. Everyone else has given up, it seems."

"What time is it?" the old man asked.

"Well, it's ten p.m., past my bedtime, but when you hear what's going on, you'll understand," said Izzy.

Then Izzy handed him a tablet that showed the earth's polar section missing the ice.

"What's this?" the old man leaned out for support, trying to sit up. "This is *terrible*." His eyebrows furrowed.

"I know, right?" said Izzy.

Izzy pulled the old man up, but it took several tries. Finally, the old guy sat on the edge of the bed. The child's eyes widened, as he had never seen a beard that long.

"Get me those slippers and robe," the grandpa said.

Izzy complied, shaking the dust off the robe.

"You can't walk with that long beard. You'll trip for sure," said Izzy.

"I see what you mean," said the old grandpa, feeling the weight on his face. "Maybe if we cut it down a bit."

Izzy found a pair of shears in the drawer, and he began cutting through the bristling tangle.

"That's better," he said finally.

Looking on the floor, Izzy saw a mass of hair that looked like a giant snowbank. A few mice jumped out, scurrying to find other shelter.

"Let's go," said the old man.

With Izzy's help, and a tall wooden staff, Grandpa Pythagoras descended the stairs. Picking up speed, he made his way into the Council's Chamber, throwing open the doors.

A gasp came from the assembly. The chairman looked stunned. And then scared.

Only Max's voice was heard. "**Izzy! What have you done?**"

But Grandpa Pythagoras glared at the group.

"Izzy is the only one here with an ounce of sense. Why did you let me sleep so long?"

His voice boomed, shaking the glassware on the table.

"We couldn't find the wheel so we didn't think you could do anything if we *did* wake you up," said the Chairman.

"Do you think I would leave that wheel laying around?" said Pythagoras.

No answer came from the Council members.

Clearly, there had been a *massive* breakdown in communication.

Grandpa Pythagoras clapped his hands, and the engraved oak table began to spin. When it stopped, a wheel, shaped like the nine-pointed enneagon, floated above the table. It looked to be made of platinum.

A rumble of approval erupted from the room.

"So *that's* where you keep it?" The chairman said.

"Knock it off," Grandpa Pythagoras said, glaring at him.

Then the old man commanded, "The Chain of Nine must be assembled."

A hush settled in the room. Immediately, the Council members filed out, leaving a core group.

Joseph Spencer, Izzy, and Max remained among the designated few. Hildegard of Bingen, Tolstoy, DaVinci, and the tall red-headed woman in pink silk also stood in the circle. Without needing a cue, Max and Izzy removed their blue contact lenses, exposing their dazzling green eyes.

"That's good," the grandpa said. "Now, we just need that kid. What's his name?"

"Jack Abernault," said Izzy.

Max and Izzy moved fast.

Several hours later, they entered the house on Orrington Avenue. Moving quietly, they didn't want to wake Grace.

Bleary eyed at this midnight hour, Jack sat in the cube. Max and Izzy had rushed him out of the house into the glass vehicle before he could object, stopping only to grab a jacket. As soon as the cube passed through the time portal, Max explained what was going down.

"**Pythagoras!** The *real* Pythagoras?" Jack asked, clearly flummoxed at hearing the extraordinary events that had occurred that evening on Sophia.

Then Max and Izzy removed their sunglasses.

Jack was startled by their emerald-green eyes.

"You see, we're distant cousins. And now, a group must assemble. Only a few of our relatives are part of the Chain of Nine. Seems we are neurodivergent. Has something to do with a mutated gene that alters our electromagnetic chemical makeup. The special feature can skip many generations, and then just pop up," said Max.

"Pythagoras says it's likely from a higher power," said Izzy.

"Bottom line, it's a mystery." Max said.

"Woah," said Jack. "That *is* crazy," he added. "But why did you wear the blue contact lenses?" Jack asked.

"The focus group felt our emerald eyes would be off putting to Earthlings. The chirps and clicks in our speech pattern were already pretty strange for you all," said Max.

"It's weird, but I kind of got used to it," said Jack.

When Sophia finally came into view, Jack thought of the doctors on this planet who had saved Izzy's life with their medicines.

Jack wondered if his brother and parents were still alive.

Izzy nodded. "They're back home. Two of our agents rescued them from the subway. When the traffic in the Loop snarled, they abandoned the car, and tried to take the train."

Then the glass cube slowed, and they landed near a fountain. They made their way over to the Council's rotunda where Max and Izzy led Jack into the chamber.

There, eating dinner, sat his ancient great grandfather.

"Oh, good you're here. Nice to make your acquaintance, Jack Abernault, I'm your great, great...et cetera, et cetera, grandpa," said the very, very old man.

Pythagoras lifted his crystal goblet in a greeting. Wiping his mouth with a linen napkin, the old man rose.

Astounded that he was meeting Pythagoras, Jack looked around at the assembly, trying to get his bearings. Max and Izzy had filled him in about the others with this gene mutation. The news that Tolstoy, DaVinci, and Hildegard of Bingen were among his ancestors just blew his mind.

A smiling Joseph Spencer gave him a long hug, and the sixteen year old, finally felt connected to his legacy. After all, he had gone on the quest and taught the *Anamchara Text*.

Grandpa Pythagoras announced that the apple pie would have to wait, and he gestured the group to circle the platinum wheel.

"Extend your hands toward the center, like this," he said.

Obeying instructions, the nine assembled around the wheel, and raised their arms. They were amazed to see a river of golden mist flow from their palms and blend into a spinning disk.

A river of energy lit up the paths and points on the circle, illuminating the enneagram pattern.

Pythagoras slowly lowered his arms, and the group followed, until the lighted paths merged with the platinum wheel.

"There we go," he said with satisfaction. "Locked and loaded," said Pythagoras. "Isn't mathematics wonderful?"

A bell rang and the door to the chamber opened. The entire Council took their places.

"You may all sit down now. Prepare to be dazzled," he said, with twinkling green eyes.

CHAPTER TWENTY

Integration

T he overhead lights dimmed, and a hush settled on the group. Pythagoras pushed a button on a console, and a large curtain of something resembling a panel of stardust appeared, creating a large screen. The planet Earth came into view. Growing larger, the image tipped and rotated, until the North Pole rested in the center.

"Let me be clear. The wonders you will witness would be impossible without the work of Jack, Izzy, Max, and Joseph. They are the ones who prepared Earth with technology and with teachings from the *Anamchara Text*. Millions of enlightened minds now function as an actual conductor. Like a webbed radio channel, or morphogenic field, vibrating at a harmonious frequency."

Pythagoras blotted the tears from his eyes. His voice cracked as he continued. "For many centuries, I have dreamed of this night."

"Let me show you an infrared scan of the earth's consciousness two years ago, compared with how it looks today. This shift shows the change in how citizens view each other and the planet. Old caste systems are falling away as people gain dignity and respect."

On the split screen, the first image showed a dreary mist of red and dark grey ominously hanging above the earth's atmosphere.

The recent scan showed a soft glow of turquoise and pale yellow now hovering above the Earth. The contrast was stunning.

"Our efforts here this evening would be useless if the Earth had remained in the dark. So, may we have an applause for our champions," Pythagoras said.

The chamber erupted with enthusiastic whelps of "Hear! Hear!"

Jack choked back tears as Izzy grabbed his hand.

Pythagoras rose, and placing his hands on the wheel, he began to turn it until a golden beam rested on the North Pole.

"OK, let's get this system powered up. Prepare to encounter the wall where knowledge smashes into mystery."

Jack could hardly believe his eyes.

Superimposed on the globe was the sculpture he had seen in Lake Geneva. The one that had touched his soul. The one with the arms powering the gear shifts. This piece of art captured his struggle, away from fear and the need for certainty, into a place of peace and courage.

Then the image of the sculpture faded away. Was he the only one who had seen it?

Like a maestro conducting a symphony, Pythagoras gripped the wheel, wailing to the universe:

"*Goodness, Kindness, Effectiveness, Creativity, Wisdom, Loyalty, Joy, Power, Peace.*"

Instantly, the virtues arose, manifesting as nine colors. Streaming in a ring that wrapped around the globe, sparks of energy flew from nine points of fire. The flashing traveled from point one to seven, to five, to eight, to two, to four, and back to one. A brilliant pulsating triangle illuminated the enneagon's center. Finally, a web of connections appeared, covering the enneagon. The design shivered and then exploded into a sphere, the symbol of wholeness.

"Come here, Izzy. You're the star this evening for listening to your heart, and for having the courage to wake me up," said Pythagoras.

Izzy stood up proudly, moving over to the wheel.

"Now!" his grandfather instructed.

Izzy pushed down on the wheel with all his strength, tipping it. A rush of silvery ice blasted out in a stream and began to coalesce on the North Pole.

The chamber erupted in applause and shouts of amazement, as they saw an immense island of fresh glistening ice cover the Arctic.

Then Grandpa Pythagoras beckoned Jack to take Izzy's place. Jack gripped the wheel, feeling an electric current pass through his arms and down into his shoes. Following instructions, he shifted his weight down on the wheel, and an emerald river blasted the Amazon, as forests magically rose on the South American continent. It reminded him of the holograms in Morningside's contemplation chamber.

The room exploded with happy shouts.

Jack wished Grace was there to witness all of this.

Champagne was poured for the crowd. Dancing broke out, and the assembly sang the Sophian anthem. When the last note sounded, strains of Johann Sebastian Bach's *Ode to Joy* filled the air.

"It's way past midnight," Pythagoras announced.

"Go sleep now. We will let the weary Earth adjust to the healing."

* * *

In a rundown motel, Vincent Marcov heard his tablet dinging an alert.

Sitting down to check it out, he set his glass of cabernet on the desk. Tapping the keyboard, his eyes nearly popped out of his head when he saw the glistening, reconstituted polar ice cap on his screen.

He laughed, "This must be a joke," as he rebooted the program.

A second ding, and the Amazon basin appeared, green and flourishing in areas Marcov aggressively had logged for decades. The rogue scientist checked the Wi-Fi signal, and his security settings to see if this was some trickster's hack. Because he knew those images couldn't possibly be authentic.

But as the truth sunk in, the pulse of frantic, off the rails keyboard music began to build in his head. Louder and louder, it grew.

Joy by Apollo, the baroque pop version of Bach's 1723 composition, was now playing an ear-splitting soundtrack in his head... the musical score for his mental breakdown.

His faculties fragmenting, Marcov felt his mind flying apart like shards of glass. Hadn't he totally obliterated the polar ice cap? How could this be? He was living a nightmare. Furiously, he grabbed the laptop, entering a code that launched a missile aimed at the hangar in Canada.

Those idiots had failed him. Minutes later the blast took out his team. All that remained was a burned-out cavern.

He heard sirens in the distance...growing louder.

Vincent knew he needed to disappear. But the music in his head was interfering.

He couldn't focus.

Images now intervened. The face of Joseph. Then Jack. And finally, the powerful sculpture in Lutetia's studio. The one with the living arms on gears. The art that had caused him to break out in hives now overwhelmed him, wrestled him to the ground. Rolling on the floor, he closed his eyes to shut it out, but the sculpture was etched in his mind. No way he could muster the attention he needed to perform his disappearing trick.

The music now seemed to be blasting from the walls and even from the trees outside. Vincent felt his auditory and visual faculties overwhelmed with incoming music and images of the sculpture. He howled in pain.

After tracking Marcov's cell phone signal, the FBI broke down his door. Cowering in the corner, Vincent rocked and whimpered. The babbling doctor cut a pitiful figure. As he was marched out in handcuffs and into an unmarked van, the neighbors looked from behind window shades, wondering what was going down. What they saw was a slender figure with wild eyes, begging his captors to turn down the music.

CHAPTER TWENTY-ONE

The Future

S everal weeks after Marcov's arrest, Jack got his driver's license. Even after his intergalactic travel, Jack found driving a shiny, new electric-powered Jeep off the lot the best ride ever.

He could hardly believe the road his life had taken, but he hadn't traveled alone. Grace, Mike, Max, and, most of all, Izzy, had been there for him. Sometimes, the path, he realized, was more of a relay race.

* * *

For the next ten years, scientists, politicians, and educators worked on the flash drive information from Max and Izzy. The environment slowly improved as new international cooperatives worked to shield the polar ice cap and the Amazon forest canopy. Green technology blossomed, but it was estimated that it would take decades for the air, water, and habitats to recover. Fusion atomic energy fueled the planet after the special generator was invented, funded by the Morningside Foundation.

Attitudes in the culture shifted, as a new generation learned the lessons from the *Anamchara Text*. Meditation and breath work were added to school curriculum. Jack and his friends took part in this huge revolution in education. Avatars made individualized instruction possible, while teachers led discussions on the material.

Jack eventually recovered from all his post COVID issues, and he went on to study science.

Jack and Grace dated through high school; however, they chose colleges on opposite coasts. While they remained lifelong friends, they understood they had admired qualities in each other that had attracted them in the first place. Over the years Grace picked up some of Jack's prudence, while Jack became more assertive and peaceful. Mike entered the Foreign Service and eventually worked as a diplomat at the United Nations. Jack became a neuroscientist, studying the mysteries of the brain. Grace joined Doctors Without Borders after medical school.

Max and Izzy continue to visit.

NOTES

The enneagram is a model of personality patterns based on nine gifts. The purpose of the system is to help an individual make a shift to balance the self. The template offers an awareness of cognitive styles and shows underlying motivations. The enneagram helps one recognize the confinement and bias in one's pattern. The idea is to develop the "inner observer," and to "wear one's style more lightly."

Twenty-seven subtypes further define variations in the nine patterns; however, no external description can ever capture an individual's uniqueness. Many people find it helpful to work with the three centers, finding how they favor one type/point in the head center (5, 6, or 7), one type/point in the heart center (2, 3, or 4), and one type/point in the gut center (8, 9, or 1). Often one of these centers (head, heart, or gut) remains less developed. Breathwork serves as an invaluable practice in grounding the lessons of the enneagram into one's life.

The enneagram system has ancient roots in many cultures, remaining mostly an oral tradition until the 1980s. Over the past forty years, hundreds of books on the topic have been published. Many corporations and government agencies use the system. For decades, psychiatrists, psychologists, and educational institutions have found the enneagram helpful. New research in the fields of neuroscience and psychometric testing offers exciting support for the nine patterns.

Teens often benefit from journaling, interactive games, panels, and listening to stories about the styles of behavior. Mentors and workshops are available through the International Enneagram Association, and the Shift Network's Global Enneagram Summit and Breathwork Summit.

Dr. Jerome Wagner, Loyola University, created the WEPSS, a standardized, reliable, and valid Enneagram inventory for individuals, age 18 and older, reviewed in *Buros's Mental Measurements Yearbook*.

Other Enneagram teachers and authors include Russ Hudson, David Daniels, Helen Palmer, Denise Daniels, Sandra Maitri, Suzanne Stabile, Daniel J. Siegel, Richard Rohr, Katherine Fauvre, Beatrice Chestnut, Jessica Dibb, Deborah Ooten, and books by Conscious Dimensions.

Anam Cara, or Anamchara, refers to a mentor or guide in the Celtic tradition.

Most of the green technology described in this book exists.

Printed in the USA
CPSIA information can be obtained
at www.ICGtesting.com
JSHW082045070823
46124JS00001B/5